RESCUING MICAH (SPECIAL FORCES: OPERATION ALPHA)

PREY SECURITY: CYBER TEAM

BOOK THREE

JANE BLYTHE

Cover designed by Q Designs

Dear Readers,

Welcome to the Special Forces: Operation Alpha Fan-Fiction world!

If you are new to this amazing world, in a nutshell the author wrote a story using one or more of my characters in it. Sometimes that character has a major role in the story, and other times they are only mentioned briefly. This is perfectly legal and allowable because they are going through Aces Press to publish the story.

This book is entirely the work of the author who wrote it. While I might have assisted with brainstorming and other ideas about which of my characters to use, I didn't have any part in the process or writing or editing the story.

I'm proud and excited that so many authors loved my characters enough that they wanted to write them into their own story. Thank you for supporting them, and me!

READ ON!
    Xoxo
    Susan Stoker

ACKNOWLEDGMENTS

I'd like to thank everyone who played a part in bringing this story to life. Particularly my mom who is always there to share her thoughts and opinions with me. My wonderful cover designer Amy who did an amazing job with this stunning cover. My fabulous editor Lisa for all the hard work she puts into polishing my work, and Detra who does an amazing proofread. My awesome team, Sophie, Robyn, and Clayr, without your help I'd never be able to run my street team. And my fantastic street team members who help share my books with every share, comment, and like!

And of course a big thank you to all of you, my readers! Without you I wouldn't be living my dreams of sharing the stories in my head with the world!

CHAPTER 1

FINALLY, she felt like she could take a deep breath.

It had been a whirlwind of action these last few months, starting when her best friend had been snatched off the streets.

Never in a million years would Teresa Dash have expected it to turn out to be this bad when Ava hadn't come home that night. Of course, she'd known any abduction was bad, but an organ trafficking ring would never have entered her mind if her friend hadn't told them herself that's who had taken her.

Crazy.

And from there things only went from bad to worse.

But now her teammate Tobias' new girlfriend Isabella was home safe and sound, the couple no doubt tucked away in Tobias' apartment doing what new couples in love did. Same thing Ava and her new boyfriend Nathaniel were likely doing at the apartment in Prey Security's building where Ava had moved to feel safer.

The complete opposite of what she'd be doing when the elevator finally reached her floor.

There was no one waiting for her in her apartment, despite the fact that she technically shared the place with Ava and their other best friend and Prey Security Cyber Teammate, Chelsea. Even after the organ trafficking ring was finally dismantled, it wasn't likely that Ava was going to move back in.

Not with how close she and Nathaniel had grown and the fact that Nathaniel was still an active-duty SEAL and didn't have the freedom to pack up and move. That meant Ava would be the one who would have to move.

While everyone knew her as practical and no-nonsense, there was one thing she struggled with.

Change.

Something she made sure people weren't aware of, because she didn't like to admit weakness. She was independent and she'd had to grow up quickly after her dad died and her family had been thrown into poverty. Since her mom had to work three jobs just to keep them afloat, Teresa had taken over most of the household duties, including caring for her two younger brothers, at the tender age of nine.

Despite how rough it had been, there had been one bright spot.

Well, there had been from when she was fourteen up

until seventeen, when he dumped her at the very worst time in her life.

"Stop thinking about him, Teresa," she muttered aloud. Glad no one else was in the elevator to hear her talking to herself. It was a bad habit her brothers used to tease her about, and one she'd done her best to hide from her best friends and roommates. Although she was sure that both Ava and Chelsea had heard her do it on several occasions over the years they'd lived together.

Thinking about the boy who had broken her heart was counterproductive. While they could all take a momentary breath and give themselves a tiny little break, this case was far from done.

Bringing down this trafficking ring was personal to Teresa and to all of Prey. It had been a mistake that would become their undoing when the trafficking ring had snatched a Prey employee off the streets. There was nothing she and the company she worked for wouldn't do to end the ring's reign of terror.

Nothing.

But thinking about a long-ago broken heart wasn't going to help her.

"He wasn't who you thought he was, he wasn't who you wanted him to be," she reminded herself as the doors to the elevator dinged open on her floor. It was empty, and she was glad because she needed to remind herself of all the reasons thinking about her ex was a bad idea.

Dumping her and breaking her heart was one thing, but to just cut off complete contact with her because she'd been gang raped was another. It was unforgivable, and she hated that sometimes when she was at her loneliest, she still wished he had been the man she'd dreamed of spending her life with.

"Well, he wasn't, and you need to get over it," she ordered herself as she marched down the hall, pulling her keys from her purse as she did.

It was true, she really did need to get over it, but so far that hadn't happened. Even though she was twenty-nine years old, no longer a traumatized and confused seventeen-year-old girl, she still shied away from anything that hinted at a relationship. She just didn't have it in her to hand her heart over to another person ever again.

Not a boyfriend anyway.

Her friends and her family had her heart, and she knew it was safe with them.

As she approached her front door, Teresa's steps slowed.

Something looked off.

Felt off.

While she worked with former special forces operatives all day every day, both Tobias and Josiah, who were part of Cyber Team, and all the men and women serving on Prey's other teams, she'd heard of a gut feeling but never experienced it for herself before.

If she was being honest, she'd never quite believed it was a thing. Thought it was more just the operative's training and experience rather than some sort of undefinable feeling deep inside you.

It turned out she'd been wrong.

It existed.

At least it did if this weird anxiety inside her was anything to go by.

Doing her best to brush it off, Teresa let her gaze roam over the front door. It was closed, just like it had been when she and Chelsea left this morning. Normally, she would have headed home with her friend, but Chelsea had decided to bunk at the office tonight because she was coming down with a cold and hadn't felt like making the trek home only to make the trip back to the office a few hours later.

Maybe the knot in her stomach had less to do with her front door and more to do with the fact that she had allowed her ex to creep his way into her mind. It might have been more than a decade since he ghosted her, but that didn't mean the pain was completely gone. How could it? He hadn't just left, he'd left when she was broken and hurting. Without a word, without an explanation. Without a goodbye. Just gone.

"Get over it, Teresa," she coached herself. "It's time to stop letting that man rule your life. Maybe it's time to actually move on. Properly move on. As in, put yourself back out there in the dating scene."

It was a terrifying thought, and one that had her hand actually trembling as she slid the key in the lock and swung the door open.

Right as it was opening, she finally got why she'd felt weird.

Seemed a gut feeling *was* a real thing after all.

Because it wasn't thoughts of her ex that had her feeling like a rock was sitting heavily in her stomach, it was the fact that the Easter wreath still hanging on the door was upside down. Even though Easter had come and gone, they'd been so busy working on taking down the organ trafficking ring that she and Chelsea hadn't had the time to spare to take down the decorations she had insisted they put up.

Decorating for holidays was one of her favorite things to do, but now the cute little wreath, with colorful eggs and a white bunny sitting on them, was nothing more than a foreshadowing of what was to come.

What was to come turned out to be stepping inside her home and finding it had been trashed.

The expensive pieces of art that made up Ava's collection had been ripped off the walls and shredded with a sharp object. The TV lay on the floor, the screen shattered. Red paint—at least she prayed it was paint— had been poured all over their beige lounges, and the Easter decorations that she had lovingly put up were lying scattered about the room.

Worse than that was what had been painted along one of the walls.

Just two words, but they spoke volumes.

Back off.

There wasn't any need to say more than that. The warning was clear. The threat was clear.

It was the organ trafficking ring, it had to be. Who else would go to the trouble of breaking into their apartment and trashing the place? They already knew the ring was aware of where they lived because they'd abducted Ava from this very room just last month.

Now they'd come back.

Were they still here?

Panic hit then as Teresa realized she might not actually be alone in the apartment. Part of her wanted to go running through the place. Check to see what damage had been left in the kitchen and their bedrooms.

But the other part—the sensible part—knew she had to leave now.

Otherwise, she'd wind up like Ava had, tied to a bed, helpless to do anything to stop those people from removing her organs one by one until there was nothing left.

Already pulling her cell phone from her purse, Teresa gave one last glance around her apartment, then she turned and ran back down the hall, calling her boss' number as she went.

* * *

April 28th

10:30 P.M.

Stepping out of the elevator, Micah Hart walked across the lobby, wondering what he was going to do for the rest of the night.

The SEAL had flown out with his teammate Nathaniel Trevino, who was visiting with his new girlfriend, Ava. He'd intended to hang out with the couple for a while, then find a hotel to crash in.

Unfortunately, the evening had been cut short when the couple received a call from Ava's friend and roommate. Apparently, there had been a break-in at the apartment Ava shared with her friends and colleagues. Something to do with the organ trafficking ring that Prey had been hunting.

The same ring that first connected Nathaniel and Ava.

His buddy was supposed to tag a ship being used by the organ traffickers, but got sidetracked when he discovered a life raft floating alone in the ocean. Inside that raft had been Ava, and the two had clicked immediately, and were now well on their way to falling in love.

If they hadn't already.

Love.

What a lie that was.

Micah shook his head in disgust. While he was happy that his friend was happy, and Ava seemed like a great person, he wasn't sure he believed in the whole concept of falling in love anymore.

Not since he'd been betrayed by the girl he thought he loved. The girl he thought loved him back. Turned out she'd get on her back for anyone, including multiple anyones at the same time.

Writing the whole thing off as a youthful blunder, he'd moved on with his life. Joined the military and made it into an elite SEAL unit, he hung out with his friends, and hooked up with women, any woman. It didn't matter to him who the woman was as long as she was single and not looking for anything serious.

Life was good and yet …

As he crossed the quiet lobby of the world-renowned Prey Security, Micah found it hard to admit that something was missing. Something he'd been doing a great job of ignoring right up until Nathaniel caught the love bug.

Seeing one of his best friends suddenly smitten with a woman, a woman that Micah admitted was every bit the tough warrior as any of the men he served with, possibly tougher since she'd fought so hard without the benefit of the same training they had, had forced him to confront his unresolved feelings.

It might have been over a decade since he realized love was a lie, he might be older now, wiser, but when it came down to it, a part of him had died that day, and he was now having to accept that he hadn't moved on at all. All he'd done was ignore the whole mess and pretend that it hadn't meant anything at all.

But it had.

When he was a teenager, it had meant everything.

And now …

"Oommff."

The startled sound came from the person on the other side of the building's front door as she pushed it open at the same moment he pulled it open.

Caught off-balance, the person stumbled, and it was purely automatic for him to reach out to steady them.

"Sorry," Micah apologized. "Didn't see anyone on the other side. Guess I was a little lost in thought." As a special forces operator, he should know better than that, his life relied on him being aware of his surroundings, as did the lives of his teammates. But he was off duty, in a secure building, and a little messed up by watching the happy couple upstairs.

What he needed was to get out of there, find a bar,

hang out for a while, check out the women there, then find one who was down for a fun night and nothing more. Maybe that would get all thoughts of love and forever out of his head. Love wasn't forever, it barely lasted any time at all, he knew that from personal experience.

"That's okay, I wasn't looking either," the person said as she gently tugged herself out of his grip.

Again, it was instinct that had his fingers tightening around the shoulders he'd grabbed a moment ago to steady the person he now knew was a woman. A beautiful woman with flawless olive skin, huge chocolate brown eyes rimmed by the longest lashes he'd ever seen, and full lips currently parting to form an O as she looked up at him.

That voice.

It was one he'd never forget.

Not for as long as he lived.

If he could go back in time, the one thing he would change was that the last time he heard it, it wouldn't be moaning as another man had sex with her. He wished he'd never gone over to her place that night, then he never would have seen it. Then again, he also wouldn't have known what kind of woman she was.

Now here Teresa Dash was, all grown up and even more stunning than she'd been as a teen.

But what was she doing *here*?

At Prey Security?

This billion-dollar private security company was the best in the world, and he couldn't imagine that someone like Teresa would have any business being there.

"Think you might be in the wrong building," he told her, pushing back ever so slightly. Just because he didn't work there didn't mean he wouldn't call Nathaniel in a heartbeat to tell him that someone was on the property who didn't belong.

"Actually, I'm not," Teresa said, trying to pull free from his grip, and he reluctantly let her go.

This woman might have shattered his nineteen-year-old heart, but he knew he'd never gotten over her and knew he never really would. Young love, first love, she'd been his from the time they met when he was sixteen and she was fourteen. For those three years, they'd been nearly inseparable, and he'd never had anything like it since.

"Come on, Teresa, what would you need to be here for?" he asked. The girl he'd known back then had no plans to join the military or law enforcement, so he couldn't imagine that she'd have a job there. She had no cleaning supplies on her, and the receptionist who he'd met earlier had already left for the day, so she wasn't there for administrative purposes.

Slowly, those big eyes of hers blinked. "Sorry, do I know you?"

For a moment he froze, caught off-guard by the cool tone of her voice and the lack of recognition in her gaze.

Did she really not know who he was?

Was he that insignificant a part of her past that she'd already forgotten him?

Back then, she'd been his everything, and he

JANE BLYTHE

couldn't forget her no matter how badly he'd wanted to, yet she didn't seem to have that same problem.

No.

There was no way she wouldn't recognize him. They might have been teens back then, but he still looked the same, just older. She did too. Micah would recognize her anywhere.

Besides, the way her lips had parted to form that O told him she knew exactly who he was.

"Nuh-uh, not buying it. You know who I am," he said confidently.

"I really don't, sir, and I'm going to have to ask you to step aside," Teresa said, her voice calm and detached like she was telling the truth.

"You shouldn't be here, Teresa. This is private property. This building belongs to Prey Security."

"I'm aware of who my employer is, sir. Now, please move immediately or I'll have to call security and have you removed from the premises."

What the hell?

Teresa worked there?

It wasn't that he didn't think she was smart enough. She'd been a straight A student in high school while also juggling a part-time job, running the home because her mom was always working, and looking after her two brothers, one of whom was in trouble with the law more often than he wasn't, and the other who was developmentally delayed.

Stepping back, he watched as Teresa moved past him. If it hadn't been for the fact that she made a very clear effort not to so much as brush against him, he

12

might have bought what she was trying to sell. But she knew him, hadn't forgotten him, he knew it deep down in his soul as he watched her scurry across the quiet lobby and swipe a keycard to access the elevator.

That blast from the past was the last thing he expected tonight, but he couldn't deny the timing was crazy. Here he was watching a friend fall in love and thinking about the past and the girl he'd once thought he would spend his life with, and then she popped up at the same place he was, quite literally walking right into him.

A sign, it had to be. But a sign for what?

That he should remember the lesson she'd taught him as a teenager and steer clear of relationships for the remainder of his life? That the past could be fixed, and that he shouldn't give up on it just yet? Or that there was no right or wrong answer, and what his future looked like was up to him?

CHAPTER 2

TERESA LET OUT a shaky sigh as she sank against the doors of the elevator the second they closed.

Of all the people in the world, she had to run into Micah Hart in the lobby of her workplace.

What the heck was he doing there?

And why did she have to run into him for the first time in twelve years after she'd just been through another trauma?

Granted, this one wasn't nearly as horrific as what had happened to her when she was seventeen, but nonetheless, walking into her home and finding it trashed was definitely violating. After calling her boss, Raven Oswald, head of the Cyber Team and the second-oldest of the six Oswald siblings who owned the company, she'd called the cops. When they arrived, she went up with them to her place, they cleared it, found it was empty, and took her statement.

A crime scene unit was coming to look for finger-prints, DNA, or anything else that might lead them to the perpetrators, but Teresa wasn't holding out any hope that they'd actually find anything. Leaving them to do their thing, she'd called an Uber and come straight into the office. There was no way she was going to risk walking or taking public transportation, not after what had happened to Tobias and Isabella a couple of days ago.

Now she was there, and all she'd wanted was to be surrounded by the people and things that made her feel safe, and get to work doing what she could to identify the people who had invaded her home and destroyed it.

The absolute last thing she needed was to run into that particular blast from the past.

Micah.

There.

At Prey.

Why?

It wasn't because he knew she was there, because if he did, he wouldn't have been shocked to see her. There would be no reason for him to care where she was anyway. After all, he hadn't even cared that she'd been violently gang raped by her brother's friends just so he could sell her body for money to buy drugs. Micah had wiped her out of his life like she'd never existed while she was still in the hospital, attempting to come to terms with what had happened to her.

Nope, no chance he was there for her.

So what was he doing there?

That question was still running through her mind as she reached the Cyber Team floor and headed out of the elevator and down the corridor to their shared office space. Although they all technically had their own offices, they never used them, preferring instead to work together in different corners of the larger space.

At least she'd done her best to convince Micah that she didn't remember him.

Wasn't likely to fool him forever, but so what? She needed to save face at least a little bit, and what better way to do that than pretending like he meant so little to her back then that over a decade later, she no longer knew who he was?

"You okay?"

Caught off-guard by the sudden voice and figure rushing toward her while she was still shaken up by everything that had happened that night, Teresa took a panicked step back.

"Hey, it's okay, it's only me."

Blinking, she saw Ava's worried face come into view. Behind her friend was Ava's boyfriend Nathaniel, also looking at her with concern.

"Uh, sorry, guess I'm a little preoccupied," she murmured, hoping there was no way they could know it wasn't just the break-in that had her on edge.

Of course, they couldn't know.

How could they?

While her friends did know what had happened to her when she was a teenager, she'd never added in the part about how her boyfriend at the time had bailed without a word. Refused to see her, blocked her on all platforms, and moved away, never to return. They assumed her reluctance to date was because of the fact she'd been raped, and while that was definitely part of it, it was more the broken heart that had her locking up her heart to protect it.

There was no way they could know the man downstairs had once meant something to her. Once meant *everything* to her.

"I'm so sorry you had to see that on your own," Ava said.

"I'm not. I'm glad you weren't there, you've already been through so much," she told her friend, snapping out of her Micah-induced stupor to hug Ava. Personally, Teresa was more of a no-touch kind of person, but Ava and Chelsea were like her sisters, and both of them loved hugs, so she was always happy to hand them out when the occasion called for it.

Like right now.

"Still, you shouldn't have been there on your own. What if they'd still been there?" Ava continued, hugging her back, hard.

"Then I would have turned and run, or defended myself," she replied. After her assault, even before she'd come to work with Prey and taken part in mandatory self-defense classes, she'd learned how to use what she had to her advantage. She couldn't grow her five-foot-one frame any taller, and she couldn't out-muscle most men, but she could make the most of what she had.

"Well, I for one am glad you didn't have to defend yourself," Ava said as she pulled back. "Nathaniel had a guy from his team over to hang out, but he left when we got the call from you about what happened. We assumed you'd want to jump right into going through footage from the building and surrounding streets to see if we can find these guys."

So that's what Micah was doing there.

When they were younger, he'd always wanted to follow in his dad's footsteps and become a cop. Somewhere along the way, he must have changed his mind and decided to go into the military instead and become a SEAL.

That was not good news for her.

Not the SEAL part, but the fact that Micah was on the same team as Nathaniel. Ava was falling in love with the man, and that meant he was sticking around. If Nathaniel was sticking around, that meant sometimes his teammates might be around, too, and Micah already knew she was there.

Pretending she didn't know him didn't mean he hadn't immediately realized who she was.

Just because he was a horrible person who had walked away rather than stand by her side as she recovered from her ordeal, didn't mean he was going to walk away now and never come back. Since she was certainly never going to walk away from one of her best friends, they might have to find a way to co-exist.

Although she had no idea how she was supposed to do that.

Already, she was a mess, and she'd just bumped into him and spent sixty seconds or so in his presence.

Hanging out in the same place as him for hours on end would be next to impossible.

No, it *would* be impossible.

"Teresa?"

A gentle touch to her arm had her jumping again, and she realized she'd zoned out, preoccupied with thoughts of a man from her past who had hurt her when she had much bigger things to focus on.

There was a dangerous organ trafficking ring out there that had already killed hundreds of people. They were ruthless and determined, and they weren't afraid to take risks. They knew that Prey was after them and were making attempts at threatening them into backing off.

Only that wasn't going to happen.

What she absolutely needed right now was something else to focus on so she could shove Micah Hart right out of her mind. She'd done it before, and she could do it again. The trafficking ring was the perfect distraction, and it was important work, something that needed to be done, and she had the time and resources to do it.

"Sorry, guess tonight was more of a shock than I realized," she said, which was true enough even if it meant more than Ava realized.

"Of course it was," Nathaniel told her.

"At least you're safe," Ava said, taking her hand and squeezing.

That was true. She hadn't arrived home when whoever had trashed their place had been there, and while seeing Micah was a shock, she'd worked hard to get over him and shred every last feeling she had for him so they no longer existed. He couldn't hurt her anymore because she no longer cared about him. Maybe he'd be back to see Nathaniel, but there was also a chance that now he knew she was there he wouldn't bother, since he obviously found being around her so repulsive.

"Safe and ready to get to work." Teresa brushed past Ava and Nathaniel, heading for their office.

What she needed most right now was to do something practical, the busier she kept her brain the better. That method had been working well for her most of her life, and she prayed it wouldn't fail her now.

Because for the first time in a long time, she felt vulnerable, and she despised that feeling.

* * *

April 29TH
   7:52 A.M.

SLEEP WAS FOR THE WEAK, Micah decided as he glanced up from his laptop, surprised to see light streaming around the edges of the curtain in his hotel room.

Seemed like he'd been up all night.

Forgoing sleep hadn't been his intention when he got to his hotel late the night before, he'd just been too keyed up by running into a woman from his past.

Not *a* woman.

The woman.

Because there were no other significant woman from his past other than Teresa Dash. Which was kind of pathetic, he supposed, given he was thirty-one and the only girl he'd ever had anything serious with was one from when he was a teenager.

But having your heart broken in the way his had been when he was so young had made enough of an impact that he just wasn't interested in trying again.

Better to protect his heart than allow it to get smashed to smithereens all over again.

While their relationship had been serious back then, they'd been young, so there was no way to know how things would have turned out between them. Teresa had still been in high school when he ended things, he'd only been in his second year of college. Maybe as they got older, they would have found they weren't compatible in an adult relationship.

Only ...

It hadn't felt like that would happen.

Young or not, his feelings had been strong back then, and he believed they only would have grown with time.

Of course, they never got the chance to find out.

Now, looking back, with the benefit of age and wisdom, he wondered whether what Teresa had done was just part of experimenting and being a kid. After all, she hadn't been a legal adult at the time, and that time of your life was supposed to be about finding out who you were.

Had he been too harsh, cutting her off without a word?

Ending it was the right thing to do, after all, she'd cheated on him even if she was just experimenting, but he hadn't gone about it in a very mature way. Hadn't even had a confrontation with her.

Embarrassed and devastated, he just got back in his car and drove back to his college. Then he'd blocked her number, blocked her on all social media, and even refused to open the letter she'd sent him about a month later.

He still had that letter. Unopened. Tucked away in the bottom of his underwear drawer back home.

Opening it had never been his intention, and he wasn't sure why he'd kept it, maybe in the hopes that it was the apology he knew she owed him, but now he was wondering whether maybe when he got home, he should pull it out and see what she'd written to him.

It wouldn't change anything, but it would be nice to know she regretted cheating on him.

Or maybe it would change something?

Right now, he wasn't sure.

Everything he'd just read about the girl he used to love with every fiber of his being said she'd turned out to be the woman he knew she would be.

Teresa had taken on a lot of responsibility from the time she was nine years old. Despite not even being in double digits yet, with her father gone and her mother the sole provider for their little family of four, a lot of the responsibilities of caring for the apartment they lived in and her brothers had fallen on her.

Her youngest brother had suffered a stroke shortly after birth and had been left with some permanent disabilities. Caring for him was a big ask, but Teresa had tackled it the same way she approached everything else in life. With compassionate determination. She was a hard worker, organized, and juggled handling school, housework, and her brothers with the skills of someone much older than her tender years.

While her middle brother, two years younger than Teresa, grew angrier with having to help out, his grades slipped, and he started to get in trouble. She worked harder to pick up the slack and show him that he was important, too, just like their little brother was.

Not that it had helped.

By the time he met Teresa when he was sixteen and she was fourteen, her then twelve-year-old brother was progressing up the criminal food chain. Moving on from stealing from local convenience stores to knocking down elderly women and stealing their purses.

In fact, it was because of those crimes that they'd met.

His father was a cop who had arrested Teresa's brother while they were out having a father-son day. Micah had still been with his father when Teresa brought her youngest brother to the police station to find out what was going on and wait for their mom to show up. The beautiful, strong, intelligent girl had immediately caught his eye, and when her mom had finally arrived to take over, he'd struck up a conversation with her.

Despite their ages, it had been love at first sight as far as he was concerned, and that love had only grown over the three years they dated.

Which was why it had come as such a blow when he drove home to surprise her that Friday night and instead found her on the couch in her family's living room, naked, with four other guys.

It was such an un-Teresa-like thing to do.

But maybe the stress of having so much on her plate finally caught up with her, and she just buckled beneath it.

Who could blame her?

She was seventeen years old, a senior in high school, but instead of hanging out with her friends she studied, worked a part-time job, did the majority of the cooking, cleaning, and laundry, cared for her thirteen-year-old disabled brother, and tried to watch over her juvenile delinquent fifteen-year-old brother.

Even adults could crash and burn with that kind of stress on their shoulders.

Had he been too harsh on her?

While he'd tried to ease a little of her burdens, helping out wherever he could, he'd still had school and his own job as well. Maybe he hadn't been a good enough boyfriend, maybe she'd needed more from him than he'd been prepared to give, and that's why she'd done it.

Back then, he'd spent a lot of time analyzing their relationship. Wondering where it had gone wrong. Trying to decide if some of the blame could be placed on his shoulders. But he'd decided that it couldn't. He'd been a kid, too, and while he could have helped out more, he had tried to do his best.

They weren't kids anymore, though. And everything he'd just spent the night reading up about Teresa told him that she was exactly the kind of intelligent, hardworking, compassionate woman he'd always thought she would be.

What if that night was just a one-off? A way for her to blow off steam?

If the girl he'd once known was now the woman he'd always expected, did that change anything?

Teresa had graduated at the top of her class in both high school and at college. She worked for the world's best private security company. She didn't just pay all her own bills but contributed enough that her mom only had to work one part-time job and covered all her disabled brother's expenses.

She was everything he'd always wanted, everything that had slipped through his fingers, and he didn't know how to feel about it.

They couldn't go back, that was for sure. Even if he could give her a second chance, his trust in her had been damaged, possibly beyond repair. Just because she'd been young didn't excuse her cheating on him, she'd known right from wrong, and if she'd needed to blow off steam or he wasn't giving her something she needed, she should have communicated that with him.

But …

Damn.

He didn't know the end to that sentence.

It wasn't like Teresa had been falling all over herself to apologize last night. She'd been cold and dismissive, pretending she didn't even know who he was. If there was going to be any real forgiveness on his part, she needed to own up to her mistakes and sincerely apologize.

After that …

He wasn't sure.

All he knew was that, other than that one night, Teresa had been the perfect girlfriend and now she was the perfect woman. For the moment, it didn't have to mean anything more than that.

Last night, she'd turned up at Prey right as he'd been leaving after Nathaniel and Ava got a call that one of their teammates was in trouble. Teresa worked for Prey as part of the Cyber Team, if her college degree was any indication. That meant she was the teammate in trouble.

Shoving away from the small table, Micah grabbed his keys, cell phone, and headed out the door. Regardless of their past, if Teresa was in danger, he was going to be there.

CHAPTER 3

APRIL 29TH
8:11 A.M.

"ARE YOU SURE?"

"That I'm hungry and want to go out and get something to eat? Absolutely," Teresa told her friend, hating that the idea of her going out upset Ava, but the truth was, she couldn't stay cooped up in the room, surrounded by her teammates for a single second longer.

She needed a break.

Last night had been too much.

The break-in, the trashed apartment, running into Micah Hart, realizing he was part of the same SEAL team as the man one of her best friends was in love with. Having to pretend for hours that the only thing that had her on edge was the fact that the apartment she shared with her two best friends had been broken into.

Without a break she was going to lose her mind.

"We have plenty of food here," Chelsea added. Despite being sick, she'd dragged herself out of bed and come to help as soon as she'd heard what had happened.

Teresa appreciated having her team at her back more than they probably understood.

Growing up, she hadn't had much of a team. Their dad's death left her mom no choice but to work three jobs to cover all the bills and for her youngest brother Arthur's care. She was the oldest, it was on her to step up and be the mom, not that it had ever worked for her other brother, Simon.

From the time he hit ten onward, he just got angrier and angrier. The way he treated Arthur was terrible, to the point where she'd moved Arthur into her room because she was genuinely concerned for his safety. Simon had zero respect for her, didn't listen to any of her rules, didn't do the chores she assigned him, didn't do his homework, and started doing worse and worse in school.

Then he started to get into trouble with the law.

It was a lot for a young girl to handle, and she'd hidden as much of it from their mom as she could because she knew how exhausted she was just trying to keep a roof over their heads and food on the table. With so much on her plate, Teresa hadn't had a lot of time for friends. There were girls she would talk with at school, but she was never able to hang out with them outside school, and there was no time or money for her to do extracurricular activities.

Besides, she'd realized from an early age that as soon as she was old enough, she had to get a job to help ease the burden a little, and she had to work hard so she could get scholarships to college. It was the only way she'd get the education she wanted, so she could get a well-paying job and take care of her mom and Arthur.

Which she'd done.

Which she was doing.

Having these people to do it with, these loyal and amazing people, had her tearing up a little.

Since her no-nonsense reputation said she absolutely was not going to cry in her office surrounded by her team, she quickly shoved away from her desk.

"I know there's food here, but I want to go get something," she told Chelsea.

"We could order food, or you could cook," Tobias suggested. That he had dragged himself out of his apartment to come into work after just getting Isabella back, meant a lot to her. He should definitely be at home resting his back, like Isabella should be resting in bed, but the two of them had come when she called to let them know what had happened and that they needed to be careful.

As much as she would usually jump at the chance to do some cooking, it just reminded her of the fact that almost every single one of her many kitchen appliances had been destroyed by the person who broke into her apartment. That just left her feeling sad and empty, so she shook her head and reached for her bag.

"I know you guys are all just looking out for me, but the truth is, I need a little bit of fresh air and a few minutes to myself." The admission was hard for her to make because she never asked for some time for herself.

As a kid, there wasn't time for her to check out. Chores always needed to be done, and Arthur was like an over-sized toddler who had to be watched constantly so he didn't get into anything dangerous.

But today she was too tired to worry about being selfish. She needed this break if she didn't want to fall apart in front of her friends. And she absolutely did not.

"Okay, but don't go far," Ava said. "It's not safe out there."

"Definitely isn't," Isabella agreed. Even though she wasn't part of the team, she'd come with Tobias and remained sitting at his side while he worked, offering silent support not just to her boyfriend but to all of them. After all, Isabella had every bit as much reason to want the organ trafficking ring shut down as the rest of them since she'd been held captive by them for seven months as they exploited her nursing skills.

"I'll be careful," she promised. "Besides, I was only planning to go across the street to the deli that sells those croissants that I like. What does everyone want? I'll get us all something. Then we can eat some breakfast together, brainstorm our next moves, and get back to work."

Ten minutes later, she stepped out the front door of Prey's main office building with a list of orders on her cell phone.

The fresh air immediately relieved her of a little of the stress she was carrying. There was no going back and putting it in the box. Micah had popped back up in her life and brought with him all those memories she'd long ago buried deep and forgotten about.

Well tried to forget about.

They were always at the back of her mind, of course, but she'd built a good life for herself. One where she was happy, where she excelled, and even had time to enjoy her hobby of cooking. She took care of her family, had money left over after paying all her bills to enjoy herself, had friends and a job she loved, and had everything she needed.

So why was she letting old memories of a long-ago boyfriend ruin that?

There was absolutely enough on her plate right now. Between the organ trafficking ring and all the other intel they still needed to gather for the other Prey teams to do their job, she had more than enough to keep her busy and occupied.

Yet it was Micah on her mind and not the traffickers as she checked both ways before darting across the street to her favorite deli.

His timing couldn't be worse.

She had to keep her focus on the ring, finding who was running it, the mysterious woman in the skirt suit, both Ava and Isabella, and many of the other people they'd rescued, had mentioned. Just because Micah might be a part of her life going forward didn't mean he would be a big part.

He didn't live in the city and Nathaniel didn't live in the city. Chances were, once they had the trafficking ring dismantled, Ava was going to want to move to be closer to Nathaniel. That meant she'd only have to possibly see the man when she flew out to visit with her friend.

That was doable.

Wasn't it?

That was highly debatable because she didn't know how long she could spend around the man who had abandoned her when she so badly needed him, without the lid that boxed up her emotions bursting open.

What happened then?

Of course, she'd done therapy after her assault, and she'd certainly talked about it enough with all the cops and lawyers involved. But she couldn't say that she had actually dealt with any of it. Not if she was being honest anyway.

There were two doors to her favorite little deli. The front one on the street, and a second one off the small alley that ran beside it. Usually, she went to the side door so she could chat for a few moments with the owner. The older couple was lovely, and she'd given them a few ideas when they opened their business several years ago. She hadn't been trying to overstep, but croissants were a favorite of hers, and she had given them her secret tip to making them flakier on top and softer inside. In thanks, they always made her a special order if she felt like something they weren't selling that day.

With her mind occupied by the six-foot-plus mountain of muscle she'd run into last night, she didn't catch the darkening of the alley the second she walked down it. Didn't see the van that had blocked the entrance until she heard the footsteps.

Because of that, she was caught off-guard by the two men running toward her.

Even if they hadn't been wearing masks that covered

their faces, she would have known they were there to hurt her.

Hurt her or abduct her.

She wasn't sure which was on their mind.

At the last second she pivoted, managing to avoid the meaty hand that reached for her.

Barely.

And the move set her slightly off-balance. So when the man lunged for her again, he managed to snag a hold of her hair, which hung loosely around her shoulders after she'd pulled it out of her usual ponytail last night when she got to Prey.

Teresa cried out at the stinging pain in her scalp as the man used his hold to yank her toward him.

Once again, she was pulled off-balance, and she knew if she didn't do something and quick, it was going to be too late.

So she didn't try to catch her balance, instead she allowed her forward momentum to send her bumping into the man. He was much bigger than her, but he hadn't been prepared for that, and he staggered back a step.

It was enough for his hold on her hair to loosen, and she rammed her knee up and into his groin.

Satisfaction rolled through her as the man's face turned bright red, and he groaned and let go of her to nurse his injury.

Served him right.

The other man was right behind him, though, and he glared at her, slamming his fist into the side of her face right as she opened her mouth and screamed, partly cutting off the sound as pain spiraled out from her cheek through the rest of her face.

Dropping low as he reached for her again, she slammed her fist into the first man's groin again, and he howled and doubled over. On her hands and knees, she ignored the stinging pain as debris cut into her palms and quickly crawled away from the two men.

The first had blocked the path of the second, and she pushed to her feet and started running. Someone would have heard her scream, someone in the deli had likely seen the scuffle and already called the cops.

All she had to do was get around the van and back onto the busy street, and she should be safe.

But a hand grabbed her hair before she could make it.

Yanked her back and swung her sideways, into the wall, her head connecting with a sickening thump that had her seeing stars.

She'd done her best to escape, but it hadn't been enough.

* * *

April 29TH
8:36 A.M.

Micah knew the second the van pulled up in front of the alley he'd just seen Teresa turn down, that something was wrong.

The problem was, he was still too far away.

It took mere seconds to commit an abduction if you knew what you were doing. He should know, he and his team had performed plenty of them. Always picking up someone who was either dangerous or someone they thought they could persuade to help them get to someone who was dangerous.

But Teresa was neither of those things.

Sure, she'd made a youthful mistake when she was seventeen, and in doing so broken his heart and permanently damaged his ability to trust the opposite sex, but she was a good person. One who loved hard and worked hard. She was dedicated and cared about the people in her life.

He didn't need to know everything that had been going on with her or Prey to know that she was in trouble, and if he didn't get to her quickly he could lose her.

Dodging around people as he broke into a dead run, he prayed he made it there in time. As he approached, he could hear a muffled scream, and his heart about jumped out of his chest.

Even though he'd stared down hundreds of armed militia, been captured along with his team, been caught up in explosions, and even survived a helicopter crash early in his career, Micah was pretty sure he had never been as terrified as he was in this moment.

As he rounded the van, he saw a man grab Teresa by the hair and swing her into the nearest wall.

Her head bounced off the brick, and he saw red.

There was not a conscious thought in his head as he closed the distance between them, grabbed the man's head between his hands, and twisted in such a way that he snapped the other man's neck.

Then he dropped the body and left it where he lay, so he could advance on the other man. This one was hunched over, clutching his groin, and Micah smiled as he realized that had to be Teresa's doing.

Little spitfire.

Needing to incapacitate the man completely until help came, Micah slammed a fist into the side of his head and watched with great satisfaction as the man's eyes rolled back and he dropped as well. Still alive, so the cops could interview him when he came round.

Now, though, he hurried to Teresa who was leaning propped up against the wall, still on her feet, her wide chocolate brown eyes watching his every move.

"You killed him," she murmured as he approached.

"Rather I'd left him alive?"

She shook her head quickly, then winced, pressing a hand to the side of her head, gently probing the lump on her forehead and the gash on her cheekbone.

"They tried to abduct you," he said, his voice coming out in a harsh growl that made her flinch.

"They did," she agreed. Then abruptly she straightened, swaying slightly. "I have to get back to Prey. Have to search the security cameras to see if I can get an ID. That guy is probably going to be out for a while, and we need to know who they are so we can try to find who sent them."

"Whoa." He caught her elbow as she staggered past him, still swaying on her feet. "I think you should sit down before you fall down."

"No time. They followed through on their threats pretty quickly."

"Their threats?" he growled, wishing he hadn't left last night. He should have stayed and offered to help Nathaniel and Ava with their friend who had the problem. Definitely should have decided to stay once he bumped into Teresa and realized she was the teammate with the problem.

If he had, Teresa sure as hell wouldn't have been out there alone and unprotected, completely vulnerable to an attack.

"I don't have time to explain," she grumbled, trying to pull free of his grasp.

Tightening his hold just enough to keep her in place without hurting her, he met her gaze squarely, doing his best not to focus on the blood and already forming bruises. "Make time."

"Come with me then. You already know Nathaniel, right? You're on his SEAL team, so you already know about the trafficking ring."

"I know about them," he agreed with a sharp nod. "I just don't know why they attacked you in an alley."

"Call the cops, tell them where we'll be, and come with me. Either that or you can stay here and wait for them, but I'm going back to work."

Realizing she wasn't going to back down, Micah muttered a curse under his breath and released his hold on Teresa. Untying the laces of the man he'd knocked unconscious, he used the shoelaces to bind his hands and feet, then dialed 911, quickly explaining who he was, what had happened, and where he and Teresa were going to be.

Then he followed her back across the street to her building.

The way she wobbled slightly had him aching to reach out and scoop her into his arms. But since he was pretty sure that wouldn't be well received, he settled for remaining close, ready to catch her if she fell.

Swiping her keycard as they went into the elevator, they headed up to a different floor than the one he'd been on last night when he visited Nathaniel and Ava in the apartment they were staying in. This floor was quieter, with closed doors lining the corridor when they stepped out of the elevator.

Like she hadn't just been attacked and injured, Teresa walked with purpose and determination toward the only open door. Micah couldn't not be proud of her, she was a warrior, tough enough to compartmentalize what had happened and still be able to focus on what needed to be done.

The room went deathly silent when she stepped through the door, then everybody began to talk at once. Cries of concern and demands for explanations came from all four of the women and two of the men, including Nathaniel, who hurried toward her, their concern evident in their voices and expressions.

While it might have been unnoticeable to the others, he caught Teresa's small step backward, and that look she got in her eyes when she was overwhelmed.

"Quiet," he snapped, surprising everyone into

silence. "She'll explain what happened, just give her a chance."

Shooting him a quick glance of thanks, she nodded to her team. "I came right back to explain, and we've already called the cops. Well, Micah did."

Nice to know she was no longer pretending that they didn't know one another.

"How did you two meet?" Nathaniel asked, his gaze bouncing between them.

"He saved me," she said quickly, clearly not wanting to get into their past, which given what had just happened, he didn't argue against. "Two men got out of a van and tried to grab me."

"Always with the vans," Ava muttered.

"I managed to get away from one of them, but the other grabbed me. He probably would have gotten me into the van if Micah hadn't shown up." Teresa swallowed audibly, and there was no probably about it. If he hadn't arrived when he did, those two men absolutely would have been successful in their abduction attempt.

"I killed one of them, the other is restrained, and cops are on the way," he quickly added.

"Didn't take them long to follow through on their threat," a pretty brunette with gray eyes said.

"What threat?" he asked.

"Last night, someone broke into the apartment Teresa, Ava, and Chelsea share," Raven Oswald replied. While he'd never met the woman before, Raven's brother, former SEAL Eagle, was an absolute legend in special forces circles. "They trashed the place and left a message painted on the wall. It told them to back off. As you know, the ring abducted Ava a couple of months ago, then came back for her a second time. Isabella was also taken by the ring." Raven nodded at a blonde with a wild mop of curls. "They know that Prey is involved in hunting them, and that we've managed to locate several of their facilities. I'm betting they're scared we're getting too close and they thought threats would work."

"As if they would." Teresa scoffed like she hadn't just been almost abducted by ruthless traffickers who would lock her up and remove her organs one by one if they managed to get their hands on her.

"You can't keep looking for them," he blurted out, drawing the attention of every person in the room, including Teresa, who glared at him as though she'd love nothing more than to punch him in the groin the same way she'd done to the man who'd tried to kidnap her.

"Excuse me?" she demanded, her voice all frosty.

"They tried to kidnap you," he said slowly.

"And I'll be more careful in the future, but we're not going to back off," Teresa told him.

"We'll all be more careful," Raven added. "From now on, no one goes anywhere alone. I'm going to assign bodyguards."

"Done," he quickly agreed.

"What do you mean done?" Teresa eyed him suspiciously.

"You need a bodyguard. I'm on leave, I'm already here, and I'm more than qualified. I already know about the trafficking ring, so I'm volunteering for the job."

CHAPTER 4

April 29ᵀᴴ
8:49 A.M.

SHE MUST HAVE HEARD him wrong.

Because there was no way her ex had just volunteered for babysitting duty.

No way in hell.

Why would a man who had deliberately abandoned her because he didn't want to deal with her ordeal now decide he wanted to help out when she was in trouble?

Of course, Teresa assumed he'd grown over the years, she had too. He was a SEAL, so he'd obviously matured. He put his life on the line to protect their country and its people, and make the world a safer place. It wasn't that she thought Micah was a bad guy, but she still harbored a lot of anger and resentment, and it was hard for her to see him as anyone other than the boy who had abandoned her.

Which meant he absolutely would not be playing her bodyguard.

No way, no how.

"I don't think that's a good idea," she said slowly. It wasn't what she wanted to say. What she wanted to say would be, in actual fact, screamed at full volume, and it would be a demand to know how he could have been so cruel and heartless, so incredibly selfish. She'd also demand to know if it had all been a lie, if he'd ever loved her, or if he'd never intended to honor the youthful promises they'd made to one another.

But none of that was a conversation she wanted to have in public.

Actually, none of it was a conversation she'd have at all.

Because as much as she'd love to have some answers to see if they could help smooth over the rough edges her ordeal had left behind, she also knew they would open a Pandora's box of emotion she wasn't ready to handle yet.

"Why not?" Micah asked, arching a brow at her, knowing that she wasn't going to bring up her trauma and call him on it right there. Smug jerk.

It would serve him right for everyone in this room, including one of his teammates, to know just what kind of man he used to be. Maybe still was. She didn't know him, hadn't seen him in over a decade, so she really didn't know if he was a good guy now or not. Being a SEAL didn't automatically exclude someone from being a terrible human being.

"Because Prey hires its own bodyguards, we have

people on staff who are paid to do this kind of thing," she replied.

"No need to pay me. Consider this a favor. For a friend," he added with a little emphasis, and she hoped everyone assumed he was talking about Nathaniel.

He had to be.

They weren't friends anymore, and his abandonment had made her doubt if they ever really had been.

After he bailed on her, she'd spent a lot of time going over every interaction they'd shared in the three years they'd known one another. It beat obsessing over her assault, and it was the only way she could handle Micah disappearing, pretending, convincing herself that none of it had been real. Over time, each memory of him she had became tainted, as she began to believe what she told herself, the sweetness of her moments with Micah becoming sour.

They were still sour, and she had no desire to spend any more time with him.

"Actually, I would love to assign someone to you who is already familiar with what we're up against," Raven told her, a slight apologetic note to her tone like she got that there was more going on than either she or Micah had said out loud.

"But—"

"No buts. It's done. Consider Micah your new bodyguard," Raven said firmly, cutting off her objection. "Nathaniel, I assume you and Ava will be remaining here?" When Nathaniel and Ava both nodded, her boss shifted her attention to the others.

"Isabella and I already talked on the way here, we're

going to move into one of the apartments as well," Tobias said before Raven could even ask.

"I think I'm going to stay too," Chelsea piped up. "I don't think I can go back home. It was hard enough after Ava was kidnapped from there a few months ago, but now with the break-in, it doesn't feel safe anymore."

So she'd just lost both her roommates.

Great.

There was no way she could afford the rent for an apartment like that on her own. Especially not while she was also paying some of her mom's bills and paying for Arthur's care. She got why neither Ava nor Chelsea wanted to be there, and Ava was going to move soon anyway, they all knew it, but Teresa wasn't ready for everything to change.

She *hated* change.

Knowing nothing in life lasted forever didn't make it any easier for her when those inevitable changes came.

Her brother's life-altering stroke.

Her dad's death.

Her rape.

Losing Micah.

It felt like she was losing Ava and Chelsea, even though she knew they would forever be part of her life.

If she was going to be forced to endure Micah's presence in her life for the time being, then there was only one thing left inside her control, and she had no intention of letting it go.

"I'm going back home," she said, aware she sounded stubborn and borderline petulant. But she couldn't stand another change right now, not even one as simple as staying in Prey's building.

"That's not—" Micah started.

"I'm not asking for permission. I'm informing you. Informing everyone. If I have to have a bodyguard, then it doesn't matter if I stay here or go back home. Micah will presumably get caught up on all the details, so he'll know how dangerous these people are and will ensure he doesn't make mistakes. Therefore, I don't see the problem in going home. Besides, it needs to be all cleaned up anyway."

There was a chance Raven could veto the idea, she was the boss, and she'd already pulled rank with Tobias about his injury before, so she silently implored the older woman to understand that this was about her mental health. She literally could not handle another change when Micah's presence was stirring up so many bad thoughts and memories.

"Fine," Raven agreed. "We'll have extra cameras set up in your apartment and in the hallway outside to be safe."

Teresa nodded her assent. "Thank you. Now we should get to work trying to ID the guys who attacked me. The cops are going to be here soon, and I'll have to give statements. Micah will too. But until they arrive, we can bring up the camera footage and see what we can do."

"Nuh-uh," Micah announced.

"What do you mean no?"

"I mean you're bleeding, and you've barely taken a breath since I found you, let alone taken the time to inform us of any other injuries and have them taken care of."

"I'm fine." Brushing off his concern, Teresa went to move around him when his hands darted out to grasp hers. His touch was gentle, and she absolutely loathed the warmth that spread through her body at the contact.

She didn't want to feel anything when it came to this man.

How could her body betray her like this?

After everything he'd done, she should hate him. She *did* hate him. Problem was, a lingering part of her heart still loved him.

"You should go to the hospital," Micah said, the pad of one thumb brushing just under where her cheek was throbbing.

"I don't need to."

"You have two head injuries." His thumb shifted to sweep across her forehead, where she was sure a knot was developing from having her head slammed into a brick wall.

"I don't have a concussion. I'm a little dizzy, but no nausea, and no trouble concentrating, I didn't even pass out," she reminded him.

"You're bleeding." He didn't seem to like that very much, if the expression on his face was anything to go by.

"We have a first aid kit," Tobias said, producing the one he must have retrieved from the bathroom down the hall.

"If you want to go back to work and not take a trip

to the hospital, you need to at least let me clean you up," Micah told her.

Teresa opened her mouth to argue. To inform him that she could do it herself, and even if she couldn't, he was the absolute last person in the world she would let tend to her wounds. Not when the most serious wounds she'd ever had were inflicted by him.

Taking her silence as assent, Micah guided her to a chair and gently pushed her down into it. Then he proceeded to open the kit and with soft, almost tender strokes, cleaned away the blood on her face and placed butterfly bandages over what she was sure was a small wound.

Why was he being so nice to her all of a sudden?

After all, it wasn't like he had thought favorably of her all these years. The first thing he'd done upon seeing her again was assume she wasn't good enough, or smart enough, or whatever the heck it was that made him think she couldn't possibly be in a building belonging to such a prestigious company.

Soft touches aside, Teresa knew that her assault had changed the way Micah looked at her. He obviously saw her as dirty and broken, the same thoughts she had battled over the years. The same thoughts she still battled.

It didn't help to know that the man she'd fallen in love with reinforced her darkest thoughts.

How was she supposed to survive spending time around Micah with her sanity intact?

Teresa was pretty sure she wasn't going to.

* * *

April 29th
6:49 P.M.

To say that Teresa wasn't happy with their current arrangement just might be the biggest understatement in the entire history of the world.

Although she'd allowed him to clean up her wounds, bandage her cut, and give her some painkillers, after that, Teresa had done her best to pretend he wasn't there. While she hadn't been outright rude, she had mostly ignored him while working alongside her team, and he was pretty sure it was because she didn't want to arouse suspicion with her friends that they shared a past.

They'd both given statements to the cops, and they'd ordered in food and eaten together while brainstorming ideas. The kidnapper left alive had turned out to be a mercenary who had taken money to abduct Teresa and deliver her to an as yet unknown person. Pretty much the same thing that had happened with Isabella Baker's abduction. A bounty had been placed on her head, and a mercenary had accepted the job. Now there appeared to be a bounty on Teresa's head, and it was driving him crazy with worry.

Unlike her.

She seemed more annoyed with his presence than afraid for her own safety.

At first, Micah had assumed that the animosity he felt coming from Teresa was a product of her guilt. She knew that she'd done him wrong, but she wasn't at a place yet where she was willing to own up to it, apologize, clear the air, and move forward as adults.

It almost seemed like she believed that *she* had a reason to be angry with *him*.

Which made zero sense.

He was the wronged party here, not her.

She might have only been a seventeen-year-old girl at the time, but she'd made the decision to cheat on him, knowing they were in an exclusive relationship. Maybe he'd handled the aftermath of finding out in a slightly childish way, but he'd only been nineteen. Running, blocking her, then shifting gears and deciding to drop out of college and join the military had seemed like the best plan at the time.

But his bailing without a confrontation certainly didn't warrant this level of hostility from a girl who had spread her legs for a bunch of men all at the same time.

As badly as he wanted to bring it up, Micah was trying to be respectful of the fact that Teresa had bigger things to worry about than a teenage love affair gone wrong.

Which was why he was down on his hands and knees scrubbing paint off the wall of the apartment Teresa shared with her friends rather than confronting her with the past and demanding an explanation.

Beside him, Teresa was desperately trying to wash the red paint off the white carpet. That was a pointless task. The carpet was ruined. It would have to be ripped up and replaced, there was no saving it.

Not that it seemed to matter to Teresa.

She had a bucket of soapy water beside her and scrubbed at the carpet with a towel, trying her best to rid it of the bright, red paint with carpet cleaner that wasn't up to the task.

Because she seemed to be getting increasingly desperate as she scrubbed and the paint didn't come off, he stopped what he was doing, set down his own towel which he'd been using to clean paint off the soft gold walls, and turned to face her.

"I think you've done all you can," he said gently. Even though there was definitely lingering anger on his part, Micah could see that while she might have hurt him deeply, Teresa was still a good person who cared about others and worked hard. She was good at her job, had a great rapport with her team, and they all seemed to respect her, Nathaniel as well, and she'd fought for her life that morning, almost succeeding in saving it.

Almost.

But if he hadn't decided to go back to Prey and talk to her, she would have been abducted.

The thought of her in the hands of such ruthless people, who wouldn't hesitate to cut her open and take her body apart, was sickening.

Just because he'd spent most of the last decade doing his best not to think about the girl who had ripped out his heart and stomped all over it, didn't mean that from time to time, thoughts of her wouldn't sneak back in. Sometimes at the most inappropriate of times, too. But memories were like that, anything could trigger them, and it was only Teresa's betrayal that had tainted most of those memories. If she hadn't, they would be the highlights of his life. Even those that weren't special in and of themselves were special because they were moments shared with such an amazing girl.

An amazing girl who even he could admit had turned into an amazing woman.

Why did you do it, Teresa?

Why did you ruin what we had?

Why wasn't I enough for you?

The questions ran through his mind, but he didn't ask them out loud. Later he would, once the trafficking ring was disbanded, those involved in prison, and the threat hanging over Teresa's head eliminated.

Teresa hadn't stopped scrubbing at the carpet, clearly ignoring him.

Needing to put a stop to her near manic behavior, he reached out and grabbed her hands. Physically stilling them. He got that this was a major violation, and he understood her need to clean it all up and make it like it had never happened. But that wasn't happening.

The couches were ruined, the TV was ruined, the paintings that had hung on the walls were ruined, the carpet was ruined, the beds in the three bedrooms were ruined, most of the clothing was ruined, the kitchen table and chairs were ruined, and the Easter decorations were ruined. Basically, the entire place was trashed beyond repair. The best they could hope for was washing the paint off the walls. Everything else was going to have to be replaced.

"In the morning, why don't we call a professional, see if they can clean it up?" he suggested. Micah wasn't sure even a professional could get the paint out of the carpet, but he was willing to try if it helped Teresa.

"I can do it myself." She huffed, tugging her hands free.

"You can't," he said, gently but firmly. Letting her come back home had been a mistake. She wasn't in the right mental headspace to handle it. But he wasn't the boss of her, and he couldn't outright refuse. She wasn't a prisoner. He would just feel a whole hell of a lot better having her tucked safely away at Prey.

"Can so." Angry fire danced defiantly in the chocolate brown eyes that stared back at him.

There wasn't just defiance there, though.

Unshed tears shimmered in Teresa's eyes.

His heart ached to find a way to make this better for her. In this moment, he didn't care about the past, about the pain she'd caused him, she was hurting, and there was a part of him—a bigger part than he'd admitted to himself—that still loved her.

"We need to take a break. How about we cook some dinner, and then we can try again. Together," he offered, willing her to take the olive branch he was offering and meet it with one of her own.

If they could talk through the past, maybe they stood a chance.

At what he didn't know yet.

All Micah knew was that his feelings for this woman weren't as dead as he'd pretended they were all these years.

"Cook," she echoed softly, the defiance seeping out

of her gaze, replaced with something he didn't like. Something that looked like defeat.

That was not the Teresa he knew. That Teresa had stepped up when her dad died and supported her family every way she knew how, despite her young age. That Teresa had never met a problem she wouldn't attack with logic and reason until she figured it out.

But the Teresa before him looked dangerously broken.

"I know you love cooking, but if you're too tired or in too much pain, then I can make something," he suggested. He was nowhere near as good a cook as Teresa was, but then again, he'd never enjoyed it the same way she had. Cooking for her family was the one chore that she'd actually enjoyed back when he'd known her, and she was always experimenting with something new.

With a desperate shake of her head, she dropped the towel and staggered to her feet, knocking the bucket beside her. It sloshed some water onto the already ruined carpet, but Teresa didn't appear to notice.

"Not hungry," she mumbled. "I'm going to go take a shower and try to get some sleep."

Snatching up the bag of clothes, toiletries, and the air mattress they'd picked up on the way back from Prey, she hurried out of the room, leaving him staring after her, wondering what had just happened.

Obviously, he'd said something that had upset her, he just didn't know how suggesting they eat some dinner had done it.

This Teresa was different from the one he'd known,

he supposed he shouldn't be surprised by that, given the amount of time that had passed since they'd been together. There was a hardness to her that hadn't been there before. She'd always been a bit of a softie, someone people could easily take advantage of because she wanted to help, wanted to ease their burdens, even if that meant adding to her own.

Now she still had that same heart, but it had been cooled somewhat. She was able to find emotional detachment as she worked, he'd seen it today and been struck by the fact that the teenage version of Teresa would never have been able to handle this job.

What had changed her?

And why did he feel so compelled to fix whatever it was and bring back her softness, when he'd already been burned by Teresa before?

Walking away should be easy, yet Micah was finding it impossible.

CHAPTER 5

She was ready to put this mess behind her and move on.

While there was no way to pretend that her home hadn't been trashed beyond repair, Teresa was ready to accept that this wasn't something she could just fix.

The future was uncertain.

Change was coming whether she liked it or not.

Ava was going to wind up moving across the country to be with Nathaniel, and Chelsea didn't want to come back to the apartment after all that had happened. So she was going to have to get on board with the idea of cleaning the place up, finishing up their lease, and then finding a new place to live. Maybe with Chelsea, maybe without.

She'd love to keep living with her friend, but watching Ava meet Nathaniel and fall in love, and then Tobias meet Isabella and fall in love, she had to also accept the possibility that Chelsea could be the next to fall.

Perhaps it was time for her to move to a place of her own.

As a child, in the darkest of times, when she felt completely overwhelmed by everything she had to handle and take care of, she'd wish that she didn't have a single responsibility in the whole world save for taking care of herself. She'd live alone, only have to cook and clean for herself, no one else's bills to pay, and no one counting on her or relying on her.

Despite her desire for freedom, she also knew that she didn't do well on her own.

She'd tried it when she first went to college, and the sound of the empty house, or rather the lack of sounds, had bothered her way more than she thought it would. She thought she would have loved being on her own, but she didn't. She craved company and companionship.

But she wasn't that eighteen-year-old traumatized girl anymore. She was almost thirty, and maybe it was time she faced that fear head-on. Sooner or later, Chelsea would meet someone and fall in love, or she'd finally convince the grumpy loner of their team, Josiah, to finally see her and give her a chance.

When that happened, it would just be her.

"Time to get used to that idea," she muttered as she gave herself a final scrutinizing once-over in the bath-room mirror and then stepped out into the hall.

Since she'd skipped dinner last night, Micah's inno-cent words about cooking the final nail in her coffin as she remembered all her specially chosen kitchen appliances were all destroyed had sent her spiraling, her stomach grumbled a little. Needing to be alone, she'd taken a steaming hot shower where she'd cried out all her emotions, then completely wrung out, collapsed onto the air mattress. Exhausted as she was, she hadn't even cared that it wasn't very comfortable, she'd slept right through until her alarm woke her up.

Now it was time to start her day, and she was ready to shut down any last lingering feelings for Micah and stop allowing his presence in her life to throw her off her game.

"Only temporary," she reminded herself as she walked into the living room.

"Did you say something?" Micah called out, sticking his head out of the kitchen doorway.

With his hair all messed up from sleep, and wearing nothing but a pair of gray sweatpants hanging low on his hips, he looked better than she remembered. Back then, he'd been little more than a boy, but now he was a man. A man who spent a lot of time working out and had the body to show for it.

Too bad the inside of the package didn't look as good as the outside.

If it did, they never would have broken up.

"No, I didn't say anything. I'm ready to go," she announced. She certainly was not going to inform this man that she'd been giving herself a pep talk on how to survive his intrusion in her life. Knowing Micah, he'd probably find some way to use it against her.

"It's only six thirty, Raven said not to be in before nine."

"I have a stop to make on the way."

"A stop? I don't think that's a good idea, Teresa. The trafficking ring has put a bounty on your head, you should be staying out of sight as much as possible, giving them as few opportunities to get to you. I'd bet anything that they're tailing you, or at the very least watching your apartment. If we go anywhere other than right to Prey, we give them the opening they're waiting for."

That was all true, yet she was still going.

"This stop is non-negotiable, and it won't take long."

"It's more important than your safety?"

"Yes," she replied without hesitation. Already, she didn't make as much time for this as she should, but once a week, she went to her mom's house to check in with her and Arthur. Sometimes they'd have breakfast together, sometimes they'd go for a walk, sometimes they'd just say hi and have a quick catch-up. Today would be a quick catch-up, but she wasn't missing out on it. Not for anything, and certainly not to cower to some trafficking ring that thought they could threaten her into letting them continue committing crimes.

With a sigh, Micah leaned against the door jamb. "Where is this life-risking place you have to go at this hour of the morning?"

"My mom's," she answered simply.

Another sigh fell from his lips, but he didn't offer another protest, just disappeared into the kitchen and a minute later reappeared with something wrapped in parchment paper.

"Breakfast," he said as handed it to her. "French toast sandwich. I found some fruit in the fridge, they didn't touch that, so I put in some strawberries, blueberries, and raspberries. I know French toast used to be your favorite. Give me ten minutes to shower and get dressed then we'll head to your mom's."

Teresa watched as he grabbed his bag and headed for the bathroom. She was pretty sure her mouth was hanging open in shock.

He'd remembered that?

French toast was her favorite. Arthur's too. Not Simon's, though. Her brother would always complain when she made it, which would make her feel guilty about doing something she enjoyed, just for herself, even if it was kind of for Arthur, too. So she'd make sure to cook pancakes as often as she did French toast, even if she didn't really care for pancakes.

When Micah found out she loved French toast, he would make it for her all the time. Often, he'd bring a French toast sandwich for her to school, usually with fruit, although occasionally he'd put bacon or eggs. But he knew fruit was her favorite.

And he'd remembered that.

Remembered it and made it for her.

What did that mean?

Why was he being so nice to her?

It wasn't like she'd been welcoming in any way to him yesterday. His presence was like nails on a chalkboard, and she already had too much to deal with. She was trying not to be outright rude to him, but she was also not going out of her way to be polite, much less friendly.

Yet he'd worked side by side with her yesterday, trying to clean up the mess the intruders had left behind. And then this morning he made her breakfast.

Was this his way of trying to apologize?

Honestly, she'd rather he just came right out and told her he was sorry for bailing, but it had been too much for his nineteen-year-old self to handle.

That might make a difference.

Would it?

If he apologized, would it make things better?

Going back to the way they'd been before was impossible. How was she supposed to ever trust him to be there for her in the future when he'd left her in the past while she was at her most vulnerable?

The simple answer was that she couldn't.

But that didn't mean she had to hold onto the anger and resentment. Maybe if he apologized for leaving, she would be able to lay to rest some of the past. That might even help her move forward. Possibly even allow her to try dating again, put herself out there, and try to believe that not everybody was like Micah. Most people supported those they claimed to love when those people were hurting and needed help.

As much as she didn't want to initiate that talk, it was embarrassing to have to bring up what he'd done, and it made her feel weak and pathetic to have to explain how much it had hurt, maybe it was something she needed to do.

For so long she'd run from the past, done everything

she could to avoid thinking about it or dealing with it. But that hadn't helped. Not really. She was still deeply affected by her rape and Micah's abandonment, and it was getting in the way of her living.

Ava was moving forward, sooner or later Chelsea would too.

Did she want to be left behind?

Did she want to spend the rest of her life being tied to the worst thing to ever happen to her while everybody else found happiness?

Of course, the answer to that was simple.

She didn't.

Maybe Micah's unexpected arrival in her life was exactly what she needed to finally cut the ties of the past and be free to move on.

* * *

April 30th

7:18 A.M.

"Maybe you should wait in the car," Teresa suggested when he pulled up outside her mom's place thirty minutes later.

That caught him by surprise.

Micah had had a good relationship with both her mom and her brother Arthur. In fact, Arthur had looked up to him almost like he was a big brother, and he'd enjoyed that role. Back then, Arthur had been ten, but his mental age had been closer to three. He wasn't sure if that had changed over the years, but he knew the now twenty-five-year-old man would still be as sweet as he'd been all those years ago.

Was that why Teresa didn't want him to see her family?

Had she lied to them about why they'd broken up? Was she worried that if he was there and saw them, spoke with them, that her lies would unravel?

While he hadn't offered to be her bodyguard to cause her trouble, he wasn't going to make this particular accommodation. He'd been looking forward to catching up with Arthur and Mrs. Dash, and he intended to do that.

"Nope, I'm good to come in," he told her, making it clear that he wasn't going to back down. While he'd had a good relationship with both his parents growing up and still did, Mrs. Dash had been like a second mom to him for those three years he'd dated Teresa, and Arthur was like the sibling he'd wanted when he was a kid.

It was clear that Teresa didn't like that idea, and was shocked by his decision by the way her mouth dropped open and anger sparked in her wide, chocolate brown eyes. "Wow. That's … I don't even know what to call that. They know."

"Okay," he said slowly. If she'd already told her mom, and possibly Arthur, although he doubted she would have talked about having an orgy with her mentally disabled little brother, then why did she care if he came in? Embarrassment?

That couldn't be right, because she looked furious, not mortified.

No matter how hard Micah tried, he couldn't understand where her anger was coming from. She'd cheated on him, she had no right to be angry. Yet she was. More than angry, it was like she hated him.

Which was hardly fair.

So he could have handled things better back then, confronted her and ended things rather than ghosting her, blocking her, and then dropping out of college and joining the military. But he'd been young and devastated. His handling of her betrayal was no reason for her to hold this much hostility toward him. Certainly not over a decade later.

After all, he was the wronged party, and he was willing to lay the past to rest and look to the future instead.

Wait.

Was he?

The thought had come out of nowhere, but the more he pondered it, the more he realized it was true. Teresa had hurt him deeply, but he couldn't deny that those feelings from when he was a teenager still existed. He just wasn't sure what to do with them. If nothing else, he'd like to maybe be friends with Teresa again. With Nathaniel and Ava being together, it was inevitable that occasionally their paths were going to cross. May as well make that as pleasant for everybody, themselves included, as possible.

"I don't mind them seeing me," he added, hoping that reassured her that, from his end, things could be okay again, if she was willing. They would talk later, sort out everything, but for now he wanted to keep his focus on the job he'd signed up for. Protecting her from any threats.

"Umm, all right then?" It came out sounding like a question instead of a statement, and confusion swirled in the chocolatey depths of her eyes.

There was something else there, too.

Something that almost looked like ... hope?

Did she regret what she did back then? Wish she hadn't ruined what they had? Was she really angry at herself and not at him at all?

They both climbed out of his rental, and Micah quickly rounded it to stick close to Teresa's side in case there was a problem. Not that he expected one. There had been a tail when they left her place this morning, but he'd easily lost it. They'd argued on the way there about her moving into Prey, but she'd been adamant that she didn't want to. When they got there, he'd circled the block twice to make sure no one was watching the building, and only once he was confident there wasn't, he parked.

Still better safe than sorry.

"What's your mom doing these days?" he asked, partly to make small talk and partly because he just liked the sound of Teresa's voice. He'd missed it a whole lot more than he would let himself accept.

He had no idea what it was about this woman who still had the ability to tie him up in knots, but he regretted more and more that he hadn't confronted her back then and talked things through. Who knew, maybe there would have been hope for them, even though it had been impossible to see that back then.

"Mostly, she takes care of Arthur full-time. Takes him to his appointments, and his job."

"What does he do?"

"Helps out at a local thrift store run by a charity. Mostly just putting clothes that people donated onto hangers so they can be set up in the store, but he loves it. He's so social, and he's really popular there, lots of the customers make time to chat with him. It's nice, makes him feel special, and he deserves that."

"He does," Micah agreed.

"Mom was able to quit two of her jobs when I started working at Prey. She stuck with teaching singing lessons because that was always her passion. But it's nice, now she doesn't have to work as hard, and she can focus more of her time on Arthur, who is thriving."

It *was* nice that her mom didn't have to work as hard, but Teresa was working hard.

Still supporting her family, only in a different way now. Contributing to her own living expenses, which even split three ways would be a fair bite of her salary, she was then taking care of her mom and brother as well. Did that leave enough for her to take proper care of herself? Treat herself?

He could guess it didn't, and that she hadn't thought twice about her decision to keep looking after her family.

That was who she was. Kind, thoughtful, responsible, hardworking, and selfless.

Which made catching her cheating such a shocking blow. He had quite literally never seen it coming. Of all the people in the world who might cheat on a partner, Teresa Dash had seemed like the least likely.

"It's amazing that you still take care of them."

"They're my family and I love them," she said simply.

"How is Simon doing these days?"

They were almost at the front door of the building, but Teresa froze, the color drained from her face, and pure terror danced across her features.

For a second, Micah thought she'd seen something, and his hand reached for his weapon as he scanned the area in search of whatever had scared Teresa. When he found nothing out of the ordinary, nothing he would consider a threat, he returned his gaze to her to find that fine tremors were wracking her body.

She swallowed audibly. "He's out of prison, still on drugs, though," she whispered.

Something in her voice had the hairs on the back of his neck standing up. He hadn't kept up with anything that she or her family had done over the last decade, and his focus the other night was finding out about Teresa, not her family. Within a week of catching her cheating on him, he'd quit college and enlisted, shipped out to basic training, so he had no idea what the fallout from his disappearance had been.

Had things with Simon spiraled over the intervening years?

Honestly, he wouldn't be surprised if they had. Simon Dash had already been on a path to ruining not just his own life but others as well. By the time he was in his early teens, he'd already progressed from petty theft to assault, and he was sure those crimes had continued to escalate, especially since Teresa said he hadn't gotten clean.

"I'm sorry," he said, not exactly sure what he was apologizing for, but he hated that her brother's criminal activity had obviously taken such a toll on Teresa.

"We don't talk about him," she said, her voice earnest now, her eyes pleading with him to understand, only he got the feeling he didn't really understand any of what she was trying to convey. "Please don't bring him up in front of my mom or Arthur. Arthur, he … he doesn't fully understand, but he gets enough to be upset. And my mom. What Simon did broke something inside her. So please, don't mention him when we're with them. Not at all."

"Okay," he quickly assured her, wanting to calm her growing panic. "I won't say anything," he promised.

But he couldn't promise that he wouldn't look more into Simon Dash as soon as he had the opportunity to, because the level of fear and desperation Teresa had just demonstrated was more than excessive. Something was going on that she hadn't told him, and he wanted to know what it was.

CHAPTER 6

"Sooooo." Chelsea drew the word out, and when Teresa turned to look at her friend, she saw that Chelsea's big gray eyes were wide, and she was watching her expectantly.

"So, what?" Teresa asked, returning her attention to her computer screen.

This morning had been weird, having Micah be so insistent on coming to see her mom and brother, even after abandoning her, had thrown her off-guard. Had he wanted to see them because he felt bad about what he'd done and was figuring out how to apologize to her?

There hadn't been an apology yet, but that didn't mean one wasn't coming.

And she couldn't think of another reason why he would want to come and spend a bit of time with her mom and Arthur after she'd let him know that they knew he'd bailed on her after her assault.

At least he hadn't brought up Simon.

After Simon set her up to get gang raped, not just set her up, but actively pimped her out, her mom had basically had a breakdown. Knowing that one of her children, one of her little baby boys, had done something so horrific to one of her other children had left permanent scars on her soul.

They didn't talk about Simon.

Ever.

For any reason.

Even Arthur knew enough to understand that his big brother had done something bad, although he didn't have the capacity to grasp just how evil a thing Simon had done.

Her brother had served six years for his crimes, and although she had a permanent restraining order against him, he had turned up at her door a few times asking for money to feed his habit. She never gave him any, and she called the cops, but in the end, the system didn't seem to really care because he never spent much time in prison for violating the order. He had been in and out a couple more times over the years, and she was sure at some point he'd do something that would wind up getting him a life sentence.

If Micah hadn't listened to her plea this morning and mentioned Simon, it would have upset the delicate balance her family precariously maintained. While it pained her to be grateful to him for anything, she was thankful he hadn't been a jerk and done it to spite her.

Actually, he hadn't been a jerk at all these last couple of days.

He'd been the Micah she'd known back when they were teens.

Why couldn't he have stayed that way? Why did he have to change? Why did he have to ruin everything?

If he hadn't bailed on her, they'd likely be married by now, have a couple of kids, and have built a wonderful life together. Instead, she was alone and too afraid of getting hurt the same way he'd hurt her to try her hand at love a second time.

"We're not going to talk about it then?" Chelsea asked.

"Talk about what?"

"Hmm, I don't know. Maybe the super sexy SEAL who seems to have the hots for you and is currently playing your bodyguard."

When she threw a quick glance Chelsea's way, she saw her friend was wiggling her eyebrows and grinning despite the fact that she still looked pale, her nose was all red, and she sounded stuffed up with her cold.

"He doesn't … he's not …" Teresa stammered, feeling her cheeks heat in embarrassment as she tried to explain it wasn't like that. She still hadn't told her friends that she knew Micah, there hadn't been time, and she didn't want to dig into old wounds, reopening them.

Besides, she'd been hoping everyone would just assume the reason she was a little off was because of the break-in and almost being kidnapped. That was certainly enough to throw anyone off, even someone like her who had a reputation for being calm under pressure, and practical in her approach to everything, including the dark and often disturbing work they did.

It wasn't that the things they saw didn't affect her, they did, deeply. It was just that she had learned early on how to compartmentalize and just do what needed to be done. That's what she did every day, and when it got to be too much, then she had a good, long cry in the shower where no one would hear her.

"Lunch just arrived. Why don't we take a break and eat?" Ava suggested, popping up beside Chelsea.

"I'm right in the middle of something, I'll take a break in a bit," she said, refocusing on her screen. She wasn't really in the middle of anything that couldn't wait, but she didn't want to give Chelsea a chance to pursue her line of questioning.

"You'll take a break now," Micah informed her, appearing seemingly out of nowhere even though she knew he'd been in the room all along.

She'd just been doing her best to ignore his presence.

Something that was becoming increasingly harder to do.

The way he ordered her, swooped in, and tried to take over irked her, and she tossed him a glare. "I said I'd take a break later," she ground out, doing her best not to let on how deeply this man affected her and knowing she was failing, which only irritated her more.

"But you won't. You'll just keep working, pushing yourself too hard, and completely forgetting that you were injured yesterday."

"Boy, does he have your number," Chelsea whispered.

"Take a break. Eat some lunch, drink plenty of water, and then take these." Micah set two white pills on the table beside her, then added a bottle of water and a sandwich.

While she knew she could refuse, Teresa also knew that if she put up too much of a fight, she'd only draw more suspicion. Already, Chelsea was hinting at there being something between her and Micah, and Ava wouldn't be far behind. If she wanted to nip that in the bud, she couldn't go overboard.

"Fine," she huffed, closing her laptop. "I'll take a short break."

"Good. You're a hard worker, and that's amazing, but taking care of yourself is also important," Micah said, and the warmth and genuineness of it made it hard to stay mad at him.

Her focus as a teen had always been taking care of her mom and brothers, making sure the housework was done, Arthur was entertained, and there was food on the table. But ever since they met, Micah's focus had been on taking care of her.

It had been sweet back then, but now it was … she wasn't even sure.

Unsettling.

Truth was, she'd spent a whole lot more years hating him than she had loving him, and that was hard to undo, even if she wanted to. Which she didn't. Definitely didn't. Although that smile did do things to her. Things she didn't want to admit, even to herself.

"He's so sexy and protective," Chelsea whispered as

Micah disappeared out the door, leaving Teresa thankful for the respite.

Not that it seemed she'd be getting much of one. Chelsea seemed determined to see things between her and Micah that just didn't exist. Probably the one way to shut it down was to tell them the truth, or at least some of it.

"Nathaniel likes him, says he's a good guy. Has a bit of a reputation for sleeping around, but nothing excessive, and he's never had a serious relationship in the time Nathaniel has known him," Ava told her.

The thought of Micah with other women, even though he hadn't been hers in a very long time, had a knot forming in her stomach.

These two weren't going to let up until they knew, which left her with no other choice.

"Look, there's nothing between us and there's not going to be," she told them, keeping her voice low, glad that Tobias had disappeared somewhere to have lunch alone with Isabella, and Josiah was off in his own world in the corner, fingers flying furiously across his keyboard. "I already knew him. Before this. Back when we were teenagers. We dated but it didn't work out. I hadn't seen him until the night of the break-in. I bumped into him downstairs, he was leaving as I was arriving. I can assure you that absolutely nothing is going to happen between us, so you two can take your romantic little ideas and place them elsewhere. Like on Ava and Nathaniel, and Tobias and Isabella."

Those were couples in love, she and Micah just shared an unpleasant past.

Well, not all of it had been unpleasant. Most of it had been wonderful. Perfect. But that ending had ruined everything.

Both her friends stared at her with their mouths hanging open. They obviously hadn't been expecting to hear that.

"Are you sure Micah feels the same way? Because the way he looks at you …" Chelsea trailed off.

Knowing her friend meant well, and that Chelsea was a sweet romantic who saw the best in everyone and everything, she didn't get frustrated, she just nodded. "Positive. Let's just say that things didn't end well between us. His popping up again is just the universe's way to make sure I have plenty on my plate." Same way it always did.

"Or," Ava said gently, "it's the universe's way of righting past wrongs, and offering you both a chance to make the future whatever you want it to be."

* * *

April 30<small>TH</small>
12:34 P.M.

"So," Micah started hesitantly as he led Nathaniel into a quiet room and set their lunch on the table.

This was an awkward conversation, but he wasn't going to back down from it.

They'd known each other for years, serving on the same team for over four years now. Nathaniel was every bit as much a brother as if they'd been born to the same parents. They'd spent countless hours together, both in the field and at home, but they'd never had a conversation like this before.

Still, this was a conversation that needed to be had. Just because Nathaniel hadn't known Teresa for long didn't mean he didn't know more about her than Micah himself did. He'd known Teresa the girl, not Teresa the woman. But it was that version of Teresa that his friend had met, and while he was definitely feeling awkward about this conversation, he was going to have it anyway.

Because pretending he could keep his distance from Teresa was like pretending he could grow wings and fly. There was zero percent chance of either one of them happening.

May as well admit that and at least feel things out to see if a friendship between him and his ex could be a possibility. If it could, then maybe over time trust could be rebuilt, and if Teresa was willing to own up to her actions back then maybe they could start over.

A fresh start.

Micah liked the sound of that way more than he should, considering he'd only reconnected with Teresa a couple of days ago.

"So, what? And why are you staring at me like that?" Nathaniel asked as he pulled out a chair from the table and took a seat.

There hadn't been time yet to talk to his friend, so nobody knew that he and Teresa shared a past. Maybe there had been some guesses about it, because Teresa had been pretty adamant that she did not need a babysitter, but they could also have assumed that was because she was wildly independent.

Explaining their past without painting Teresa as the bad guy might take a little bit of work, but the last thing Micah wanted to do was tarnish her relationships with her friends over something she'd done as a stupid seventeen-year-old kid.

Taking a seat opposite his friend, he unwrapped his sandwich and took a deep breath. Talking about Teresa definitely made him feel like a teenager again. His confidence wavered, and he was forced to admit the deep wounds she'd left him with.

"Teresa," he said, like that explained everything.

A wide smile brightened Nathaniel's face. "You like her. I thought I sensed something there, the way you watched her the other day. I'm not the only one who picked up on it either. Ava is determined to try to play matchmaker. She thinks it would be really cool if one of her best friends started dating one of my friends. If she can get you and Teresa together, I think I can expect every single guy on the team invited out here for auditions to see if they match with Chelsea."

"It's a little more complicated than someone just playing matchmaker."

"Why? You guys not hit it off last night?"

"It's not that," he said, although they hadn't hit it off last night, not that he'd expected them to. He had expected more hostility from himself and less from Teresa. After all, he'd done nothing wrong, and she'd ruined everything they shared. "We have a past."

At his revelation, Nathaniel almost choked on the

mouthful he was chewing. Coughing and spluttering, he opened his bottle of water, swallowed a few mouthfuls, and then stared at Micah like he'd just announced he was the king of the world.

"You and Teresa know each other?"

"We do."

"When did you meet? How did you meet? Why did neither of you say anything?"

"We met when I was sixteen and she was fourteen. My dad arrested her brother."

"Simon," Nathaniel muttered like he was aware of Teresa's criminal brother. "Ava said he's bad news. Also said he occasionally pops up to try to demand money from Teresa. Apparently, it always freaks her out, although she tries to hide it. According to Ava, anyway."

"Started getting into trouble before he hit his teens," Micah explained. "Always thought he was going to drag his family down with him one day. I'm glad he didn't. Teresa is doing well for herself, and she's taking good care of her mom and Arthur."

"Haven't met the kid, but Ava said Arthur is the sweetest."

"He is. There's something so innocent and charming about him. I know he was a lot of work for Teresa back when they were kids, with her mom working so much she did most of the caring for him when he wasn't at school, but she did good."

"She did great," Nathaniel agreed. Studying him in such a way that Micah wanted to squirm, he wasn't surprised by the question his friend asked next. "You and Teresa dated?"

"We did. For three years."

"Who ended it?"

That was a difficult question to answer. He supposed technically he had ended the relationship, but he'd only done so because Teresa had cheated on him. So he supposed in reality she'd been the one to end things through her actions.

"That's complicated. We were young, and stuff happened, and neither of us handled things like we should have." Micah felt that was fair. The majority of the blame lay on Teresa's shoulders. If she'd been having doubts about them, needed something he hadn't been providing, or wanted to let loose and be free, then she should have come to him and talked it through. But a little bit of blame rested with him for not confronting her before bailing.

"Fair enough. Relationships are hard enough as an adult, let alone when you're just a kid," Nathaniel said, and Micah knew his friend was thinking about how he'd kept messing up with Ava by allowing his past to get in the way of his future.

"I was wondering if you could tell me a bit more about what Teresa is like now."

The smile was back on Nathaniel's face. "You want a second chance with her?"

"Maybe. I'm not sure. It wouldn't be easy with her working here and us on the other side of the country."

"Ava and I are going to find a way to make it work."

"Don't doubt it for a second." But that was different. Nathaniel and Ava were falling in love. Teresa didn't seem to want to have anything to do with him.

"I haven't spent a huge amount of time around Teresa. I barely have enough time to spend with Ava with being back on the team, and everything going on here with the trafficking ring, but from what I can see and what Ava has told me, she's a great woman. Loyal and protective, she definitely made it clear she wouldn't stand for me hurting her best friend. She's smart, practical, logical, and no-nonsense. She's probably the best on the team at maintaining emotional distance."

Everything else he'd already known, but the last part shocked him. He'd already thought that young Teresa could never handle a job like this, so he'd known she'd changed somehow over the years, but no way would he have thought she was the best at compartmentalizing.

"Better than Josiah Fleet?" he asked, positive that couldn't be true. He knew what the former SEAL had been through and the psychological toll it had taken.

"Josiah just channels everything as anger from what I hear and what I've seen. But Teresa is able to take a mental step back and not allow her personal feelings to get in the way. It makes her an amazing analyst."

That might be true, but Micah was stuck on what had made her change. How had she gone from having such a big heart that she hurt for others, took on way too much responsibility, and allowed herself, but never Arthur, to be bullied by Simon just so as not to cause her mom extra stress, to a woman who could take an emotional step back?

So much had changed over the last decade, and he wasn't sure what that meant for him and Teresa going forward.

Chances were, he was kidding himself that there was anything for them going forward.

After all, she didn't seem to like him much anymore.

"Has she …? Does she …? What's her dating life like?" He forced himself to shove aside his embarrassment and come right out and ask the question he was dying to know.

"Pretty much opposite from you as far as I know," Nathaniel replied.

"Hey, I don't sleep around that much," he protested. He had sex when he felt like it, and okay, he was a young, healthy man with an equally healthy sex drive, but it wasn't like he had a different woman in his bed every night of the week.

"More than Teresa does. From what I've gathered from Ava, Teresa hasn't been in a relationship in all the years they've known one another. Doesn't bring guys back to the apartment and rarely sleeps over at a guy's place. That's part of the reason she's so into the idea of you and Teresa, she thinks her friend needs someone to help balance her out. To make sure she doesn't overload herself with too much on her plate."

Now that sounded like the Teresa he knew. He'd always worried that she would forget about herself because she was so busy taking care of everyone else.

Micah liked knowing there hadn't been many men in her life, but he was having trouble correlating that with the cause of their breakup. Had things changed for her when she realized her choices had cost her him?

He was so confused about the whole thing, but most of all, he worried he was no longer what Teresa needed to balance out her life. He should have contacted her before now, or at the very least read the letter she sent so he could better understand what had happened back then.

Because it felt like he was missing a whole lot of pieces.

CHAPTER 7

April 30th
    6:46 P.M.

"You ready to leave?"

Teresa tensed at Micah's question, wishing she had something that could delay their departure, an excuse as to why they had to stay a little longer, so she didn't have to face being alone with him again.

But there was nothing she could think of, and if she said no just to say no, then she'd be the one who looked like the silly, petulant child. If she let herself look like the crazy one and Micah the sensible, calm, rational one, then she would let on that she didn't just have a past with Micah but that it was a dark and painful one.

While she'd told Ava and Chelsea about her history with Micah, and they already knew about what her brother had organized to happen to her, and they knew that the two of them broke up after her assault, she

82

hadn't told them that Micah just straight-up abandoned her. It felt wrong to cover for the man who had let her down so badly, but Micah worked with Nathaniel, their lives depended on trusting one another, and she didn't want Ava to hate Micah, cause trouble between her boyfriend and his friend, and someone get hurt because of it.

Ava deserved happiness, and so did Nathaniel. Micah ... well, he didn't deserve to die because he hadn't been able to handle supporting her through trauma when he was only nineteen.

If she didn't want the truth to come out, she had to watch how she acted around him.

To that end, she gave a nod, shut down her computers, and pushed back her chair.

Pain pounded between her temples, but she wasn't sure if it was because of the blows to her head she'd taken the day before, or because of all the stress she was under. Having Micah there really was the absolute last thing she needed. The fact that he was pretending to be interested in taking care of her when she knew that absolutely wasn't the case only made it worse.

Maybe she should just agree to stay at Prey. Then there would be no need for a babysitter, and Micah could fly back home and get out of her hair. Perhaps then she could finally relax and begin to process all that had happened.

But she didn't mention anything about staying there.

Just moved away from her desk and pushed her chair back in, scanning the space beside the keyboard and screens to make sure she hadn't left anything behind.

"Here, you should take these. I don't think you took anything since lunch, and I can see you're hurting," Micah told her, holding out his hand with two small white pills nestled in his palm.

Why was he being so insistent on looking out for her? Helping her clean up last night, making her breakfast this morning, ensuring she kept hydrated and fed throughout the day, and offering her painkillers when she would have just powered through without them. It all felt like it meant something, but she had no idea what that could possibly be.

She did know she didn't want it to mean anything, though.

What she wanted was for him to get out of her life again as quickly as he'd entered it. Only, when her fingertips brushed across Micah's warm skin as she took the pills, and she caught sight of the almost tender expression on his face as she popped them in her mouth and took the bottle of water he offered, she found herself feeling almost … bereft at the idea of him being gone again.

Which was crazy since she didn't even like Micah Hart anymore.

Still, she watched him with more interest than she should have as he scooped up her bag before she could pick it up and started across the room.

Josiah was the only one still in it. Tobias and Isabella had already left for the night and so had Ava and Nathaniel. Chelsea had made it halfway through the afternoon before she was coughing and sneezing and obviously feeling like garbage, so they'd all ganged up on her and sent her off to bed.

Neither she nor Micah spoke as they walked down the hall, got into the elevator, and traveled all the way down to the underground parking garage. She had no idea what she should say to him, she wanted to beg for an explanation that made sense as to why he had abandoned her, but this didn't feel like the time or place to have that conversation.

It wouldn't go well because there *was* no explanation that would make sense as to why he would tell her he loved her and wanted to spend the rest of his life with her, and then bail when she was at her most vulnerable.

So she said nothing and had no idea why he seemed content with the silence as well.

At his rental car, he opened the door for her, and she had to force herself not to snap that she could do it herself. It was just a door, and she was pretty sure he would open it for anyone he was protecting and that it had nothing to do with their shared past.

He placed her bag on her lap, and as he pulled his hands away, they brushed against her. Even through the layers of clothes, the brief touch seemed to sear her skin, branding it in a way she hated.

How could her body still respond to him when her heart and brain knew better?

Traitorous thing.

It was like Micah felt it, too, at least that's what his expression said as he nodded at her seatbelt. "Don't forget to buckle in."

"I never forget to put my seatbelt on," she snapped, the moment broken. "Why would I?"

While he didn't give a response, he smiled at her as he closed her door and rounded the car. She could tell from the way his head turned that his gaze was roaming the garage, looking for anything out of place, even though it would be next to impossible to break into Prey.

Still, it brought her back to reality, and Teresa once again reminded herself that there were more serious matters to think about than her hurt feelings from twelve years ago. So she checked her annoyance with Micah and boxed it away. Before he left, she'd confront him about the past, but for now, she needed to stay sharp, aware of her surroundings, and not be a hindrance to Micah protecting her.

The last thing she wanted was to wind up a victim of the trafficking ring.

Especially if it was because she'd been prioritizing her hurt feelings over safety.

Micah got into the car, turned it on, and drove them out of the garage and onto the street. They'd been driving for maybe five minutes before he spoke.

"We can pick something up on the way back to your place, order something when we get there, or I can cook you dinner, but you're eating something tonight before you go to bed."

Something about his matter-of-fact tone made her see red. He was speaking like he'd already decided, and it wasn't up for discussion. Treating her like a child who needed an adult to take care of them.

She was no child, and she'd been the one taking care of others for most of her life.

"I'm not hungry," she snapped, even though she was in fact hungry.

"You need to eat."

"You don't get to decide what I do and don't need."

"Someone has to, otherwise, you won't take care of yourself at all."

The fact there was no heat to his words had her drawing up. He didn't sound like he was angry with her, he sounded almost sad. But he didn't sound repentant, and that hurt. When they were teens, he always told her it was his job to take care of her because she took care of everyone else. Only then, he'd left her when she most needed taking care of.

Realizing there was no way she could hold off any longer on having this conversation, she shifted in her seat and fixed Micah with a glare. "Why? Why are you pretending to care now, one way or the other if I'm taking care of myself, when you didn't care enough back then to stay? If you had even called or checked in just once I ..." Teresa trailed off, but not because she was overcome with anger or even sadness.

She trailed off because the vehicle that had pulled up beside them at a red light had someone climbing out of it.

That was weird enough as it was, and would have drawn her attention, but it was the mask covering the man's face that told her this wasn't just strange, it was dangerous.

"Micah!" she screamed.

He was already drawing his weapon.

But the man in the mask held something in his hands. It wasn't a gun, but when he pointed it at them, a mist began to seep into the vehicle.

The man wasn't wearing a mask to cover his identity, he was wearing it to protect himself.

Whatever the gas was, it was fast-acting. She began to feel dizzy, sleepy, and although she fumbled with her seatbelt, it was no good.

Already she was weakening.

The world faded away.

Darkness descended, and with it the knowledge that she was going to die at the hands of the organ traffickers.

* * *

April 30th
10:01 P.M.

THERE WAS NO WORSE FEELING in the world than waking up and not knowing where you were and what had happened to you.

Yet that was exactly how Micah felt when he regained consciousness.

His body felt heavy, like his limbs had been encased in concrete, and although he tried to move them, he found that he couldn't. His head also felt heavy, only in a different way. More like it had been stuffed with cotton wool and it was clogging up his thoughts so he couldn't quite get them to focus.

Even his eyelids felt heavy as he attempted to pry them open.

Despite feeling so odd, he had no memory of what caused it.

One minute he'd been …

Flying out with his teammate Nathaniel to visit his friend's new girlfriend. No, that wasn't right.

He'd bumped into the only girl he'd ever loved in the doorway to the Prey office building. No, that wasn't right either.

Teresa had been attacked, and he'd stopped the men from taking her. One had been killed, and the other had acknowledged that there was a bounty out on Teresa's head and that he'd tried to collect on it, but he didn't know the name of the person who wanted her.

Their rocky history had seemed like nothing in comparison to losing her.

So he'd agreed to play bodyguard.

There was no way he wouldn't have taken every precaution necessary to make sure she stayed safe so they couldn't have been caught.

Could they?

What else could explain the feeling that he'd been drugged?

Only, how would anyone have gotten close enough to drug him?

If anyone got that close to him, then they were too close to Teresa. And if anyone who was a threat to her got that close to her, he would have killed them, or at the

JANE BLYTHE

very least, incapacitated them, since he did know they needed intel.

But it *did* feel as though he'd been drugged, even though he knew he wouldn't have let anyone inject him with anything.

A hazy memory forced its way through the cotton wool inside his skull.

A mask.

A mist.

Why are you pretending to care now, one way or the other if I'm taking care of myself, when you didn't care enough back then to stay? If you had even called or checked in just once I ...

Teresa's words echoed through his mind. That's what she'd been saying right as he caught sight of movement out of the corner of his eye. She'd seen it too because she'd trailed off and then screamed his name.

The terror in her voice as she did so sent a rush of burning panic through his veins, and just like that, everything snapped back into focus.

They had been abducted. Whatever the man in the mask had used had knocked him out before he could get his weapon free and fire it. He'd been unconscious, hadn't protected Teresa when she needed him, and now ...

As Micah opened eyes that still felt a little too heavy, he saw that he was lying in what looked like a hospital room. He might have believed it really was a hospital room and the man with the mask and the mist were nothing more than an injury-induced hallucination if it weren't for the leather straps binding his wrists and ankles to the bed.

90

The reason he couldn't move his body wasn't just because he'd been drugged, it was also because he was tied up.

Fury scorched through him just like the panic had, pushing more of the drug out of his system.

He'd failed.

Failed Teresa in the worst possible way.

Because if he'd been taken, there wasn't a doubt in his mind that she had been too.

After all, she was the one the trafficking ring wanted. Although, why they thought going after another Prey employee was a good idea he couldn't figure out. That was only going to make Eagle Oswald and the entire Prey family angrier and more determined than ever to destroy the trafficking ring and make sure everybody involved was punished to the fullest extent of the law.

Whoever was left alive anyway.

If Micah had his way, that would be none of them. Sitting in a prison cell for the rest of their lives was too good for the people who had decided to go after his Teresa.

It didn't matter what had happened in the past, what she'd done, how he'd reacted, because deep down inside him, Micah had known from the time he was sixteen years old and first laid eyes on the pretty girl with the thick mane of dark hair and big chocolate brown eyes, that she was his.

His, and he'd failed her.

Let her get taken by people who weren't just going to kill her, but do it in a torturously slow manner while they took her body apart piece by piece. It would be a horrific death, one that he would suffer as well, but he would rather suffer it a million times over than let it happen to the girl he had never stopped loving, no matter how hard he'd tried to convince himself he had.

A soft moan close by had his head lifting as far as it could with his body restrained, and he saw her. There was another bed in the room, a hospital bed like the one he'd been strapped to, and it was a mere two feet away.

So close yet so far.

In it lay his girl, and she must be waking up as well.

Another moan, this time a little stronger, there was an edge to it as well, like she knew something was wrong.

Wanting her to know that she wasn't alone, Micah called out her name. "Teresa, hey, pretty girl," he crooned. She'd always blushed the most adorable shade of pink when they were teens, and he used to call her pretty, which of course made him want to do it all the time.

Only she wasn't just pretty. Teresa was beautiful, inside and out. Whatever had happened to make her decide to cheat on him, he didn't even care anymore, not when they were faced with this kind of horrific death.

If he found a way to get them both out of this alive, he was going to forgive her, truly and really forgive, and move on. With her if she'd have him.

"Can you hear me, Teresa? I'm right here, you're not alone."

"Mmm … Micah …?" she mumbled.

"It's me and I'm right beside you, pretty girl," he assured her.

She moaned again, only this time it turned into a groan. "I don't feel so good."

"I'm sorry, honey, I'm so sorry." This was all his fault. Everything from them being kidnapped to Teresa feeling sick because of the drugs they'd been given. He'd wanted to be her bodyguard because he hadn't been able to resist the pull he felt toward her, but what he should have done was insist that she remained locked up behind Prey's doors.

She might have been angry with him for it, but at least she'd be safe right now.

Not bound to a bed feeling ill.

"The man … in the mask … he … drugged us." She said the words like she couldn't quite believe them, and he was right there with her.

It was hard to accept they'd been on the cusp of having the conversation he'd intended to have once the ring was dismantled, and then the next moment they were drugged and waking up there.

He had no idea where they were, or how long it had been since they'd been taken. However, he did know that Prey would be looking for them. The cocky kidnappers had taken them right in the middle of the road, so he had no doubt Prey would be scouring CCTV footage to learn where they'd been taken.

"He did," Micah agreed.

"And they … took us?"

"They did." It killed him to say the words, but not saying them wouldn't make them any less true.

JANE BLYTHE

"We're … we're trapped." Beside him, Teresa began to pull on the straps binding her to the bed.

"For now."

Her head lifted, tilted in his direction, and her terrified eyes found his. "For now?"

"I will do everything within my power to get you out of here." Including sacrificing himself if it bought her enough time to escape. He didn't know how he'd get her out, he didn't have enough intel to formulate a plan, but he would. He'd find a way to save her. He had to.

"I want to believe you, but …" Teresa trailed off, not finishing her sentence, but then she didn't need to. Her words from earlier once again echoed in his mind.

You didn't care enough back then to stay.

Whatever had happened in the past, it seemed they had different recollections of it, but it was clear that she no longer trusted him. He'd let her down by ghosting her the way he had, and while he didn't quite see it the same way, he wanted her trust back. He wanted to prove that this time he could be what she needed.

The problem was, he had no idea how to do any of that.

CHAPTER 8

May 1ˢᵗ
   8:03 A.M.

THE NAUSEA WAS DIMINISHING, but the fear wasn't.

It was only growing.

Teresa could hardly believe this was really happening.

She was really there. Tied to a bed, in a room that could quite easily pass as a real hospital room. She was going to be operated on, her organs taken.

For the last couple of months, she'd done her best to be as empathetic toward Ava as she could be. Everything her friend had been through was so horrific, and she wanted Ava to know that she was there for her, even if she could never completely understand the horror she'd lived through.

Now she could, though.

Now she was living through it herself.

Only it wasn't just her, it was Micah as well, and she couldn't help but blame herself for the fact that both of them had been captured. After all, he was only there because of her.

If they hadn't unwittingly timed things to bump into each other as he was leaving Prey and she was arriving the other night, he wouldn't be there right now. There was zero doubt about that. He would have likely flown back home while Nathaniel's attention was focused on Ava, the break-in, and the trafficking ring. It was because of their past that he had offered to step up as her bodyguard, and because of her stubbornness they hadn't remained safe at Prey. They'd been out and about where any mercenary who wanted to try to get the bounty on her head could make a move.

Now she wasn't even sure why she'd been so stubborn.

She'd been trying to keep her life as stable as she could in the midst of an emotional storm, trying to change as little as possible, but now that just seemed so silly.

Change or dying a horrible death, it shouldn't have even been a choice.

But she'd made it one, not just for herself but for Micah as well.

"You're okay, pretty girl, try to take a deep breath for me."

The calm, soothing voice came out of nowhere, and she hadn't even realized that air had begun to saw in and out of her lungs at much too fast a rate. It was only natural to hyperventilate at the thought of what was to come. So far, they hadn't seen any of the people who had abducted them, no nurses or doctors had come into their room, but it didn't mean they weren't aware of who had taken them.

Still, she did her best to calm down. Panicking wasn't going to change anything, certainly wasn't going to fix anything. The only thing that gave them a chance was maintaining control of their emotions and looking for weaknesses.

Ava had done it. She'd escaped.

Isabella had done it too. While all her attempts at escape had failed, she'd gotten a woman out, and that had led to her rescue and the rescue of all the other nurses, doctors, and patients the ring was holding there with her.

Could they escape, too?

If anyone could do it, she believed it was Micah. He was smart and highly trained, he knew how to work under pressure, and he would be significantly stronger than anyone working there, including the armed guards.

She knew how to work under pressure, too, only the pressure had never been this. Had never been life and death. Having to step up at nine years old to take over most of the household responsibilities and childcare had been rough, nothing a child should have to do, but it didn't compare to this.

"I'm good," she wheezed as she managed to get her breathing mostly under control.

"I know you're scared, Teresa, but Prey is looking for us, and I'm not giving up. Not while you're in danger, not until you're safe."

The words were said so fiercely, with such determination that her gaze couldn't help but snap to his. Fire danced in his dark eyes, and his jaw was set. He wasn't just willing to fight for her, he was primed and ready to go.

"I'm sorry," she whispered.

"Sorry?"

"This is my fault. You're going to die because of me." Somehow, she swallowed down the emotion that threatened to choke her.

Actually, she was sorry for more than that. She was sorry about their past, that things had ended the way they had, maybe she hadn't tried hard enough to reach him, maybe she'd let go too easily. When no response came to her letter, she'd stopped trying to reach him. While she knew it wasn't her fault he'd abandoned her, Teresa couldn't help but think she should have done more.

"Good morning."

The voice coming from the man strolling through the door to their room drew both their attention, and they saw a man dressed in a white coat with a stethoscope hanging around his neck. They already knew that some of the medical personnel working for the ring were doing so by choice, presumably for the money. Others had been blackmailed into doing it, and others still were like Isabella, who had been abducted, trafficked, and forced to do it against their will.

It was clear which category the doctor belonged to. His cheerful attitude and the cold, calculating gleam in his eyes gave him away.

But another person trailed after him. A woman. She was older, maybe in her fifties. A bruise was on the side of her face, and she kept her head down, looking at the ground as she walked into the room following the doctor. This woman wasn't there by choice, Teresa would bet anything on that.

Did that mean anything good for them?

Could they use that?

Convince her to help them?

"We need to draw some blood for testing," the doctor announced. "We already have a potential match based on the preliminary tests we ran on the blood we took when you first arrived."

Since he walked over to her bed first, she had to assume he was talking about her. They had a match for one of her organs already? Did that mean she didn't have long to go before they started stealing her body parts?

Ava had been gone for two weeks and only had one organ taken. Then again, her escape had changed everything, and all that had happened over the last couple of months had shaken up the trafficking ring. If they wanted to keep in operation after taking hit after hit, it was no wonder they had to work fast. Otherwise, they risked a raid that would cost them more organs, more money, more guards, more nurses and doctors.

"The nurse is going to take more blood," the doctor informed her. "I'm just going to check your vitals."

As the man's hand touched her wrist, recoiling was pure instinct. Only there was nowhere for her to go, and his amused smirk told her he knew it and liked it. Teresa wanted to do something, lash out however she could, but she couldn't see any benefit in doing that.

Beside her in the other bed, Micah's body was still and tense, fury radiating off him as the doctor touched her, taking her pulse and then taking his time to brush her hair out of the way as he pressed the stethoscope to her chest.

She was pretty sure he did it slowly just to bother Micah, who let out a small growl.

"Your boyfriend wasn't a planned addition, but there was no need to be wasteful, especially since you and your company seem so intent on destroying our work."

"Of course we are," she snapped, a moment of anger drowning out her fear. "What you're doing isn't just illegal, it's cruel and psychotic."

The doctor tutted. "And to think I was nice enough to let you two share a room and you speak so disrespectfully."

"There's nothing about you worthy of respect," she spat out, and when the doctor laughed and brushed the pad of his thumb roughly across her bottom lip, Teresa didn't think, she merely acted.

Clamping her teeth down on the digit, she refused to let go even as the man howled and blood dribbled into her mouth.

Served him right, treating people like they were nothing more than a bag of organs to be sold so they could profit. He was a monster, and she absolutely would not show him an ounce of respect.

Teresa kept her teeth closed around the man's

thumb until he swung a fist into the side of her head, and she saw stars.

"You'll pay for that," the doctor snarled as he cradled his injured hand to his chest. "Your little display of defiance will be punished, and it won't change anything. We already have someone lined up to take one of your organs, it won't take long to sell off the rest. Take the blood," he snapped at the nurse before disappearing out the door.

With apologetic gray eyes, the woman made quick work of drawing blood, and then she too disappeared.

"You shouldn't have done that," Micah said once they were alone again.

"Why not?"

"Because now you're on their bad side."

"I don't care," she said simply, and it was true. That moment had reminded her of her promise to herself after she was raped that she was never going to be a victim ever again.

While she couldn't stop these people from taking her organs, and she was in a way a victim, being a victim was more than just having someone do something terrible to you, it was something that permeated your soul. She wasn't going to let these people do that to her.

They could take her body, but they couldn't take her mind.

She was going to work with Micah, and they were going to find a way out of there. Then they were going to destroy the trafficking ring and make every one of those smug, sociopathic people pay.

* * *

May 1st
    8:20 A.M.

Seeing Teresa fight back was both the most terrifying thing he'd ever witnessed in his life, but also the most amazing.

His girl was a fighter. Whatever life threw at her, she found a way to take control of it and not let it beat her.

As much as he didn't want her to draw undue attention to herself, wanted her to fly under the radar for her own safety, he was so proud of her for not just holding her own but actually knocking the smarmy doctor down a few pegs.

"Don't do that again," he murmured as he glanced at the door the nurse had just departed through. While the doctor absolutely wanted to be there and was fully involved in the trafficking ring's operation, the nurse was not.

Something they could possibly use if they could get the woman alone again.

"I told you I don't care," Teresa said with fire burning in her chocolate brown eyes, and a determination that told him she was going to survive this ordeal if he could just keep her alive long enough.

"I care." More than he'd realized. For a decade he'd been positive that he'd moved on, that he hated Teresa for betraying him, that even if he ever saw her again, it wouldn't change anything.

But he'd been wrong.

It changed everything.

Seeing her reminded him of what they used to share, and he wanted that again. If he could let go of his anger, then he didn't see why he couldn't learn to trust her again.

When it all boiled down to it, being confronted with her imminent death, he knew he'd rather find a way to have her in his life than hold onto his wounded pride.

"I don't want them to hurt me, but more than that, I won't let anyone make me a victim ever again," Teresa vowed fiercely.

"Not asking you to be a victim again, I'm just saying that you can't …" Micah trailed off, her words clicking. "Wait, what do you mean you don't want to be a victim again? You mean after they almost abducted you the other day?" His gaze roamed the healing wound on her cheek and the bruise on her forehead. As much as he hated the marks marring her perfect skin, they were vivid reminders of her ability to fight.

She hadn't given up then, and he prayed she didn't give up now.

"You know I don't, Micah," Teresa answered, an edge to her voice that confused him. She sounded angry with him, but he had no idea why.

"I don't know what you mean," he said honestly. Had she been hurt sometime within the last twelve years? Was that where she learned to harden her heart a little and distance herself from her emotions?

"Don't do that," Teresa snapped. "Don't pretend anymore. I can't take it. You've spent the last few days acting like we didn't break up because you left without a word."

Seemed like they were going to have this conversation now.

There couldn't be worse timing. They had more important things they needed to focus on, only … was there really anything more important than clearing the air with the girl who had tangled herself up in his heart, and he wasn't sure it was possible to get her out?

They might die there.

Just because he would do anything he could to save her life, there were no guarantees. Prey would be looking for them, and while he believed in them, they weren't miracle workers. If they were going to die there, he didn't want anything left between them. No bad feelings, no anger, no hurt, no betrayal. He wanted to get rid of all the bad so only the good remained, and there had been so much good.

"Leaving the way I did was the wrong thing to do," he admitted. "But what did you expect me to do after what I saw?"

Her brow furrowed. "What you saw?" Now she was the one who seemed confused.

"That weekend I came home to surprise you."

All the color drained out of Teresa's face, and if she hadn't already been lying down, he was pretty sure she would have fallen. "Y-you w-were there?" she whispered, her voice barely more than a breath of air.

He was hurting her, and it wasn't what he wanted, but Micah also knew they had to have this conversation. It was better to just do it and get it over with. "The door was open when I got to your place. When I saw ... I didn't stay. I got in my car, drove right back to college. A couple of days later, I decided to join the military. My parents were shocked at my sudden decision, but I never told them it was because of you."

"Y-you were th-there," she stammered once again. "And y-you didn't s-stop them."

"Stop them? Did you find out I was coming? Did you want me to see it? Were you trying to get some sort of message across?" That didn't sound like the Teresa he'd known, but what else could she mean? If she'd wanted him to see and stop them, stop her, then why hadn't she come after him? She'd have to have been watching for him, and he'd seen her on the couch with the four young men, there was nothing stopping her from having seen him in the open door.

"You l-left me w-with th-them." Teresa's eyes filled with tears, and she sounded so heartbroken that his heart cracked along with her, but he still wasn't sure why she would want him to see her having sex with other men.

It made zero sense, and he hated things that didn't make sense.

"I didn't know what else to do."

"Didn't know what else to do?" she hissed, anger shoving away the devastation. "How about stopping them? How about calling the police? How about doing something to make them stop hurting me?"

The bottom dropped out of his world.

It felt like it literally disappeared, and he was falling.

Falling.

JANE BLYTHE

Falling.

Finally, everything clicked into place.

All the pieces snapped together to form a picture.

A terrifying picture.

What he'd thought he'd seen was wrong.

So very wrong.

He hadn't walked in on his girlfriend cheating on him with four other men, he'd walked in on his girlfriend being gang raped.

"Tell me it's not true," he croaked.

It couldn't be.

Because if it was, he'd wasted the last twelve years being angry with the woman he loved for no reason. She'd done nothing wrong. He had.

Teresa hadn't betrayed him, he had betrayed her in the most sickening of ways.

"It's true," she whispered, looking away.

Micah couldn't breathe. All the air had been sucked out of his lungs, and he couldn't seem to find more to drag in.

What had he done?

Why had he ever believed for a single second that Teresa would cheat on him?

It had always felt wrong, the opposite of what a girl like Teresa would do, but he'd never considered another possibility.

Why hadn't he considered another possibility?

"They raped you," he said, the words tasting bitter in his mouth.

Teresa's gaze moved slowly back to his. "You didn't know?"

"Hell no! If I'd known, I never would have left."

It was clear from her expression that she didn't quite believe him, and he couldn't fault her for that.

She'd needed him and he hadn't been there. Not only that, but he'd blocked any way she had of contacting him, and he'd never even opened the letter.

The letter.

Did she tell him everything in it? If he'd just not been a coward and opened it all those years ago, could he have avoided more than a decade of pain for both of them?

"Simon," he growled as another piece of the puzzle clicked. That's why she'd been so freaked out at the possibility that he mentioned Simon when he went with her to visit her mom and Arthur.

"Drug money," she said softly.

So many emotions swelled inside him. Rage, unlike anything he had ever felt before was directed toward her heartless brother. How could Simon have pimped out his own sister for drug money? And how could he be so ruthless at just fifteen years of age?

The rage wasn't just directed at her brother, though.

A large portion of it was directed at himself. He'd thought the worst when he saw Teresa and those boys that night, he could have stopped her assault, could have saved her at least some of the pain she must have suffered. He could have been there beside her every step of the way, holding her hand, cradling her in his arms while she cried, and reminding her every day how strong she was. Been there with her during the court case because he knew her brother had been charged, convicted, and imprisoned for his crimes.

It was cold comfort to know that she had her mom and brother, because he knew Teresa would have done everything she could to downplay her own trauma so as not to be a burden.

No wonder she hated him, no wonder she'd been so angry with him.

How was he ever supposed to make this up to her?

How was he ever supposed to make things right?

CHAPTER 9

May 1ˢᵗ
2:39 P.M.

As BADLY AS she wanted to believe this wasn't happening, she couldn't.

Because it was.

Everything was horrifyingly real.

Teresa felt like she was trapped in some sort of dream state. Around her, everything was kind of hazy. Her emotions were there, bubbling beneath the surface, but they'd also been dulled. She recognized them, she felt them, but they were distant, and she was glad for that.

With the bustle going on about her there was no emotional space inside her to feel the full assault of emotions brought on by her talk with Micah.

He hadn't known.

But he'd been there.

The dichotomy of that was enough in and of itself to send her into a tailspin. Then add in all her fears about being kidnapped and her impending surgery, and it was all just too much.

Never before in her life had she checked out just because things were hard. She'd always been the kind of person to embrace the hard and make the best of it. When her dad died and her mom had needed her to step up, she'd done it, she hadn't complained about wanting to continue her previously carefree childhood. She'd done what needed to be done.

Same thing after her assault. She'd managed to salvage as many of her pieces as she could and put them back together. They hadn't fit the way they had before, but she was still her, just a slightly harder version of her old self.

But this changed everything she thought she knew and tipped her world upside down.

Until Micah had told her, she had never known he'd actually been there in person that night. She'd assumed he'd heard what happened to her, possibly from his dad since his father was a cop, and decided she was damaged goods and dumped her.

Knowing he'd seen her like that, that he'd had the power to do something to help her but hadn't, hurt more than she would have guessed if the idea had ever occurred to her. It would have been too late to prevent her from being hurt, but it would have ended it sooner. Knowing that the first thought in his mind when he saw her being raped was that she was cheating made their entire relationship feel like a lie.

Had he ever loved her?

If he didn't know she loved him, respected him, and would have spent the rest of her life with him, then she didn't think he could have.

Not *really* loved her.

Not the way she had loved him.

They hadn't spoken after his apology. If she didn't know better, she would have believed the apology was sincere. There was devastation in his eyes, and he'd actually cried as he told her how sorry he was for abandoning her, for not finding out the truth before ruthlessly cutting her out of his life.

What else was there to say?

Was he sorry?

Maybe.

Did it change anything?

No.

Not at all.

Well …

Maybe a little bit?

Honestly, right now, Teresa felt too raw to figure out if she cared that he felt bad now that he knew the truth. From the looks of things, he felt more than bad, he felt gutted, and it probably made her a terrible person to feel an ounce of satisfaction at that.

Gutted was exactly how she felt when Micah didn't answer her calls or texts, and she then realized he'd blocked her.

When the door to their shared room opened once

again, she glanced in that direction, tensing when she realized it was the doctor from earlier, the one she'd bitten. They hadn't seen him since he'd stormed out, but the nurse had been in a few times. Micah had tried talking to her, but she refused to respond. She was scared, Teresa got that, but she hadn't had the energy to try to calm the woman or convince her to help them.

"Good news, Ms. Dash, we do indeed have a match, so you're heading off to surgery," the doctor told her, a wicked gleam in his eyes. No doubt he had something planned to punish her for hurting him.

Still, Teresa couldn't find it in her to care when she saw the bandage covering his finger and most of his hand. She'd done that. She might be their prisoner, but she'd fought back and that brought her immense satisfaction.

"Don't take her," Micah said. His voice didn't come out strong and confident, it wasn't an order, and if you weren't aware of his training and experience, you wouldn't guess he was a special forces operator.

He sounded terrified.

He was begging.

Like if he pleaded hard enough, he could change what was going to happen.

One thing Teresa had learned early on in life was that you couldn't change the hand you were dealt. It was what it was. You had to make the best of it, work with what you had, and find a way to accept it.

It seemed like it was time for Micah to learn that same lesson.

There was no changing this. No going back in time

to the night of her assault and erasing it. No way for him to change how he'd blocked her from his life. No changing the fact that they were both going to be cut open and taken apart. No changing that her fate was now going to become his as well. Just because they were there for her didn't mean that they wouldn't soon be coming for him, too.

"Please," Micah continued even as the doctor ignored him. "Take me instead."

The doctor snorted. "Doesn't work that way, Mr. Hart. Certain people match other people, there are no substitutes."

Hands clamped around the metal rails of her bed, and she began to move, rolling toward the door. For a moment, she thought she should say something to Micah, ease his guilt and regret, but there wasn't really anything to say. He'd made his choices, and they'd both had to live with the consequences.

"Teresa, I'm sorry. So damn sorry, if I could go back, I'd do it all differently. All of it. I never stopped loving you. Never. Not for a single second. I spent the last decade wishing I had you by my side, that we'd made all our plans a reality. I'm sorry I ruined them. It's all on me, all of it. I promised to always be there for you. I promised to always take care of you. I failed. I let you down in the most horrific way. I'm sorry, pretty girl."

His words were the last thing she heard as she was wheeled out of the room, and the door swung closed behind them. As she was taken down the hall, away from the man she'd once loved, she knew she should have said something.

Anything.

Now it might be too late.

Her opportunity could be gone.

Forever.

While she was assuming the trafficking ring would keep her alive until they'd sold everything they possibly could, it was just that. An assumption.

She was taken into a small room, an operating theatre, and the reality of her situation struck hard and fast. This was happening. Really happening. She hadn't just been kidnapped, she was tied to a bed, and she was about to be put under and have one of her organs removed.

There was no stopping it.

Help wasn't coming.

Micah was as helpless as she was at that moment.

Whatever they took from her wouldn't kill her immediately, but if a miracle happened and she made it through this alive, it could drastically impact her for the rest of her life.

Doctors and nurses bustled about her, wires were hooked up, and the nurse from earlier shot her an apologetic look before setting up an IV.

With a smile that could only be described as malicious, the doctor she'd bitten stood beside her bed, with a syringe in his hand. "You know, there are certain body parts that aren't really necessary to what we do here."

Reaching out, he picked up one of her hands, lifting it off the mattress as far as he could with the leather cuff around her wrist. Her fingers had been curled into a fist, but he forcefully grabbed hold of her pinkie and straightened it.

"These fingers, for example. Wouldn't it be fun if you woke up to find one of them missing?"

A shudder of fear had her feeling like she'd been doused with a bucket of ice water, but she didn't look away. Didn't flinch or cower. He could cut off her finger if he wanted. He could cut off all her fingers, her hand, her entire arm, but it wouldn't change the fact that she'd hurt him, and he was never going to forget that.

"Something fun to think about as you go off to sleep," the doctor said as he released her hand and injected the syringe into her IV.

Teresa's last thought before the drugs took effect and washed her away into unconsciousness was that she really should have said something to Micah while she still had the chance.

Because despite everything, she still loved him, too, as much as she hated him.

* * *

MAY 1st
5:21 P.M.

HAD seconds always felt this long?

Micah would have sworn that they hadn't.

Then again, he'd never been forced to lie on a bed while the girl he loved, the girl he had horribly betrayed, was operated on against her will.

115

He would give anything in the world to swap places with her.

Trade his life in a heartbeat.

Anything to save Teresa. Anything to try to make up for what he'd done to her.

What he'd done … it made him sick to think about. Never before had he hated himself, not like this, this soul-deep loathing that made him want to crawl out of his own skin. Growing up with a great family, he'd never known what it was like not to be loved, and while his parents had expectations that he helped out around the house, he'd never experienced the crushing sense of responsibility that he knew Teresa had.

It was why he had appointed himself in charge of taking care of her.

Yet he had failed so thoroughly.

Something which he vowed never to do again.

There was no way Teresa would ever forgive him for what he'd done. Nor should she. What he had put her through was the ultimate betrayal, something completely unforgivable, and regardless of whether Teresa could ever accept his apology, Micah knew he would never, for as long as he lived, forgive himself.

But he also knew he was going to live, hopefully for a long time, long enough to dedicate the rest of his life to making up for his mistakes.

Dying couldn't be an option, because he was all that was standing between Teresa and death, and the woman he loved was not going to die there.

Ignoring the sharp pricks from the syringe he had balanced precariously in his fingers, he forced the horrific truth of his abandonment out of his mind and focused.

This had to work.

He had to get out of this bed.

That was all he needed, from there, he would kill anyone who got in his way.

Earlier, after Teresa had been taken away from him, the nurse had returned. It was clear that she was affected by his impassioned plea to Teresa, a plea his girl hadn't responded to. Not that she owed him any sort of response. He'd broken her heart, and he deserved her fury.

Although the nurse hadn't spoken a word, he had, he'd gone all out trying to convince her to untie him. He hadn't kept anything from her, he'd explained who he was, his training, and his years of experience, and promised to make sure she got out, too.

But it hadn't worked.

The woman was too afraid to get out of her own way and assist in her own rescue.

So he'd picked another option. One he wasn't as comfortable with, but desperate times called for desperate measures. Screaming at the woman, he'd scared her enough that she'd dropped her syringe on the bed before hurrying out.

It wasn't much to work with, but it was something.

At first, he'd hoped he might be able to use it to cut through the leather, but although the needle was sharp enough to pierce the leather, trying to use it as a saw brought little progress.

Not giving up, Micah had shifted gears. Now he was trying to use it to undo the buckle.

Already, he was close. He had it mostly lifted, all he had to do was thread it back through and …

Success.

Hope soared inside him.

With his right hand free it didn't take long to free his left hand, and then both of his ankles. Then Micah threw himself off the bed. The drugs had already left his system, and while he hadn't eaten anything or had any water since before he was abducted, his body was still stronger than anyone else's there.

Having nothing to wear but the flimsy hospital gown was annoying, but he'd do this naked if he had to. Searching the room for something he could use as a weapon, all he could come up with was a scalpel. At least it was sharp, and his hands were a weapon all of their own, but neither allowed him to take out multiple targets all at once like he could if he had a gun on him.

Still, he'd work with what he had, and he'd come out on top.

Teresa's life depended on it.

Gripping the scalpel in his fist, he headed for the door. While he was yet to see anything outside this room, he knew from Ava, Isabella, and the teams that had raided several of the trafficking ring's properties that there would likely be armed guards about some-where. If he wanted to gain the upper hand, he would have to be careful and smart.

All he had to do was get one guard alone, kill him, and take his weapon. After that, it should be easy enough to take out the rest of the guards and any of the doctors or nurses who were there by choice. Once he'd done that, he could find Teresa, make sure she was okay, and call in backup.

Right as he was reaching for the door, he heard a sound on the other side of it.

The only reason he'd survived years as a SEAL was because he had learned quickly to trust his instincts. They could be the difference between life and death. They weren't something to be second-guessed or examined too closely. If they told you something was wrong, then something was wrong.

Hanging back, placing himself where he'd be hidden by the door as the person stepped through it, he watched and waited.

Soon the door opened, with more caution than he would have expected from any of the guards who must be there, or any of the doctors, and he wondered if it could be the nurse he'd scared back to check on him.

But it wasn't a woman who stepped through the doorway.

It was a man.

Dressed all in black with a weapon in his hand.

Had to be a guard.

Knowing he was only going to have one chance to strike, he made the most of it. Darting forward, he wrapped an arm around the man's neck and jerked him back, the blade of the scalpel pressing into the other man's skin, ready to slice through his carotid artery.

"That any way to thank your friend for coming after you?" the man drawled, and Micah froze.

That voice.

It belonged to Nathaniel.

At least he thought it did.

But his heart was thudding in his chest, and he was so afraid to move in case he was imagining it.

"Can't mess this up," he murmured, unaware he'd spoken aloud until Nathaniel spoke again.

"Then let me go and we'll find her. She's not dead. They don't want her dead yet. They want to keep her alive until there's nothing left for them to take. Let's go find your girl."

Find Teresa.

Yes.

That's what he had to do.

He couldn't fail her again.

Slowly, he removed the scalpel and released his hold on the other man. Nathaniel. It was his friend's eyes he saw when the man turned around, so full of empathy, an understanding that came only because Nathaniel had also messed up with the woman he'd fallen for and almost lost her to this same ring.

"They can't have her," Micah murmured.

"No, they can't," Nathaniel agreed.

"Where are we?"

"Believe it or not, about an hour outside the city."

"Still in the US." If they were, Nathaniel shouldn't be there. Navy SEALs weren't allowed to operate on US soil.

"Better not tell anyone I'm here then." His friend winked and then grinned. "Come on, man, let's go find Teresa and get you both the hell out of here."

That sounded perfect, and he kept his grip on his scalpel as he followed Nathaniel to the door. "Who else is here?"

"Tobias, and a couple of other Prey people they could pull together at short notice. Enough of us. We got this."

Holding onto that belief, they both slipped back out into the hall, and he saw he was in one room off a long corridor. There were so many doors, and Teresa could be behind any one of them.

A shout sounded down the hall, and Micah didn't think.

He started running toward it, ignoring Nathaniel's yelling at him to stop.

Locating the room where the shout had come from, inside he found Teresa lying unmoving on a bed. The doctor she'd bitten stood beside her, a scalpel of his own in his hand as he held it to one of her fingers, a couple of nurses were huddled in the corner, and a man he had to assume worked for Prey held a weapon on the doctor.

The doctor watched them with crazed eyes and from the little he'd interacted with the man, Micah knew he wasn't one who could be reasoned with.

Besides, the man had taunted Teresa, and for that, he deserved what he got.

Which was why he didn't feel an ounce of regret about tossing his scalpel and watching with satisfaction as it sank into the doctor's neck, piercing his carotid artery.

Stepping over the dying man as he dropped to the floor, Micah went straight to Teresa's too still body.

There was a bloody wound on her stomach, a line of stitches haphazardly holding it closed, and a much smaller cut on her finger. What the hell had the doctor been playing at?

Not that it mattered, the man was dying, and the bright red gash on Teresa's otherwise pale skin was a taunting reminder of the fact that he'd failed her all over again.

CHAPTER 10

May 2ND
10:42 A.M.

She was still in shock.

Was it ever going to pass?

It wasn't like Teresa was new to the feeling of being violated, after all, she had been gang raped by four boys when she was seventeen. She knew what it was like to feel as though she were going to be ripped in two, to have something forced inside her body that she didn't want there.

But this was a different kind of violation and it hit differently.

Which sounded sort of silly.

Of course, something different hit different.

She just hadn't expected to feel this way.

When she'd first woken up, in an ambulance with Micah at her side, she'd realized that she'd been saved, and her first hope was that they'd gotten to her before the doctor could perform surgery.

That hope had fizzled out in a split second when the pain hit.

They'd operated on her.

Stolen from her.

And she'd come dangerously close to losing her finger as well.

For some reason, the little cut on her pinkie finger, not even an inch long, not even deep enough to be categorized as anything more than a scratch, bothered her more than the wound on her stomach where they'd cut her open. The wound on her stomach was business, but the one on her finger was pure cruelty. The doctor had been going to amputate her finger as payback for her biting him, it had nothing to do with selling organs.

Micah had been heartbroken to inform her that he'd been too late.

That the Prey team had gotten to them after she'd already been operated on.

When she heard the words, she'd felt like she wanted to burst into tears, but those tears wouldn't come.

Even now, hours later, after being poked and prodded in the hospital, learning that she'd had part of her liver removed, her wound properly restitched, she couldn't seem to get the tears to come.

They hovered inside her, burned the backs of her eyes, but they wouldn't fall.

Maybe because the shock was yet to wear off.

How could her tears fall when she felt so numb?

There were *too* many emotions raging inside her, and

it was almost as if they'd tangled together and gotten clogged. They couldn't come out because there wasn't enough space to let them out.

"How are you doing?" Micah asked as he walked back into her hospital room.

As badly as she wanted to go home, she had yet to convince a doctor that she would feel better and heal better if she was back in her own environment.

What nobody else could understand was that the entire fabric that she'd built her adult life on had just been ripped out from underneath her. Her belief that Micah had known about her assault and decided not to stand beside her as she battled through the aftermath was false. He hadn't known, and that changed nothing, and yet somehow it also changed everything.

How was she supposed to deal with that *and* being abducted and operated on against her will?

She couldn't.

Simple as that.

All her life, she'd been the person who took problems and found a way to make them work. She didn't complain, she just took what life gave her and worked with it. But she didn't know how to do that now.

Didn't know what to do with all the fear, and anger, and terror that simmered inside her.

What was going to happen when it started to boil?

Was it going to destroy her from the inside out?

"No one expects you to be okay, you know that, right?" Micah asked.

When she turned her head to the side, she saw that he'd resumed his spot in the chair beside her bed. The same chair he'd been sitting in almost the entire time she'd been in there. Not only had he ridden with her in the ambulance, but he had insisted that he would remain in her room while she was examined in the ER, then, when she was taken for further tests, he had refused to leave her side. Other than the occasional brief trip to the bathroom or to get her something to eat, he'd stayed.

It wasn't that she wanted him there … not exactly anyway, but she had become accustomed to his presence, and that worried her. He wasn't staying in her life. Even if he wouldn't have to go back to the other side of the country as soon as his leave was over, she didn't want him to be part of her future. Just because he hadn't known the truth, the fact that he could write her off so easily and block her out of his life like she meant nothing meant she could never trust him again.

His apologies weren't enough to fix the mess he'd made.

Nothing was.

So why was he even bothering?

Whatever else he was, Micah was smart, always had been. He had to recognize the fact that in life you could never go back, only forward, always forward. And there was nowhere for them to go. If they went forward, they would just hit block after block. There was no way to travel back in time to when things were perfect and then freeze them.

"What you went through was … beyond horrific," Micah continued, even though she hadn't spoken a word. "It's going to take time for you to heal. While you do, you shouldn't be pushing away the people who care about you. Ava has been through what you have, you should have let her come in to see you."

Ava *hadn't* been through what she had.

Her friend had been abducted, yes, and had one of her organs removed, but Ava had escaped. Ava had been strong enough to get herself out, to save herself, whereas Teresa would still be back there in that hellhole if Prey hadn't been able to find them.

The fact that it was Micah who was there telling her she shouldn't shut others out when that was precisely what he'd done to her was ironic. Frustratingly ironic. She hadn't asked him to stay with her, and she was tired, hurting, and wanted to go home. It was time for him to go away so she could work on getting over him for a second time.

Not something she was looking forward to.

But she'd done it once so she could do it again. It didn't matter if she wasn't sure how she could do it this time around, she'd find a way. The alternative was to never get him out of her mind, and that wasn't happening.

Already, he'd left lingering marks that haunted her every so often, there was no way she was going to put up with more than that. If anything, she now wanted to rid herself of those lingering marks so she could move forward with a fresh start. Now she knew the truth about what had happened, maybe she really could move on.

"I'm so sorry, Teresa. I wish I could go back and do it all over. Call the cops that day, get those men off you, and stand by your side. That was where I belonged, and

I've had an ache in my chest ever since. My heart knew what I was missing before my head caught up."

If his apology was supposed to help, it didn't.

All it did was serve to remind her that she'd had that same ache, only she'd had it because of his choices and not her own.

"Go," she said softly, her voice hoarse. She'd only used it to answer direct questions from medical personnel.

"Not leaving you alone."

"Go," she repeated, stronger this time as she pushed herself up in the bed a little, wincing as it pulled on the wound on her stomach.

"Not leaving you alone," Micah said again, standing and reaching for the bed's controls, elevating it a little so she could still rest against the mattress while also sitting up.

"I don't want you here," she hissed. It was too much. If she was going to figure out a way to get out of the mess of emotions she was mired in, she needed to focus on one thing at a time. Since the trafficking ring was still operational, dealing with that mess was more important than her boyfriend from when she was a teenager abandoning her.

Micah winced at her words, but he nodded, and his tone was soft as he spoke. "I know you don't want me here, but that's not enough to make me leave. I almost lost you. They took you, operated on you, and I failed you all over again. I will not fail you again. Will not lose you. My own stupidity cost me more than a decade with you, and I understand I might never get you back, that you might never be mine again. But understand one thing, Teresa, I will always be yours. Always. Nothing can change that. So I am not leaving your side, no matter what you say, or what you want, until I know that you are safe."

* * *

May 2nd
    11:00 A.M.

Shock was painted over every one of Teresa's features as she stared back at him.

Obviously, his impassioned speech had been the last thing she expected to hear, but hopefully it had gone a distance toward convincing her that he was serious about making up for his past mistakes.

Even if she didn't want him in her life going forward —something Micah could absolutely understand and would not blame her for at all—he could still do this for her. He could make sure she was safe, make sure she was taking care of herself, eating and sleeping, taking her painkillers, and not overdoing things.

If someone wasn't there to watch over her, he knew she would push too hard and make herself sick. And in addition to her physical health, the last thing she needed was to be alone with her thoughts.

Knowing what he'd done to her, the pain he'd caused, had him feeling like he needed to claw his way out of his own skin. The guilt and regret were so strong that it was impossible to think of anything else. He had to do something, and this was the only tangible thing.

Did it make anything better?

Not at all.

Not even a teeny tiny little bit.

But it was at least something.

Better than doing nothing.

When Teresa had been raped, he hadn't been there to take care of her, to tend to any wounds she had, to hold her while she cried, to keep watch over her while she slept in an attempt to keep the nightmares at bay.

Literally nothing was going to keep him from being by her side now.

She'd suffered a violation of a completely different type. Someone had once again taken something from her that she hadn't willingly given, and he knew what the cut on her finger meant because she'd told them.

At least he'd saved her from something.

Well, not really him, it was more Prey than anything he'd done. While he had gotten himself out of the bed, he knew he might not have gotten to Teresa in time to save her finger. The doctor had been quite literally starting to slice through her skin when he'd been stopped.

Another failure.

There had been too many for him to make up for, even if he lived a thousand lifetimes.

But he could and he would do this.

Nothing was going to stop him, not even Teresa herself.

If she tried to block him out of her life, he would do

whatever he could from a distance. He'd cook for her, clean for her, do her laundry, hire a nurse to tend to her wounds when she was released from the hospital, and sit outside her door with his weapon in his hand so nobody would get to her.

"Y-you're serious," she stammered, clearly thrown off-guard.

Micah had to remind himself that while he had spent the last decade sulking over the girl he'd loved cheating on him, harboring bad feelings over something that he now knew had never existed, she had been dealing with a very accurate grudge. She thought he'd abandoned her because he didn't want to deal with helping her through her trauma, and while that wasn't quite true, he had abandoned her all the same.

She had every right to hate him, which was why he knew there was every chance she would do whatever she could to forcibly remove him from her life. He had no doubt that Prey would back her up, and Eagle Oswald had enough clout to crush Micah's career if he wanted to, probably to have him locked up for some sort of stalking charge.

Still, he hoped that wouldn't happen. Prayed that Teresa could at least accept this from him as a very meagre step toward making things up to her. If nothing else, he hoped Eagle might understand messing up with the woman you loved, since rumor had it that once upon a time the man had messed up pretty majorly with his now wife and mother of his children, Olivia.

"Dead serious," he agreed. "I failed you in the most horrific way, and I want to make it up to you however I can." Lifting his hands and dragging them through his hair, his fingers tangled in the short locks, and he tugged hard enough to make his scalp sting, a mere drop in the bucket compared to the pain he'd inflicted on Teresa. "What I did to you, you must hate me. I hate myself."

"I don't … I didn't …" She trailed off, not finishing either sentence. Maybe there wasn't hatred in the pair of eyes that looked back at him, but there wasn't forgiveness either. "I did hate you, for a long time after. I even hated you that night when we bumped into each other at Prey."

That sounded promising.

Or was he reading too much into what she hadn't said yet?

"Of course, you hated me. You should hate me forever," he told her, meaning every word. Why should she ever forgive him? He hadn't even cared enough to find out the truth. His pride had been wounded, and he'd tucked tail and run, completely blocking her from his life.

Would it really have been so terrible to confront her with what he thought he knew and go from there?

The answer to that was easy.

It would have been so easy to go to her and talk it through, but he'd been a coward. A coward then and a coward every day since. Every day had been a new one, one he could have reached out to her. One he could have opened that letter and found out the truth within its pages.

"You didn't know," she said the words like she had to force them out.

"That doesn't change anything."

Teresa nodded, but there was a flicker of something in her eyes that said maybe she wasn't so sure about that. Was that too much to dare to hope for?

"I still have the letter," he blurted out. Did that matter? He wasn't sure. It could make her more upset to know he had it but hadn't read it, or it could soften her a little by showing her that he'd never completely let her go despite what he thought she'd done.

At that revelation, she startled. Then her cheeks went bright red, standing out in stark contrast to her otherwise pasty complexion. "You should throw it out," she whispered.

"No way," he exclaimed. The first thing he was going to do when he got back home was open that letter and read it.

"It's no longer relevant."

Micah very much doubted that.

In fact, he'd say the opposite was true.

If he wanted to know every drop of the storm of emotions Teresa had been battling in the aftermath of her assault, then those words would tell him all of it. It would be unfiltered, no doubt full of the rage she'd felt back then, the helplessness and sense of unfairness, all of it would be there for him to see, read, and experience.

"There is stuff in there I don't want you to read now," she told him, her gaze imploring. "When I wrote it, I was angry. You blocked me, and I didn't understand how the boy I loved could do that to me. I wasn't kind in what I said. Not even a little bit. But now that we've talked, and you know the truth, and I know why you left, there's no need for you to read it. You should just throw it away."

The last thing he wanted to do was hurt her further, make her feel embarrassed or uncomfortable about expressing herself any way she needed to, but he also had to read those words, absorb her pain however he could.

"I deserve every harsh word you said, Teresa. I deserve it all. I deserve your anger and your hatred. I have so many wishes, so many things I want to change, to go back and redo, it kills me that I can't. Even if you stop hating me, you'll never trust me again. This will always be between us. I know there is nothing I can do or say that can ever make up for what I did to you, what I put you through, but I am damn sure going to take care of you now. I never want to let you down again."

The problem was, he felt like whatever he did, he was letting her down. It was clear she didn't want him hanging around, so staying to take care of her would cause her pain. But if he didn't stay and do what he should have done last time, then he was causing her more pain because she would know for sure that he was never going to be someone she could depend on.

All he knew with absolute certainty was that his place was at Teresa's side.

So for now, that was where he intended to be, and if after she was safe and the organ trafficking ring was dismantled, she sent him away, he was going to have to find a way to live with that the same way she'd had to find a way to live without him when he abandoned her.

CHAPTER 11

May 2ⁿᵈ
7:13 P.M.

Finally.

Home.

Teresa let out a breath as she stepped inside her apartment. It didn't matter that the place had been trashed, her peaceful little home forever tainted. Didn't matter that most of the ruined furniture had been removed, and that the carpet had been ripped up since she'd last been there, the floor underneath rough and ugly.

It didn't even matter that Micah was with her, and he sent her world into a tailspin.

This was still home.

Even ruined, it was infinitely better than the hospital had been, and she couldn't spend any more time there without losing her mind.

With the threat that hung over her, the bounty on her head, there was no way Prey was going to let her go home rather than stay at one of their apartments without amping up security until it was almost crazy high. There were Prey operatives watching the building, and cameras set up everywhere in her apartment and the hall outside. Nobody was getting inside without Prey knowing and reacting.

Since there was no way the traffickers would be able to get past Prey, she felt safe enough there, and as much as it absolutely pained her to admit it, having Micah there helped as well.

While he might blame himself for them getting kidnapped, she did not blame him. Not for that, she did blame him for ruining the good thing they'd had going when they were kids, but this one was not his fault. Because of the bounty on her head, any number of mercenaries, gangs, or any other criminal out to make a quick dollar would try to take a go at her if they saw her. Some of them, like the ones who had taken her and Micah, were creative enough that they wouldn't see the attack coming before it was too late. Which was precisely what had happened in the car with the knockout gas.

"You need to rest," Micah announced as he locked up behind them.

Someone had obviously increased the number of locks on the door as well, because there never used to be four locks. In fact, the whole door looked new, and she would bet anything it was now a reinforced steel door rather than the regular wooden door that used to be there.

It made her feel all warm and fuzzy to know that she had people in her life looking out for her. After her dad died, her mom had remained the loving, supportive parent she'd always been, but the burden of raising three kids alone, one of whom was disabled, was a tough one, and she hadn't been able to be as involved as she used to be.

When Teresa had stepped up to fill in that role, she no longer had anyone looking out for her the same way she used to because her mom started to see her as the second parent. Their relationship had forever changed. She'd gotten used to being the one to look out for others and herself when she had any energy left.

No one had ever stepped in to fill that void until Micah.

Accustomed to taking care of herself, she never expected her friends or the Prey family to take on that role. But seeing they had stepped-up, beefed-up security there rather than forcing her to be somewhere she didn't feel comfortable, and taken precautions she wouldn't have thought of herself, made her feel cared about and important.

Her mom had never made her feel uncared about or unimportant, she was overwhelmed, it was no wonder there had been nothing left for her to give Teresa.

"A new couch?" she asked, as she eyed the beige one in the corner. It was similar to what had been there before, but she knew it had to be new because it didn't have red paint on it.

"Was as close to what you had before as I could find to get delivered at short notice," Micah replied.

"You did this?" That caught her by surprise. She knew Micah had said he intended to be there for her, support her, look after her, protect her, but she hadn't realized he'd gone to this extent.

"You wanted to stay here," he said simply. "There's new bedroom furniture as well, and a new kitchen table. I tried to get everything as close to what you had as I could, while still getting it here quickly. I don't know what your plans are for the future, but I know for now you need to be here, so I wanted it to feel as much like home as it could."

That was so thoughtful, and she didn't quite know how to process it.

"Thank you." It didn't seem like enough to say when he'd gone out of his way to organize all this for her in the last twenty-four or so hours, especially when he'd been kidnapped along with her and had every right to be recuperating from that ordeal rather than worrying about getting her new furniture.

Despite her feeling like the words weren't enough, Micah beamed at her praise.

"You don't have to keep them indefinitely if you want to choose your own things, but at least you have something to use for now."

"No." The word burst out without conscious thought. An automatic reaction to the idea that she would ever get rid of such a thoughtful gift. "No," she repeated, calmer this time, not quite ready for Micah to know how much she appreciated his thoughtfulness.

After all, she honestly could not see a future for the two of them, and she didn't want to give him the wrong idea. "No need to get rid of perfectly good furniture."

If he saw through her flimsy attempt to pretend she wasn't deeply moved by the gift, he didn't say anything. Just placed his large hand in the small of her back and guided her toward the couch.

The wound in her stomach hurt with each step she took, but his touch infused her body with warmth, and although she tried to cut the feeling off, it persisted until she reached the couch and sank down onto it, tucking her feet up beneath her.

Micah looked pleased to see her on the couch that he'd chosen for her, and he was smiling as he turned and headed for the kitchen. "I'll make you some dinner."

"Normally I cook."

"I bet you do. You're great at cooking, and you're a natural caregiver. But today you don't have anyone to take care of except yourself. Whatever I make won't be as good as you could do, but you need to rest and I'm here to take care of you."

There didn't seem to be any point in arguing, it was pretty clear that Micah had already made up his mind, and if she was being honest with herself, it felt too nice to be the one who was being taken care of for a change.

So she stayed right where she was and let her head fall back to rest against the buttery soft leather. As her eyes fell closed, she listened to the bustling sounds from the other room. She had no idea what he was cooking, and it didn't really matter. He was a reasonable enough cook, and she wasn't all that hungry anyway, mostly eating because she knew her body needed the fuel.

"Here, I don't want you getting cold."

When she opened her eyes again, Micah was standing there holding a blanket in his hands. It was new, she knew that because even before her place had been trashed, she hadn't owned one like it. But it was a pretty shade of yellow, and looked delectably soft, so she didn't make a protest as he tucked it around her, fussing about like a mother hen to make sure it covered her properly.

He'd always been like that, even as a teenager.

Since he was the first person to start taking care of her again after five years of being the primary caregiver to her family, she'd fought him on it often. She may have been only fourteen years old, but she already thought she no longer needed anyone to take care of her.

She'd been wrong.

Everybody needed someone to take care of them sometimes.

If she had to take care of herself right now, then she could. Maybe she'd be a little slower and more awkward at it, but she could tend to her own needs. But having Micah there meant she didn't have to worry about it and could just focus on recovering.

Which might prove to be harder than she thought.

Definitely harder than she wanted it to be.

Ava had bounced back well after her ordeal, although Teresa knew her friend was still struggling more than she wanted people to know, because she'd forged a bond with Nathaniel and that bond strengthened her.

She didn't have a bond like that. She would have to navigate her path alone.

Only as the kitchen door swung open and Micah carried through a tray with some water and fruit, she realized she wasn't quite alone. The man who had almost destroyed her over a decade ago might wind up being her salvation.

If she could find a way to let go of her anger and resentment toward him. And that was something she wasn't sure she could do.

* * *

May 2nd

11:02 P.M.

Restless, Micah prowled the apartment like a caged tiger.

He needed to be doing something, and while he knew he was doing the most important thing he could be doing right now, it didn't mean that he didn't want to do more.

More like find where the woman who headed the trafficking ring had squirreled herself away and storm in, take her into custody or kill her, preferably kill her, then kill every other person involved. If he thought it would make her happy, he would bring Teresa their heads on stakes as a gift, an offering, a plea for forgiveness.

Although he'd set up the air mattress in the living room, he had no intention of sleeping there tonight. It was too far away from Teresa.

Sleeping in her bed was obviously out. There was no way she was close enough to forgiving him that she would even entertain that thought. Sleeping on the floor of her room would also be out. That would still be too close as far as she was concerned.

So, he intended to spend the night sleeping on the floor outside her room. Snatching up his pillow and a blanket, he padded quietly down the hall, stopping at her door and pressing his ear to it. When he didn't hear any sounds coming from within, he assumed she'd gone to sleep, so he sat down and got himself settled.

Not ready to sleep yet, since he'd already taken a quick shower after they'd both eaten and Teresa had retired to her room, there was nothing else to do, so he unlocked his cell phone and brought up Nathaniel's name. Teresa's friends knew that she had been discharged from the hospital and she was home now, with him staying by her side for the foreseeable future.

For the moment, he couldn't allow himself to focus on the fact that his team would be called in. They were supposed to be on a break, but that didn't mean things couldn't change, and their unit might be sent out some-where. If that happened, he would have to make a choice between Teresa and his job. Since refusing to follow orders was an offense that would get him court-martialed, possibly thrown out of the SEALs, maybe even sent to prison, he would have to go.

Was there any chance he could convince her to move with him?

Maybe if Ava came too?

It wouldn't have to be permanent, just until this situation was brought under control.

Hey, dude, you up?

ALMOST IMMEDIATELY, the three dots began to bounce, and he sat there, head resting back against the wall, blanket tossed haphazardly over his legs, pillow lying on the floor beside him, phone in hand, feeling lost.

He needed someone who could give him step-by-step instructions on how to fix the mistake that he'd made. Too bad such a person didn't exist.

Realistically, the only one who could tell him what she needed him to do to earn back his trust was Teresa herself, but he could hardly expect her to hold his hand and walk him through this process when he was the one who had put them in this position to begin with.

YEAH, Ava and I are up
How's Teresa?

. . .

MICAH WISHED he had an answer to that question.

She was doing as well as anyone could expect given the circumstances. But that wasn't really doing well at all. He saw the fear and pain lurking in the depths of her chocolate brown eyes, even if she wanted to pretend they weren't there.

She ate something and now she's in bed

THAT DIDN'T SEEM like enough information, but he didn't know what else to say.

Still, he couldn't help but feel that Teresa's best friend deserved more. Too bad he hadn't been able to convince Teresa to stay at Prey. Not only would it be easier to protect her, but she would be better supported with her friends around.

As much as it pained him to admit, he wasn't what she needed right now.

Wasn't what made her feel safe and secure.

Unfortunately, he'd blown that all up when he left without talking to her. While he still hoped he might be able to earn her forgiveness, maybe even her friendship, he understood and accepted that might never happen.

Likely wouldn't happen.

It was a weird feeling to be this helpless when it came to Teresa because from the moment they met, everything had always been so smooth and easy. He'd stepped into the role of taking care of her as soon as they met. Even when she'd grumbled at him for being such a mother hen, he'd always known that she secretly loved that he doted on her when she was the one who always had to dote on everyone else.

I'm outside her door if she needs anything tonight

THE THREE DOTS APPEARED AGAIN, and he watched them to distract himself from getting up and going into Teresa's room. If he wanted to try to earn her forgiveness, then the very least he owed her was to respect her boundaries.

She knew he was in her apartment, if she wanted him in her room she would have asked. She hadn't, so she didn't.

IF SHE WAKES up tell her I'm here if she needs me

Ava?

YEAH IT'S me
I wanted to come right over but Nathaniel

said I should give her the space she requested

THEY DIDN'T HAVE to be in the same room for him to read her tone perfectly. She was feeling as lost and out of her depth as he was. She wanted to do something, wanted to find the perfect words to make this better for her friend.

Of all of them, Ava was the one who could offer the most support. She'd been through the same thing Teresa had, and he didn't quite get why Teresa had been adamant that she didn't want to see anyone when she knew that Ava got it in a way none of the rest of them did.

She knows you're here for her

THE ASSURANCE WAS AS MUCH for himself as it was for Ava.

They both cared about Teresa, just in different ways, and they both wanted what was best for her, which was why they were both holding back and fighting against their instincts to flood her with love and support.

AND YOU'LL MAKE her call if she needs anything?

I will

AN EASY PROMISE TO make because he knew that Ava would be more support for Teresa than he would be.

Was there a way to get her friends over there without going against Teresa's desire for space?

Why don't you text her in the morning?

THAT WASN'T REALLY a violation of Teresa's wishes. It wasn't like her friends were going to turn up unannounced, although in reality, they could since this was still their place too, even if they were staying at Prey for now.

Chelsea too
All your team
Convince Josiah to do it as well if you can

WHILE HE DOUBTED that the surly retired SEAL would ever text anyone unless he was pressured into it, if ever there was a time to force the man to do something this was it.

147

Teresa needed to be surrounded by support. If she didn't want to reach out and grab hold of it, then they all needed to build bridges over to the island she had placed herself on.

YEAH JOSIAH WILL BE THRILLED to text

HE'LL DO it
Guaranteed

HE ASSUMED the slight pause between texts was Nathaniel taking his phone back from his girlfriend. Micah had no doubt that his friend could twist the former SEALs arm to get him to do the right thing.

Likely wouldn't be as hard as they were expecting anyway. Josiah wasn't a bad guy, he'd just been through something horrific, and it was no wonder the guy had emotionally shut down. But he'd seen with his own eyes how hard the man was working this case, he cared about his team even if he didn't want to.

Thanks
Appreciate it

It helped to know he wasn't in this alone, and neither was Teresa.

All she had to do was accept it.

For whatever reason, she seemed to want to do this alone, but she had to open her eyes and accept the fact that trying to do so would only make things so much harder on herself.

Truth was that she *wasn't* alone. Not only did she have amazing friends and a whole family at Prey, as well as her mom and brother, but she had him, too. He had no right to hold a place in her life anymore, but he was going to claw one out for himself if it was at all possible no matter what that place wound up being.

He'd lost her once, and the thought he might have to do it again terrified him.

CHAPTER 12

TERESA GROWLED in frustration as the pain flaring across her stomach had her lowering her arms.

It shouldn't be this hard to put her hair in a ponytail.

That was all she was trying to do. Nothing fancy, wasn't planning on braiding it or anything, she just wanted it up and off the back of her neck. She was feeling too hot as it was, and the added warmth of her thick hair hanging down her back was too much. Spending the last ten minutes trying to get her hair to cooperate didn't help either.

Sweat was actually dripping down her back, and she was on the verge of tears.

Over her hair.

Which was ridiculous, and yet she couldn't seem to help it.

Sleep had been fitful last night, better than she would have gotten if she'd stayed in the hospital, but still restless. Her dreams hadn't quite been nightmares, and they weren't about her abduction. They were more like memories from the past, good times she'd shared with Micah when they were both young and in love.

Now the memories were more painful than sweet because they were a bitter reminder of everything that had once been in her grasp and yet she'd lost anyway. It had felt like a sure thing back then. Why wouldn't she and Micah get married and start a life together when they were both adults?

There was no way she could have foreseen the mess her life would turn into when she was fourteen and falling in love.

With a small hiccup she refused to believe was a sob, Teresa shoved all memories of happy times with Micah out of her mind. She had no time for them right now, and they served no purpose other than dragging her down like a millstone around her neck.

As she lifted her arms to once again try to get her hair up and into a ponytail before the pain across her stomach forced her to lower them again, there was a knock at the bathroom door.

"Everything okay in there?" Micah asked as he opened her door.

Although he looked well-rested, with a clear gaze, hair combed, dressed, and ready for the day, while she felt like she was still half asleep, Teresa had a sneaking suspicion he'd slept on the floor outside her bedroom door last night. When she'd walked out of her room this morning to head for the bathroom, the floor right outside the door was warmer than the rest, like someone had recently been standing, sitting, or lying there.

Since Micah was the only other one there, it had to have been him.

Before she'd retired to her room, she'd seen him make up the air mattress in the living room, so she'd assumed he was intending to sleep there. Had he, or had he moved closer to her, watching over her in sleep?

"Just doing my hair," she muttered, suddenly overcome with emotion by the idea—that she didn't even know was true—that he might have slept on the floor just to be closer to her.

It shouldn't matter, but for some reason it did.

"Having your arms up like that will put pressure on your stitches. Come and sit down in the living room, and I'll do your hair for you," Micah told her.

"What do you know about doing hair?"

"I'm sure I can manage a ponytail." Before she could argue further, he'd snatched the hairbrush and hair tie out of her hands and was ushering her toward the door.

While she could argue the point, refuse to move, insist that she had it all under control, the warmth of his hand on the small of her back was soothing, she was tired, and it was easier to give in than stand her ground.

In the living room, he gently pushed her down onto the couch. Picking up the blanket he'd tucked around her yesterday, he now spread it over her legs, tucking it in, before moving to stand behind her.

With smooth, gentle strokes, he drew the brush

through her hair. The more he brushed, the more relaxed Teresa became until she felt like she could drift right off to sleep.

After brushing for a solid couple of minutes, much longer than was necessary, but maybe he was enjoying the moment as much as she was, he began to gather her locks together. He fiddled for a while, probably trying to get rid of all the bumps, before he seemed satisfied with his efforts and used the hair tie to secure her hair into a ponytail.

"Still a few bumps," he said with a critical eye as he came to stand in front of her to survey his handiwork. "Want me to try again? I know how much you always hated bumps in your hair."

Normally, she did hate to leave lumps in her hair, but today she didn't seem to care. It wasn't just that, though, she wasn't sure she could handle having Micah brush her hair again without collapsing into a puddle of goo. She wasn't ready to hand him that much power yet, but more than that, he'd done his best and that meant more than having her hair perfectly done.

"It's fine, leave it how it is," she replied.

His eyes widened in surprise, but then he shot her one of those winning smiles she'd loved when they were teens. He looked pleased as punch that she wanted to leave her hair how he'd done it, and that made her smile despite the anger she still held onto tightly.

Just because he didn't know doesn't mean he didn't abandon you.

It's almost worse because he actually believed you were capable of cheating.

And he didn't even care enough to stick around and talk it through. Yell at you even.

The insidious voice whispered through her mind, and the smile slid off her lips. Echoing hers, Micah's smile also fell away, and she felt a pang at its loss.

The thing was, she didn't want to hold onto her anger. It was draining, it had stolen her happiness for over a decade, and Micah was clearly devastated by what he'd done back then. There wasn't really any way to make up for it, but he was trying, and that did mean something.

"I'd better go check on the bread," Micah announced, heading for the kitchen.

"The bread?"

"You like fresh bread for breakfast. In the summer you used to try to make it every day since you had time because school was out. I'm sure it's not going to be anywhere near as good as yours. The dough was rising, though, so that's something." His smile came back, and he hurried back into the kitchen.

He was making her bread.

Because he remembered yet another thing about her from when they were together.

Was he hoping to woo her one little thing at a time?

Much as she hated to admit it, that might work. Already she was softening toward him. He wasn't watering down what he'd done, he was accepting full responsibility and apologizing without reservation. He was also doing his best to make amends while under-standing that it wasn't something you could just make right. All of that made it increasingly harder to cling to her righteous anger.

Maybe it was time.

To finally forgive, cut the ties that held her stuck in the past, and move forward.

But forgiveness was a terrifying thing because it meant letting go, and in a sick sort of way, there was a layer of stability that came with hanging onto the past.

"Dough is still rising," Micah said excitedly as he bustled back out of the kitchen. "Should be ready to go into the oven soon. I'm going to go and put on a load of laundry, and then I need to check your stitches."

He didn't wait for her to say anything, just disappeared off down the hall, and a moment later, she could hear the lid of the small washing machine in the tiny laundry cupboard lifting and then closing, and whirring to life. As much as the idea of him touching her had nerves dancing in her stomach, Teresa knew it was part of what she'd agreed to when she convinced the hospital to discharge her.

Micah was his team's medic, and he was confident in his ability to keep her wounds clean and monitor them for signs of infection. It wasn't that she didn't trust him to do that, because she certainly did, it was just his hands touching her made it hard to think all over again.

"All right, let's take a look," Micah said as he took the seat beside her on the couch, setting the first aid kit at his side.

Unable to take her eyes off his large hands, they eased the blanket down, then gripped the hem of her soft leggings and tucked them down just enough that he could get to the bandages. With nimble fingers, he pulled back the bandage covering her wound, his eyes assessing the cut with an expression she couldn't read.

She knew it wasn't pretty, it wasn't like the traffickers had cared enough to be careful with it. They'd intended to keep opening her up and taking more organs. When she chanced a glance at it, she could see it was red, not quite infected-looking, but close.

Was that why she'd been feeling so hot?

It would be exactly her luck for her wound to get infected. Especially with Micah there.

Now he knew the truth of what had happened all those years ago, and that she'd been able to rebuild her life, she felt an almost irrational need not to get sick in front of him, not to show weakness of any kind.

Ever since she stepped up to help her family, she'd worked hard to be the strong, independent, together woman that everyone else saw. Once upon a time, she'd let Micah see her weaker parts, the parts she hid so well, and he'd walked away.

Letting him in again was not an option.

Not if she wanted to survive this intact.

* * *

MAY 4th
2:36 P.M.

SOMETHING FELT off with Teresa today.

It wasn't her attitude, if anything, she'd definitely

softened toward him, which Micah was eternally grateful for, but she seemed distant in a different way.

It wasn't like they were back to being a couple, or even friends, but she was being polite, and most of the hostility from those first couple of days seemed to have disappeared. It was more than he could have hoped for, but nowhere near where he wanted to wind up.

Now that he knew all their problems from the past were his fault, he felt like he couldn't rest until he'd fixed them. Righted things, put them back to the way they were always supposed to be.

It was a weird dichotomy because Micah both knew he had no right to have Teresa back in his life in any way, shape, or form, but at the same time, he craved regaining what he once had so carelessly tossed aside. He wanted Teresa more than he wanted his next breath of air. Wanted her to smile at him like she used to, those little ones she used to shoot his way when she thought he wasn't looking. He'd always pretend to be distracted by something, preoccupied so she wouldn't know he was watching and cherishing every second.

Those smiles had been full of warmth and love. She hadn't hidden anything in them, looking at him like he was the rock in her life, the one thing she could stand on when she was overwhelmed by all the responsibilities on her young shoulders. She used to believe he hung the moon, but now she thought he guarded the gates to hell.

How could he possibly earn back her love when what he'd done was so awful?

As much as he wanted to study that problem until he

could come up with a solution, he knew he had other things he needed to focus on as well.

Like figuring out what was going on with Teresa today.

This morning, he'd covered her wounds with waterproof bandages so she could take a shower, and she'd been grateful although she'd flinched every time his fingers had brushed against her skin. At first, he'd thought it was because she was affected by his touch, but now, he wasn't so sure.

There had been something like panic in her eyes each time she flinched.

But what could she possibly be panicked about?

It wasn't like he didn't already know that she loathed him and was only putting up with his presence in her life because of the threat hanging over her. That and the fact that he was Nathaniel's teammate and Ava was one of her best friends, so their lives would be connected, and she probably didn't want to cause problems for the happy couple.

So if she wasn't just hating the feel of his touch, then what else could it be?

All she'd done at breakfast and lunch was pick at her food. At the time he'd wondered again whether it was just being around him that had her thrown, now he thought it was more than that.

There was another obvious answer as to why she wasn't keen on eating.

Nausea.

If she felt sick, it would make sense that the thought of putting food in her mouth only made her feel worse.

And if she knew she was running a fever, she might have been afraid that if he touched her skin, he'd feel that it was overheated.

A bit of a stretch maybe, but it did fit with what he knew about Teresa. She'd never been one to admit weakness. With so much to take care of as a kid, she'd always tried to push through when she was sick because people were depending on her.

Was that what she was trying to do now?

The last few times he'd checked her wounds, they had been a little red and inflamed. There had been no puss and nothing to confirm infection, and he'd been relying on Teresa to be honest with him if she started feeling worse.

A mistake.

Obviously.

She'd been holed up in her room all day, not because she needed space but because she was trying to avoid him.

Shoving off the couch, Micah hurried to Teresa's bedroom. As much as he had been trying to respect her need for space and not shove himself on her, even though he'd love to haul her into his lap and apologize over and over again until she had no choice but to accept, this wasn't the time for space.

Physical health came first. If she was trying to hide from him that she was sick, he needed to know. There was no way he was going to lose her to her own stubborn pride.

Pride already had her shutting out the people who loved her. He knew for a fact she hadn't responded to any of the texts she'd received because he was in constant contact with Nathaniel and Ava. In fact, the three of them had started a group chat, added Chelsea, then Tobias and Isabella, and even Josiah had reluctantly agreed to be part of it. If she'd replied he would have known about it, and she hadn't. If she didn't soon, she was likely going to find herself the recipient of an intervention.

Not bothering to knock on Teresa's door because he already knew she'd just tell him to go away, that she was fine, he opened it and saw her standing beside her bed. She had a hand pressed to her temple like she was dizzy, and when she turned toward the now open door she swayed and teetered precariously.

There was no conscious thought on his part.

He was just there, beside her, wrapping an arm around her waist and pulling her against his chest so she didn't hit the floor.

"I was fine," she grumbled, but her voice was thready, her protest weak at best.

"You were going to fall," he corrected. When they were kids, he'd never coddled her, he'd respected her strength and determination, but never been shy about pointing out her weaknesses, mainly her stubborn pride, and how it could negatively affect her if she let it.

"Was not," she shot back, but there was no heat to her tone.

"You're sick." It came out accusing, because, okay, that's how he meant it. She should know better than to play games with her health for any reason whatsoever.

"Am not."

Rolling his eyes, Micah pressed the back of his hand to her forehead. "Then why are you burning up?"

"Because I was in bed, under the covers." She huffed, actually sticking out her bottom lip into a pout.

Again, there was no conscious thought on his part, his thumb just pressed to her lip, trailing along it, remembering all the times he'd kissed her. Back then, he'd never thought about what a privilege it was to be able to kiss Teresa whenever he wanted, he'd taken it for granted, not realizing how good he'd had it until it was gone.

"You're sick," he said again, more reproachful this time than accusing. "You didn't tell me that you were feeling sick."

"Didn't want you to think I was weak." Her gaze dropped, and her already flushed cheeks pinked further.

"Why on earth would I think you were weak?" Micah had a feeling that the answer to that question was also the answer to why she was shutting everyone out.

"Because I didn't save myself," she whispered. There was so much pain in those few words that his heart ached.

"I didn't save myself either," he reminded her.

"You would have. You'd already gotten free. I didn't. I didn't stop them from taking part of my liver."

Smoothing a lock of hair behind her ear, he palmed her cheek, his fingers tracing along soft skin he thought he'd never get to touch again. "You held it together under the most horrific of circumstances, how can you think you were weak? How many other people do you think almost bit off the finger of one of the doctors?"

"Umm … probably none?"

"Are you asking me or telling me?"

"Telling you."

"Then say it like you believe it. Tell me that no one else dared to do what you did."

"No one else did what I did. No one else almost bit off that monster's finger." Her voice was stronger that time, and there was a flicker of determination in her eyes.

"I told you in the hospital not to shut yourself off from the people who love you. That's what you've been doing and you're letting all those bad feelings fester. You went through something horrific, but nobody thinks you're weak. Least of all me. Knowing what you've survived in life, I'm in awe of you."

Their gazes met and he knew in that moment that if he never gained Teresa's forgiveness, never got her back, there would never be another woman for him.

This woman owned his heart.

Always had. Always would.

"Please don't shut us out," he whispered. Teresa had already survived so much, he knew she could find a way through this, too. But it didn't matter what he knew, she had to know it, too.

When she gave a shaky nod, he knew she'd pulled herself back from the brink. It was far too easy to fall over that ledge and far too hard to climb back up.

CHAPTER 13

May 5TH

11:48 A.M.

"It's getting the mail," Teresa reminded Micah with an eyeroll.

Not that she really minded him being so overbearingly protective.

Just because she wouldn't admit it out loud didn't mean that she wasn't secretly pleased that he was looking out for her like he used to. Those were the good old days, the days when she had more responsibility than ever as Simon started acting out, but there was someone looking out for her, too. It had made all the difference in the world, and she'd missed that the most after her assault and Micah's departure from her life.

Of course, she'd had her mom. Her mom had *always* been a good mom, and none of them could help the fact that their husband and father had tragically passed away, leaving them struggling. They'd all done the best they could with what they had to work with, and Teresa knew her mom carried a lot of guilt about piling so many things on her daughter's shoulders.

Once upon a time, Micah had made all that pressure so much easier to manage, and it was so tempting to give in and let him take that role again.

Especially after how great he'd been these last few days. Yesterday, after he'd found her dizzy and almost passing out in her bedroom when she got up to go to the bathroom, he'd cleaned her wounds, arranged for a nurse to make a home visit, organized a prescription of antibiotics, and insisted she hang with him in the living room so he could keep an eye on her.

Which turned out to be exactly what she needed.

Admitting it kind of sucked because she didn't want to add more points in Micah's favor, but he was right, cutting herself off from everyone wasn't helping her. So after he settled her on the couch, tucked under a blanket, with one of her favorite childhood movies playing on a new TV he must have bought, with all her favorite snacks, she'd replied to all the messages from her friends.

That first one was the hardest to type out, but with each one it got easier until she was trying to keep conversations with five different people all straight in her mind so she didn't type out answers in the wrong message thread. Even Josiah had sent her a brief message updating her on the progress he'd made. It wasn't a lot of progress, but they were chipping away at the trafficking ring, closing down more and more of their operations. Sooner or later, the woman in charge would mess up and then they'd have her.

Teresa couldn't wait.

"But you'd have to go all the way down to the ground floor to get the mail," Micah reminded her as though she didn't know how her own building worked.

"Well, I'd have to walk down the hall to the elevator and ride in it to the ground floor, then cross the lobby to the mailboxes." He was acting like it was a twenty-mile hike through dense vegetation.

"You're safer in here."

"You'd be with me."

"I was with you when you were taken, it didn't help much then."

"Not your fault," Teresa reminded him firmly. Yesterday, he'd given her a little tough love. Today, she needed to do the same for him. She'd been so caught up in her own emotions that she hadn't given much thought to how Micah was handling everything. Just because they were no longer a couple, no longer even friends, she'd still once cared deeply about him, loved him, just because he'd hurt her didn't mean all those feelings had died. They'd just been tainted, turned sour.

Now maybe they were sweetening again.

At least a little.

"Come on," she wheedled, "a whole bunch of the new kitchen gadgets I ordered have arrived, and I want to cook us something for dinner. It'll only take one trip if we both go, otherwise, you're going to have to leave me here and make two trips down to get them." That was playing a little dirty because she knew leaving her alone was the last thing Micah wanted to do, but she really wanted to stretch her legs a little.

"Fine." He huffed. "Down and straight back up."

"All I can handle right now anyway, especially if I want to cook something for dinner," she quickly agreed. The medication was helping, and she felt a little better today, but still tired and washed out.

As they headed out of her apartment, Micah stuck close to her side. Close enough that she could feel the slight brush of his body against hers, and she hated that her treacherous body ignited at the slight touch.

Okay, maybe she didn't really hate it.

Resent it.

A little.

Not as much as she should.

It didn't take them long to get down to the lobby and greet the doorman, who had a whole stack of parcels waiting for her. While it might seem silly to some, replacing her broken cooking equipment had been her top priority because cooking was her happy place. One she needed more than ever.

"Package for a Ms. Dash," a delivery woman appeared in the building's doorway right as the doorman had started filling Micah's arms with the already delivered parcels.

"That's me," she said, walking toward the woman.

"Teresa," Micah hissed.

"It's fine, I'm not going to be out of your sight, and it will take literally a few seconds to sign for it and grab it," she reminded him. It wasn't that she didn't take the bounty on her head seriously, she absolutely did. The last thing in the world she wanted was to wind up back in the trafficking ring's clutches, but Micah was right there, a dozen feet away, and that made her feel safe.

Crazy since she'd spent the last decade loathing him.

Hurrying over to the woman, she signed, grabbed the package, and was closing the door when someone suddenly rushed it.

If it was actually possible for a heart to jump out of the chest, then that's what would have happened.

She gasped, stumbled forward, and probably would have fallen flat on her face if someone hadn't darted out a hand to catch her.

When she looked up, it was to meet the last pair of eyes she ever expected to see again.

"Simon," she murmured.

Twelve years might have passed since that night, but all it took to throw her right back into the past like it was happening around her right now was meeting her brother's gaze.

It didn't matter that her brother no longer looked like the same fifteen-year-old boy he'd been when he'd stood by, leaning against their living room wall, his arms crossed, a cold, calculating look she'd never seen in his eyes before.

Now he was older. His head shaved, tattoos covering the skin on the top of his head and his neck. That coldness she'd seen that night had devolved into something she could only describe as pure evil. An emptiness that said he truly didn't care that he was hurting his own sister. Being related to him wasn't going to save her.

Any humanity her brother had ever had inside him

had died when he was a fifteen-year-old boy who decided to sell his sister's body for money.

He shouldn't be there.

Wasn't supposed to be there.

There was a restraining order that was supposed to make him keep his distance.

Not that a piece of paper could ever really keep him away.

"Sister," Simon sneered the word like it was a bad one. "Ms. Perfect, always has everything together, the boss of the world, too good to be human, sister."

If she hadn't already known her brother hated her with a passion, then the utter disdain in his voice would have made that fact crystal clear.

"You shouldn't be here."

"Yet here I am," Simon snapped.

Searching his gaze, Teresa tried to find any remnant of the little boy she'd once loved. Before their father's death, Simon had been a bit of a troublemaker, but he hadn't been evil. That all changed in the car accident that took their father's life. An accident that Simon had also been involved in because he'd been in the car.

Counselling hadn't helped, and over the years, Simon just got worse and worse.

"I need money."

"You need to leave," Teresa corrected. There was no way in hell she was giving her brother money that he'd spend on drugs.

"Always were a little goody two-shoes, weren't you?" Taking a threatening step forward, the hand he still had on her elbow tightened to the point it would likely leave behind bruises, yanked her closer. "Let me make this clearer, sister. I'm not asking. I'm here for money."

If Micah hadn't been there, Teresa wasn't sure how she would have reacted to her brother's unexpected visit. But knowing Micah was just feet away, that he would notice what was happening at any second, emboldened her.

Meeting her brother's gaze head-on, she stood straight and tall, ignoring the pain throbbing in her stomach. "I never tried to be perfect, Simon. All I wanted was to be a decent human being, something you obviously don't care about at all."

Simon growled, rage pouring off him, and he drew back his fist to give her a strike Teresa would happily take because for the first time in twelve years she had stood up to the person responsible for her assault.

* * *

MAY 5th

    12:03 P.M.

"TOUCH HER AND DIE," Micah snarled as he snapped out a hand and caught Simon Dash's fist before it could slam into Teresa's face.

All he'd done was take his eyes off her for a matter of seconds, and she'd been accosted by her despicable brother.

Honestly, he'd love to kill Simon for what he'd done to his sister. Snap the man's neck like it was the twig it was. End his life so Teresa could be free of the fear that her brother might pop back up and hurt her all over again.

Killing Simon slowly would also be fun. He'd learned a lot in his years as a SEAL, and he knew how to keep someone alive while inflicting unfathomable pain. Simon deserved a whole lot worse than that for what he'd done.

If there had been any justice at all, he'd be serving a life sentence, since Teresa was certainly serving one.

Rape victims always did.

That didn't mean she wasn't living her life like the champion that she was, but it meant those scars were always a part of her, they would remain with her until the day she died. He had not a single doubt that her brother's death would bring her a level of peace she wouldn't readily admit to out loud for fear it would make her sound like a bad person.

But how could it?

Brother or not, Simon had done something unspeakably evil to her, and she was entitled to hate him for it.

Just like she was still entitled to love the little brother she'd once known before he decided to turn down a dark path.

"Who's going to kill me? You?" Simon asked with a smug smirk.

There were still parts of the twelve-year-old boy Micah had first met visible in the man standing before him, similarities that had told him who the man Teresa was talking to was without anyone having to tell him. Simon had changed, though, and not just in the normal way a person aged. Not just in the tattoos, either, several of which he could see were gang-related.

It was the man's eyes.

They were cold and hard. Heartless.

Without speaking a word, Micah merely tightened his grip on the other man's arm. Smiling as he squeezed, and Simon's face went redder and redder until he felt the bones crack, and Teresa's brother cried out in pain.

A broken bone wasn't much in comparison to what Teresa had suffered, but it was something. A small offering to her that he hoped might show her how desperately sorry he was for the part he'd played in hurting her.

"Don't remember me, do you?" he asked, holding Simon's gaze as he pressed against the bones he'd just snapped.

"Who the hell are you, and why are you playing my sister's protector?" Simon snarled.

"I'm the man who's been in love with your sister since the day I first laid eyes on her."

Recognition flickered in Simon's eyes. "Micah Hart. The boyfriend who bailed." A triumphant smile curled up the man's lips, and he knew he'd scored a direct hit even though Micah made sure he didn't visibly react in any way.

"Stop it, Simon. You know you're not supposed to be here," Teresa spoke up.

"Go back inside and wait with the doorman," Micah told her, hating her being this close to her brother. "Told the doorman to call the cops as soon as I realized something was wrong. They're going to be here any moment, and they're going to take Simon into custody for violating the restraining order. And for assault."

"Didn't assault her, *you* assaulted *me*," Simon whined.

"Actually, you put your hands on her, it's going to leave bruises. That's assault, and I'm merely defending her," he said mildly. Actually, he'd love to do a whole lot more defending, he was itching to take out some of the impotent rage boiling inside him—some toward Simon, but most of it directed at himself—by inflicting a few more wounds. Maybe then Simon would get the message and finally leave his sister alone for good.

"You broke my arm," Simon growled. Rage danced in the man's brown eyes, a much darker shade than Teresa's, but with the tight hold Micah maintained on his arm, Simon couldn't move without causing himself more pain.

"Self-defense. Cops aren't going to care that I broke your arm looking out for your sister, who you were about to punch in the face while you're here in violation of a restraining order."

Something calculated replaced some of the fury in Simon's expression. The man knew he'd lost, he was going to be arrested, and would spend some time in prison, but he wanted to get in whatever strikes he could now while he had the chance.

"She never let you touch her, did she?" Simon drawled.

Beside him, Teresa gasped, and it was instinct this time and not conscious thought that had Micah tightening the fingers wrapped around Simon's broken bones. He and Teresa hadn't had sex. She hadn't been ready back then, and he hadn't cared, as far as he'd been concerned, they'd had all the time in the world. Waiting for her had been easy because he'd always known she was his forever.

But it gutted him to be reminded that Teresa's first time hadn't been voluntary. Her innocence had been ripped away from her.

It was all so unfair, and he hated that he'd been part of the whole mess.

Instead of being the rock that steadied her, gave her respite from the storm so she could find her footing again, he'd just been another rock to strike her when she was already down.

"When my friend pulled out and saw the blood, we all laughed. He said she was so tight he knew the second he sank into her that she was pure virgin. Paid me double for getting to be the first one to tap that. The others—"

"Inside, Teresa. Now," Micah barked.

"Micah, he's not worth whatever you're going to do," she said softly, and her much smaller hand lightly closed around his.

"He's not, but you are. Inside. Please."

For a moment, he thought she wouldn't leave, but then the fingers around his pressed lightly before withdrawing, and he heard the door whoosh closed, leaving him alone with Simon.

"You don't know what I do, do you?" he asked, focusing the throbbing fury pulsing through his body with each beat of his heart. It could consume him if he let it, but if he harnessed it the right way, he could possibly ensure Teresa never had to worry about her brother hurting her again, even if she chose not to keep him in her life.

"Don't care what you do."

"You should. Because whatever you think you know about violence is nothing compared to what I know. I was literally trained to learn how to inflict maximum damage with minimum effort."

Doubt crept into the man's expression, but he didn't back down, didn't break eye contact.

The first blow caught Simon completely by surprise.

Micah had the man's broken arm twisted up behind his back, yanked high enough to pop his shoulder out of place, and shoved up against the wall in one smooth movement.

"I'm a Navy SEAL," he murmured in Simon's ear. "I eat men like you for breakfast. You think you're a big man because you and your friends outnumbered your sister that day? Hurting someone who never did anything to you but love you and take care of you, that doesn't make you big, it makes you small. Microscopic."

Using pressure points to inflict pain, Micah smiled as Simon thrashed and cried beneath his hold. Whether it made him a bad person or not, he didn't care, because he was loving every pain-filled yelp falling from Simon's lips. In a small way, he was righting the wrongs Teresa had suffered.

"You *ever* come near her again, and I will make you wish for death. Death that won't come until I decide that you've suffered enough. Understand?"

When the man didn't respond, he amped up the

pain until Simon was literally sobbing and writhing, desperate to get away from the agony flooding his body but with nowhere to go.

"Understand?" he repeated.

"Y-yes."

"Say it."

"I-I un-understand," the man babbled.

"I know how to make sure your body is never found, and honestly, who's even going to care if you go missing? Your family wants nothing to do with you. You think your little gang friends are going to cry a river over your loss?" Micah barked out a laugh. "No one cares about you, not anymore, not after what you did. The world will be a better place without you in it, so part of me almost hopes you come after her again, so I have an excuse to kill you. But that's not what she wants. Part of her still loves you, which is the only reason you're still breathing right now. But if you ever go near her again, that changes. I will end you, and I won't feel an ounce of remorse for it. You touch her again, you die. It's as simple as that."

CHAPTER 14

May 5TH
    1:39 P.M.

HER MIND WAS BLOWN.

Teresa still couldn't really believe she'd heard Micah say what she knew she'd heard him say.

He was still in love with her?

When he'd said he loved her as she was being rolled away to be operated on against her will, she'd thought that was his fear talking, not that he really did still love her.

The apologies he'd given, and his claims that he wanted to make it up to her, she'd assumed he was being primarily motivated by guilt. After all, it had been twelve years since their lives together imploded. What else would she think?

Sure, he'd talked about wanting to earn her forgiveness and wanting a place in her life, but again, she had assumed he'd meant friendship. Possibly she would stretch so far as to believe that he wanted to recreate a time in their lives where they'd both been young and happy, now he knew he was the one who had ruined what they shared and not her.

But it was more than that.

Deeper than that.

He still loved her.

Actually loved her. Not just saying it out of fear.

Did that change things?

Did it matter?

Love couldn't go back and fix what was done in the past, make it so that it never happened, but it could change her future if that was what she wanted.

The ball was in her court, Teresa was well aware of that. Micah wanted what she now realized was a second chance at a romantic relationship, not just a friendship born of guilt and shame. While he wanted that, he wasn't going to push for it. He knew that what he'd done had possibly ruined things beyond repair.

So it was up to her to decide which path they walked down.

And whether they walked down it alone or together.

There was only one way she could even begin to make a decision about that.

"We need to talk," she announced the second Micah locked her apartment door behind them.

They'd spoken with the cops, her brother had been arrested, the officer who had cuffed him had assured her that he would be serving time, and not getting bounced right back out. She hoped that was true, but even if it wasn't, she'd seen the look on Simon's face as he was loaded into the back of the police car, clearly in agony, and it was one she recognized. It was the same look of terror she'd walked around wearing for months after the assault.

Whatever Micah had done to him seemed to have worked, and she could only hope he was forever scared away from her. A lingering part of her still loved the little brother she'd known when they were small, but mostly she just wanted to keep him out of her life and heal as best she could from the trauma he'd inflicted on her.

"First, ice for your arm." Micah took her hand, and she found his was trembling as he led her over to the couch.

With extreme gentleness, he eased her into it, his hand clasping one of her ankles, and he tugged off her shoe, repeating the process with her other foot. Then, grasping both ankles and carefully lifting them, he turned her as he did so that she was sitting with her legs up. Finally, he tucked the blanket in around her and disappeared into the kitchen.

Returning with an icepack, he placed it on her lap, took her hand, and settled her arm so that the bruises on her forearm rested on the cold. It was pretty much a guarantee that she would wind up with some bruises, but they weren't the life-threatening injury Micah was treating them as.

"Second, I need to do this." His dark eyes were tormented as he stood before her for a moment before he dropped to his knees.

Her mouth fell open in shock, and she was about to ask him what he was doing when he leaned in and wrapped his arms around her waist, burying his face against her neck.

Were those ... tears ... she felt on her skin?

"I am so sorry for leaving you, pretty girl," he whispered, his voice hoarse.

The thing was, she actually believed him.

Not something Teresa ever thought would happen. But Micah seemed completely sincere in his apologies. Plus, he had no reason to keep offering them. Sure, he'd messed up, but a lot of time had passed, and he could have just said sorry, then packed his bags and gone back home.

He was sticking around for her.

Because he really did want a second chance.

Never would she have thought she would get to this place, but it felt right. Actually, it felt like a weight was lifting off her shoulders. It wasn't until right this very second that Teresa even realized she'd given herself a second burden to bear. Instead of forgiving Micah a long time ago, for her own sake, not his, and allowing herself the freedom to move forward, she'd clung to her righteous anger because she absolutely did have reason to hate him for his abandonment.

But she didn't want to.

It was time.

"I forgive you," she whispered, feeling her throat begin to clog with emotion.

Micah's head whipped up, his eyes and mouth wide with shock. "Wh-what did you just say?"

"I forgive you for leaving. That doesn't mean what you did didn't devastate me, and it doesn't mean that it doesn't still hurt. It also doesn't mean that I know where to go after this. Did you mean it?"

"When I said I loved you?"

Her nod was shaky as she waited for his answer. Whatever it was she knew forgiving him was the right thing to do for herself.

"I meant it with every fiber of my being. For a long time, I hated you for betraying me, I tried to get you out of my head, but I could never let another woman get close to me. I told myself it was because you ruined my ability to trust, but I was wrong. It was because my heart was already yours, and I could never take it back. It kills me knowing the truth now, knowing what I did to you, how badly I—"

"Shh," she murmured, touching a finger to his lips. "You apologized a million times already, and I said I accept."

His lips moved so he could touch a kiss to her fingertip. "Pretty girl, I'm telling you here and now if you let me stay in your life in any sort of capacity, I will be telling you every day for the rest of my life how sorry I am. Scratch that, I have your phone number, I'll text you an apology even if you don't let me stay in your life. And if you change your number, I'll apologize through Nathaniel for as long as I live."

"That's really what you want? To be part of my life again?"

"More than anything."

"Even if it's only as friends?" Forgiving and dating

again were not the same thing, and she honestly couldn't say she knew what she wanted right now. Too much had happened these last few days with seeing Micah again, then the abduction, the surgery, and now with her brother. It was a lot, and she couldn't process it quickly enough to make lifelong decisions.

"I won't lie, I want you back, I want to make all our teenage dreams a reality, but I truly understand that ship might have sailed. I'll take back in your life any way I can get."

"You said you haven't let women get close to you, but according to Nathaniel, you're a bit of a player." That might be a problem given that sex for her was not a fun experience. Pretty standard, she thought, given that her first experience had been horrific.

If she'd had Micah by her side, she might have been able to work through those issues, but she hadn't so she'd had to stumble her way through them on her own. She could make herself come on her own, but when she was with a guy, she usually wound up panicking and getting out of the moment. Which was why there hadn't been many guys.

"Much as I'd like to tell you there were none, there were quite a few. I was a stupid nineteen-year-old kid who panicked and took the coward's way out when he thought his girl cheated on him. Then I was stubborn and held onto that anger and pain instead of doing the mature, grown-up thing and confronting you. A million wishes—and believe me, I have them—can't change that. Have there ..." Micah trailed off and audibly swallowed. "Have there been many men for you?"

"Well, you already know that back then, unlike you, I was still a virgin, and I was waiting for my eighteenth birthday for us to sleep together for the first time. I was trying to be all responsible, not risk a pregnancy when I already had a lot on my plate. Those first few months, I wished so hard I had thrown caution to the wind for once in my life and done it. Since then, there have been a couple of guys but no relationships."

Did she leave it there or tell him everything?

It would be trusting him with a part of herself that she hadn't shared with anyone else, not her mom, not Ava or Chelsea.

Regardless of what the future held for them, there was one thing Micah could do for her now that might change her life.

Dragging in a deep breath, she held it and then jumped off the deep end. "Sex was kind of ruined for me thanks to what happened. I don't know what I can promise you for the future, but do you think you could help me learn to like it?"

* * *

May 5th
    1:54 P.M.

"Can I help you with what?"

The question exploded out of him without any sort of thought on his part, but when he watched as Teresa's gaze slipped away, and her cheeks flushed a deeper shade of pink, it was clear she had misinterpreted what he was saying.

It was obvious she was conflicted about what their future held, and he could hardly hold that against her. Not only had he not been there for her twelve years ago, but he had popped back up in her life at absolutely the worst possible time when she already had so much to deal with. There was no way her mind could settle enough to focus forward when her present was so full of turmoil.

But she'd reached out to him.

Asked him for help.

A real request, something that had taken him months to coax out of her back when they first met. His pretty girl was so stubborn and so independent that she hated showing an ounce of weakness and asking anyone for anything.

Still on his knees before her, Micah grasped her chin between his thumb and forefinger and guided her face back so it was looking at him. Slowly, her gaze once again shifted to meet his, and he saw the tentative hope in those warm brown depths as well as her strength as she was already steeling herself for his rejection.

"May I?" he asked as he maintained his gentle hold on her chin and used his pinkie to brush across Teresa's bottom lip. There was no way he had the right to kiss her anymore without her express permission. Micah knew how lucky he was that she was even allowing him to breathe the same air as her, much less offer him the gift of her forgiveness.

"You want to kiss me?"

"I would spend the rest of my life kissing you if it were possible and at the end know it was a life well spent," he answered honestly. He knew why she was hesitant to believe that after all these years he still loved her, and he didn't know how to convince her it was true.

One day at a time.

When she nodded, he used his grip on her chin to guide her face down a little to meet his, and leaned in so he could whisper his lips across hers. She tasted every bit as good as he remembered, and while he would love to jump all in, ravish her beautiful mouth, they weren't in that place yet.

Pulling back required all his resolve, and so he wasn't tempted again, Micah rose, lifted her legs, then sat on the couch beside her, settling her feet in his lap. Because he knew she was a sucker for a foot massage and he was a sucker for anything that made Teresa happy, he began to rub, keeping most of his attention on what he was doing so Teresa wouldn't feel so self-conscious as they had this conversation.

"So, you don't enjoy sex?" It was selfish of him, but a part of him was glad that even though he wouldn't be her first, he would be her first that actually brought her pleasure.

"No. Like it doesn't hurt, but I don't get off, and I'm too tense the whole time. Guys can tell and it kills the mood. Not that I ever really cared, I always just did it because it seemed like that's what I was supposed to do. Adults have sex."

"What about when you're alone? Do you ever touch yourself? Make yourself come?" These were weird questions to ask the woman he thought he hated for the last decade. He'd thought what Teresa and he could have had was gone forever, but now there was a chance to get it back, and he wanted to cling to that chance so badly it was all he could think about.

There were no guarantees, he got that. He could help Teresa with this, and she might still decide she only wanted to be friends with him, or she could decide she didn't want him in her life at all.

But it was a risk he had to take.

How could he not?

This was Teresa, his pretty girl, the woman he'd known was his soul mate since he was sixteen years old, and he first laid eyes on her.

"I do."

The thought of Teresa once again standing in for herself, doing all the work because she didn't know how to let someone else in, broke his heart. Picturing her bringing herself pleasure was hot, sure, but not with the reasons why she did it alone.

"Just yourself, or do you use toys?"

Without even looking at her, he knew her cheeks were flaming red. They might not have had sex when they were teens, but they'd been in love, there had been lots of kissing, a little touching, and he'd bought her a toy for her sixteenth birthday, one they agreed she would only use when he was on the phone with her, getting himself off.

"Teresa?" he prompted, looking over at her.

"Yeah, I have a few toys," she said in a rush.

"Why don't we start there? We can buy you some

new ones, and then when they arrive, you could use them on yourself while I watch. That way I can see what you like, anything you don't like, and we can take it from there." That seemed the safest option, because Micah doubted Teresa was really ready to jump right on in to having sex with him after she'd just forgiven him.

He might be safe in her mind given their shared past, but so many years had passed, and he feared the trust between them that he'd broken could never be fully repaired.

"Umm … we don't have to wait. I keep them … the toys … hidden in my closet in the back corner, behind a false wall. They're still there, I checked because it would have been super embarrassing for the cops and everyone else to know about them."

Leaning over, Micah grasped her chin again, ensuring he had her full attention. "Nothing about you bringing yourself pleasure should be embarrassing."

"That's easy for you to say, you're normal," she whispered back.

"And you are perfection. Who gets to decide what's normal anyway? You went through something horrific, but you didn't let it break you, and you didn't let it steal your pleasure, you're better than normal."

A smile curled her lips up at the corners, there was still tension radiating off her, but it was a start.

"You want to do this now?"

"Better do it now before I lose my nerve," she agreed.

Lifting her feet once again, Micah stood, then held out his hand. Teresa took it after barely a moment's hesitation and allowed him to tug her to her feet and guide her through to her bedroom.

As they stepped through the doorway, she straightened her spine, and he knew her well enough to know that she was steeling herself to do this. But she walked resolutely toward her closet, dropped to her knees, and then held her head high as she came back up with a somewhat large box in her hands.

She hadn't been kidding when she said she had some toys. He'd been thinking like one or two, but when she opened the box, he saw she had at least a dozen in there, maybe more.

"This is my favorite," she said, setting the box down and holding up one that worked externally. It was no wonder she preferred that to something being inside her. Even though he didn't want to, he hadn't been able to stop imagining how terrified Teresa must have been that night.

Part of him expected her to back out, lose her nerve, but Teresa walked over to the bed he'd bought for her, set the toy down, shimmied out of her leggings and panties without even looking at him, then lay down on top of the covers. This was his first time seeing her naked, and that alone would have been enough to have him growing hard, but add in the strength he knew it took for her to do this before him of all people, and he was aching with desire for this beautiful, brave woman.

"I'll delete it in front of you so you know I'm not doing anything sneaky with it, but what if I record this, then when you're ready to try sex, we can play it and you have something to focus on other than the thoughts running through your head," he suggested.

"You want a video of me doing this?" she asked, but there wasn't judgment, reproach, or anger in her tone. The opposite, in fact. She sounded almost turned on by the idea. Maybe he wouldn't be deleting it after all.

"We'll use your phone instead of mine." That way she wouldn't have a single doubt about what would and wouldn't happen with that video.

"O-okay," she agreed.

Hurrying back through to the living room, he grabbed her cell phone and returned to the bedroom where Teresa lay waiting for him. Once again, her cheeks were flushed, although this time with arousal instead of embarrassment, and when she parted her legs, baring her most intimate parts to him, Micah knew that however things between them turned out, he was one lucky guy to have a woman like Teresa trust him with something this important.

CHAPTER 15

May 5TH
  2:05 P.M.

SHE WAS REALLY GOING to do this.

There was no going back now.

Funnily enough, Teresa found that she didn't even want to.

What was done now was done, she'd stripped half naked in front of the man she'd once loved with her whole heart, and parted her legs, revealing her most intimate parts to him.

Maybe there would be room inside her for shame or at least embarrassment if there wasn't a raging fire of desire in Micah's eyes. After all these years, he still burned so brightly for her. She remembered how much she used to love their make-out sessions, how badly she'd wanted to take that next step. But the thought of risking adding a newborn to her list of responsibilities had kept her holding off at least until she graduated from high school.

Now she was an adult, and while they would use protection, if she wound up pregnant, it wouldn't be the worst thing in the world. Certainly, something she could financially handle, and even with the mess of the last couple of weeks, emotionally handle as well.

"Show me what you like, pretty girl," Micah said as he moved to the end of the bed and held up her phone.

A shiver rocketed through her as the camera caught her spread out like this. It wasn't really nerves, it was more … excitement. The thought of filming this was a turn-on even though she never would have guessed she'd be comfortable with this but turned out she was. After all, she'd have control of the video, it was on her phone, so she wasn't worried about someone doing anything inappropriate with it, and it might be all she had left of this night with Micah.

One night.

That was all she was offering herself.

Offering him.

Although at the back of her mind, she was well aware that one night was all Tobias and Isabella had planned on, and now they were falling in love and expecting a baby.

With Micah's heavy-lidded eyes watching her every move, Teresa felt her body come alive as she pressed the button to turn the toy on and then moved it between her spread legs. While she owned almost two dozen different toys, she used them sporadically at best. Getting herself off just never felt like much of a priority.

Not until right now anyway.

Now she felt like she had to come or she would spontaneously combust.

Positioning the toy against her bud, the sound of its vibrations filled the air. She jolted at that first touch, feeling much more sensitive than she usually did. Normally, she would hold the toy there, shifting its position slightly for several minutes, sometimes she never got that buzz other people seemed addicted to, and in the end would give up.

Today, though, as she held the toy against her delicate flesh, she felt something begin to build inside her.

She'd had orgasms before. Never when she was with other men, but sometimes when she was on her own she was able to get herself there with the help of one of her toys, or sometimes her own fingers. When she did come, it was nothing to write home about, pleasant but nothing earth-shattering.

In fact over the years, she'd come to believe that people were lying when they said sex was amazing and orgasms were addictive. It was mediocre at best as far as she was concerned.

"That feel good, pretty girl?" Micah asked.

"Mmm," she mumbled with a nod as the vibrations continued to build something inside her.

This was her favorite toy, and she had spent a bit on it, but she loved the way it circled around her bundle of nerves and pulsed right where she needed it to if she was even going to have a hope of coming.

"What else do you do while you make yourself come? Do you touch your breasts?"

"They're not very sensitive," she replied as her hips began to rock a little, seeking more of what the toy was offering, and she pressed it tighter against her, wanting to fall apart with Micah watching.

Maybe it was a bit of payback, showing him what he could have had, but there was much more to it than that. She was seeking a kind of redemption that she thought only he could give her. Even with his betrayal she felt safe, at least physically, when it came to her body, with him.

This was a place she could let go. Be free.

"Can I?" he asked, nodding at her chest.

When she gave a shaky nod, Micah shifted his position, keeping the camera aimed at her while he lifted the hem of her shirt. Since she hadn't been planning on doing anything other than hanging around the house today, she hadn't put on a bra, so her breasts were bared to him the moment he bunched her sweater up above her breasts.

"The way I remember it, you loved it when I played with these," Micah murmured as he took one of her nipples and rolled it between his thumb and forefinger.

Heat pooled low in her belly, and she could feel her orgasm shimmering just out of reach. Teresa pressed the toy harder, and her finger hurried to find the button that would increase the intensity of the vibrations.

Micah's fingers continued to play with her nipple, alternating between gently stimulating it as he rolled it and then tweaking it harder. Her head moved restlessly on the pillow, her legs trembled, and she felt her body grow tense.

This was what always happened.

She wanted that orgasm too much, and the more she wanted it, the more it shimmered out of reach.

It was like she could feel it, rumbling around the edges of her body, but it couldn't get past the mental block she had built without even realizing it.

"Relax, pretty girl. It's time to come for me."

With those words, Micah leaned down, and his lips closed around the nipple he'd been playing with. Suckling hard, he stole her attention right when he needed to, and without the barrier she usually kept in place even when she didn't want to, he opened her up to the most intense feelings she'd ever experienced.

Something seemed to possess her, it was the only way she could describe it. A rush of pleasure fired out through her body, starting low in her belly, then claiming every inch of her.

Words maybe, or just moans, fell from her lips, her head thrashed from side to side, the fingers not clutching the toy like a lifeline curled into the covers, needing to hold onto something as ecstasy licked along her veins.

It was almost too much.

Too overwhelming.

And if she hadn't had Micah's tongue, swirling along her nipple, suckling it gently, keeping her grounded, she wouldn't have been surprised if she'd been swept away with the onslaught of pleasure.

"So beautiful falling apart for me, aren't you, pretty girl," Micah murmured as his lips left her breast, causing her to whimper a protest as she floated back down from her high. He chuckled as he stripped out of his clothes.

Without her needing to say anything about it, she saw him hold up a condom. "You still want to do this?"

"Yes," Teresa answered without hesitation. She needed to know what real sex was regardless of whether her future was with this man or someone else. This was something she knew he could give her, and for once in her life, she wanted to be selfish and take instead of give.

Slipping on the condom, little aftershocks of pleasure were still rippling through her system as Micah climbed onto the bed and settled above her. After touching a kiss to one end of the jagged wound on her stomach, he lined up and slid inside her in one smooth move, not giving her time to think about what he was going to do.

There was a moment of slight pain as her body accommodated his size—which she had not been too blissed-out to notice was absolutely huge—but then she could hear her own breathy moans playing out through the phone he pushed into her hand.

"Watch yourself, pretty girl, look how stunning you are when you don't get in your own way," Micah told her as he began to move. His thrusts were steady, nothing too hard and fast, but he also wasn't treating her like she was made of spun glass either.

Teresa found her eyes glued to the image of herself on the phone, the way her body moved, the raw need on her face, the way she looked with her hand holding the toy between her spread legs.

Now there was a man between them, not a toy. A man who looked at her with nothing but love and tenderness as he rocked in and out of her.

"You ready to fall apart for me all over again, pretty girl?" Micah asked.

"I'm ready." It was true, she was ready to stop being her own enemy and fly high, experiencing everything Micah could give her.

"Keep watching that video, and if you need me to stop, you tell me."

"I need you to keep doing what you're doing."

Micah chuckled, then picked up his pace. Balancing his weight with one hand, his other reached between them, found her swollen and sensitive bud, and took it between his fingers. What he was doing felt so much better than the toy, and Teresa moaned in delight as the little aftershocks turned into something much more powerful.

Between his fingers and his length, pleasure built quickly. If she'd thought that last orgasm was the earth-shattering experience she'd heard orgasms could be, then this one felt like it was about to break the entire universe.

Instinct had her lifting her legs, hooking her ankles around Micah's hips, bringing each thrust deeper. The phone fell from her hand, she no longer needed it to keep her locked in the moment. Instead, her fingers tangled in Micah's hair, and she brought his mouth down to meet hers.

Kissing him was a different layer of intimacy than sex and one she probably shouldn't indulge in when she knew she couldn't yet offer him anything, but she needed to feel one of his kisses.

The second their lips met, her world fractured into a

million diamonds of pure pleasure, as another orgasm tore through her body. It flared with bright light, consuming her, and she cried out, the sound caught by Micah's mouth as he poured a lifetime worth of emotion into the kiss.

Could they still have a lifetime worth of life to live together?

Was it crazy of her to even consider a future for them, given what she'd learned the hard way in their past?

Or was this moment really all they could ever share?

* * *

May 6th
  8:46 A.M.

"THANKS FOR MAKING THIS POSSIBLE," Teresa said as they stepped into the elevator at Prey's office building in the city.

He hadn't wanted to.

In fact, when Teresa had first asked yesterday evening if she could come into Prey for a few hours, work with her team, collect some stuff she could then take home and work on, Micah's initial instincts had been to say no.

Last time he'd brought her into Prey, they'd been gassed and abducted on the way home.

But Teresa had said she understood if it couldn't happen, that she didn't want anyone to get hurt because of her desire to get back to work now that she was starting to feel better and wanted to contribute to her team's efforts to bring down the trafficking ring. She hadn't begged, and he knew she wouldn't complain if he told her it wasn't feasible.

Which was exactly why he'd wanted to make it happen for her.

So he'd talked with the guys helping watch over her, and together they had all agreed that if they made a very clear motorcade, it would deter any potential abduction attempts. They'd also used a decoy to pretend to be Teresa while they snuck her into the back of a different vehicle, just in case any mercenaries might be bold enough to try another attempt, and they might be able to turn the tables on them.

Thankfully, nothing had happened and now they were safely there. While he'd spend the rest of the morning worrying about the return journey, the smile on Teresa's face made the stress more than worth it.

"You're welcome," he told her, smiling back.

Things had been pretty good between them yesterday after they'd slept together. He'd worried it might create awkwardness, they'd taken a major step that Teresa hadn't been ready for when they'd been dating, and had only hours before forgiven him, so he wouldn't have been surprised.

But there was no awkwardness.

If anything, things had been better.

They'd talked, keeping to fairly neutral and easy topics, he'd helped her cook dinner, and they'd watched some old movies together. It had been nice and was exactly what he wanted his future to look like even as he knew that Teresa was nowhere close to even wanting to be his friend again, let alone anything more.

For a moment, she just looked at him, then she pushed up onto her toes and pressed a kiss to his cheek. "I know you didn't want to do it, so I really appreciate it. It feels good to be back out, not cowering at home, not letting them steal my power. My team and I are going to bring them down."

Her fiery determination not to be broken, to keep fighting, only made him fall even harder for her. Micah would have sworn he already loved her as much as it was physically possible to love anyone, but then she went and did something like this, and that love that already felt so full swelled a little more.

The elevator dinged open before he could say anything, and they both headed down the hall to the Cyber Team office. Everyone else was already there since they were all staying in the building, most of them in the apartments, although he had no idea where Josiah lived. Seemed like the man spent ninety-nine percent of his time at his desk working.

"Teresa!" Chelsea exclaimed, hurrying over to hug her friend. Ava was right on her heels, and even Isabella and Tobias got up to come over and offer hugs. Only Josiah once again remained at his desk, seemingly oblivious to what was going on around him, although Micah suspected he was actually anything but.

As the girls chattered away, Micah stepped away to give them space to do their own thing. Taking a seat down the opposite end of the table, Nathaniel and

Tobias immediately joined him, and when he caught their eyes, he realized they were looking at him expectantly.

"What?" he asked.

"You slept with her," Nathaniel said softly so his tone wouldn't carry and the girls wouldn't hear him.

"How could you possibly know that?" While he wouldn't have been averse to the idea of tattooing on his forehead that he was hopelessly and forever owned by Teresa Dash, he obviously hadn't done that. So how had his teammate figured it out within seconds of seeing him?

"You saying it's not true?" Tobias asked, arching a brow.

"I'm not saying it's not true, and I'm not saying it is true. I don't want to violate Teresa's privacy." He didn't care if the guys knew he and Teresa had slept together, but he wasn't sure she'd feel the same way about it.

"Doesn't look like she thinks talking about it is violating her privacy," Nathaniel said with a nod at the other end of the long conference table, where the girls had their heads down and appeared to be deep in conversation.

"Oh yeah, they're talking about it," Tobias added.

"Girls," he said with a chuckle. Still, he was thrilled that Teresa had a group of women with whom she felt safe and comfortable. Back when they'd been kids, she'd had plenty of friends, but getting close to them had been difficult given that she had so much on her plate at home, plus her studies. He could imagine her rape had made it harder to trust people, especially since she thought he abandoned her because of it, but it looked like she'd found people worthy of her trust, and he absolutely loved that for her.

"So are you two together again?" Nathaniel asked.

"No. We're not anything," he replied honestly.

"Your decision or hers?" Tobias asked.

"Hers. I'm one hundred percent in. If she'd take me back, I'd be there in an instant. But I messed up big time. Way bigger than you guys did." Maybe it would be reassuring that Ava had taken Nathaniel back after he'd freaked out on her multiple times because of his own hang-ups about growing up poor while she came from a wealthy family. Or that Isabella had been able to forgive Tobias for telling her he wanted nothing to do with her or their baby when she wound up unexpectedly pregnant, because of his back injury and his mother's illness.

But neither of those things reassured him.

They hadn't messed up anywhere close to as badly as he had.

"I'm trying to keep realistic expectations," he continued. "She has every reason to hate me forever. That she found it in the depths of that big heart of hers to forgive me is more than I could have hoped for. But ..."

"You want it all," Tobias said softly, like he got it. Which he probably did. From what he'd gotten to know of the former Delta Force operator over the last few days was that the man had given up on his dreams after being injured, much like Micah had given up on his after he'd thought Teresa cheated on him.

"Yeah, I want it all. For the last twelve years, I thought I hated her, that I was over her, that if I ever ran into her again, all I'd want was an apology. But it changed the moment I bumped into her downstairs. I still thought she betrayed me, but it became pretty clear pretty quickly that I never got over her. Don't even think it's possible to get over her. I fell in love with her when I was sixteen, and I'm going to love her for as long as I live."

"So you're going to fight for her?" Nathaniel asked.

"Hell yeah," he exclaimed. "I'm going to fight for her with everything I have, but I'm going to do it in the most respectful way I can. In the end, I wronged her, and what happens next has to be up to her. I just don't know if I honestly stand a chance or if I'm hoping for something that's never going to happen."

"I think given enough time it's going to happen," Tobias said.

"Why?" That sounded a little desperate, but he *was* a little desperate for some confidence that a future with Teresa could still be in the cards, and he'd take anything at all.

"Because she keeps glancing over at you," Tobias replied. "I know the look. It's the way Ava looks at Nathaniel, like she needs the reassurance of knowing he's close by. The way Chelsea looks at Josiah, even though I doubt he's ever going to notice that the woman is hopelessly in love with him. The way Isabella looks at me, making me feel grateful every day that she was strong enough to forgive me for my mistakes and short-comings, and wants to be with me anyway."

Did Teresa really look at him like that?

He felt her gaze on him, sure, and he could even buy

that he made her feel safer. But making her feel safe and making her feel loved and supported were two completely different things.

Fighting for her was something he had to do, it was as important as breathing, but this couldn't be a one-sided fight. The only way they could ever work was if they both were fighting for the same goal. And Micah couldn't shake the fear that after what he'd done he wasn't worth fighting for.

CHAPTER 16

MAY 6TH

8:52 A.M.

"YOU LOOK DIFFERENT TODAY."

Teresa startled at Chelsea's words, wondering if the thoughts running through her mind had also been running across her face.

She'd tried to be careful, keep her expressions neutral, it was nobody else's business what she and Micah had done yesterday afternoon, but there was every chance she could not think of sex without her face blushing, or her eyes darkening, or something else equally as obvious that would give her away.

"Uh, is that a good thing or a bad thing?" she asked, hoping that if she played it off right, then her friends would just think that it was everything going on with the trafficking ring that was weighing on her mind this morning.

And it *was* weighing on her mind.

There was no feasible way to forget about the ring and what they'd done to her when most movements still caused a tug of pain across the wound on her stomach. It was getting better, the antibiotics were clearing away the infection, and in another few weeks, all that would be left was a scar that would forever remind her of her ordeal.

It would forever remind her of something else as well.

Micah.

Not just because he'd been kidnapped alongside her, but because that was where she'd learned the truth about the past.

Despite her offered forgiveness and what she'd asked him to help her with, lingering pain remained that he could think she would cheat on him and walk away with such apparent ease. Only the more time she spent with him, the more she realized it hadn't in fact been easy for him to walk away.

When he thought she wasn't paying attention, he cast her glances that were so full of pain and remorse that it made her eyes sting with tears of her own. Knowing he was truly sorry about his past choices helped a lot. As did trying to think about what she would have done if their positions had been reversed.

If she'd walked in on him having sex with four other women, would she have thought rape or cheating? Would she have stayed and confronted him? Would she have tucked tail and run?

It was easy to say she would have confronted him,

but the truth was, they'd both been so young that maybe she wouldn't have made the wisest of choices.

Whatever the answer to that question, one thing she knew for certain.

Clinging to the pain wasn't worth it. It wasn't helpful. It was holding her back and keeping her present tied to her past. Her past would always be there, but it didn't have to be the central focus of her entire life.

Her future could be.

"Oh, it's definitely a good thing," Chelsea answered.

"A very good thing," Ava added with an amused smile, like she knew exactly what game Teresa was trying to play and had no intention of letting her get away with it.

"I think what your friends are trying to not so subtly hint at is that they want the most current gossip," Isabella explained.

"And what gossip is it exactly that you think I have? I'm not the one who's been at work every day," she said, still feigning innocence. It wasn't that she didn't want to share what had happened between her and Micah with her friends because she didn't trust them, she did, even Isabella, who she hadn't known for very long, it was just that she still wasn't sure what she wanted, or what she could handle.

Bringing others into it increased the pressure to make some sort of decision.

It wasn't like she was trying to drag things out for punishment to Micah or anything. She didn't want to hurt him, or leave him living in limbo, she just honestly had so many thoughts and emotions swirling inside her that it was too hard to still them all, put them into some sort of logical order, and make sense of them.

"There was zero gossip from here," Ava said. "All we did was work and worry about you."

"We want the *real* gossip," Chelsea told her.

"And I have that real gossip?"

"From the pink on your cheeks and the way you keep darting little glances over at Micah, I'm going to say yes," Isabella informed her.

"Little glances at Micah?" Had she really been doing that? She hadn't even realized. Although now that she thought about it, it did seem like she was constantly reassuring herself of his presence by seeking him out.

"Something happened between you two, right?" Chelsea, the romantic, asked.

Lying felt wrong, especially with her best friends. Maybe they could offer her a little perspective since she was having so much trouble figuring it all out on her own. Isabella didn't know about Teresa's past, but her newest friend had suffered a similar fate when she was abducted last year in Cambodia and trafficked, so even though they'd known each other for the shortest amount of time, Isabella might actually understand the best.

"Yeah, something happened," she acknowledged. "We talked some more yesterday, and I told him that I forgive him."

"For leaving you?" Ava asked.

"Turns out Micah thought I cheated," she explained. They hadn't had a real chance to talk since she found out the truth about everything, but now that she'd started talking, she wanted to get it all out, wanted them to help her figure out where she went from there. "He was upset, left, blocked me, and became a SEAL. While they were holding us captive, we finally talked, and I told him what really happened. He was ... devastated."

It made her sound like a bad person, but she was glad of that.

If the truth hadn't changed anything for him, or if he'd still tried to put most of the blame on her, or if he'd only been mildly apologetic but defended his actions, she wasn't sure she could have forgiven him.

"How could he have thought *you* would have cheated?" Chelsea gasped. "You barely had time to breathe back then."

"He was young, and he made a terrible mistake. One that hurt me deeply. But he's apologized a million times, he, uh, even cried." She didn't tell them that to embarrass Micah—not that she thought it actually would, she was pretty sure he would wear those particular tears as a badge of honor—but to emphasize to her friends how serious he was. "He wants me back, said he still loves me, but that he also understands there might be no going back. Forgiving him was easier than I thought it would be."

"Because he was sincere," Ava said.

"Makes all the difference," Isabella added.

"I was gang raped when I was seventeen," she told Isabella.

"Kind of figured from everything I'd put together," the other woman told her. "I'm so sorry that happened to you."

"Right back at ya. It's … indescribable, as you know. It was a long time ago now, and in some ways, I've moved past it, but in other ways I haven't. I've had sex since, and I … you know … get myself there sometimes. But it's never been fun for me. It's weird because trusting Micah with my heart seems so hard, but trusting him with my body was much easier."

"You guys had sex," Chelsea exclaimed excitedly.

"Shh," Teresa shushed, but as she looked over to the other side of the table, she saw the guys were deep in conversation and didn't seem to have heard. "We did, and it was amazing, but after …"

"After what?" Ava asked.

"Well, things weren't awkward even though I thought they might be. He helped me cook dinner, and he came up with a safe way to get me here this morning, and we watched some TV, even talked a little, about our jobs, and hobbies, nothing too deep or personal. When it was time for bed, I didn't want to leave him, wanted him to stick close, but I didn't know how to ask."

Asking for help had always been hard for her. She'd had to be a grown-up from the age of nine, but asking Micah for anything seemed particularly hard because he hadn't been there when she needed him.

"Pretty sure he'd jump at doing anything you asked him to," Isabella said.

"He would," she agreed. "But is it fair of me to ask anything more of him when I don't know what I can give him in return?" Asking for help with sex was one thing, but how did she find the strength to move beyond that?

"I don't think he sees your relationship as transactional," Ava said gently. "Part of him wants to do things for you to make up for his actions in the past, I'm sure, but I don't believe that's all there is to it. He *wants* to be there for you because he loves you. No strings, no add-ons, no anything else. Just love."

"If you want to figure out where you go from here, then all you need to do is find out the answer to one question. Do you still love him?" Chelsea asked.

Did she?

Part of her was terrified to think she might because it left her open to the chance of more pain. Part of her hoped she was because it would make everything going forward so much easier.

How did she figure out which side of the coin her heart lay on?

* * *

MAY 6th
9:58 P.M.

"OKAY, TIMES UP," Micah announced.

Teresa turned her head to throw him a quick glance before refocusing on her laptop. "Just a little longer."

"No. Not just a little longer. Do you know what time it is?"

She shrugged. "Maybe six or seven?"

"We stopped and had dinner at six," he reminded her.

"Then seven, I guess."

"Does it look like seven outside?" Reaching out, he hooked a finger under Teresa's chin and turned her head again so she could look past him to the window where it was completely dark outside.

"Oh. It's dark. I guess eight then."

"And I guess time really does fly when you're having fun," he teased. "We got home before seven. It's ten now."

"I can work for at least another hour then." Teresa tried to tug her chin out of his grasp, but he tightened his hold slightly.

"You've already been working most of the day, and you're still recovering. You need sleep. If you keep going like this, you're going to wind up missing something important because you're too tired to catch everything."

"I've probably missed something anyway." She huffed. "We all have. It's so annoying, we keep going through all the information we have so far, running different checks, focusing on different things, and we still wind up with nothing. I knew these guys were good, but I also know they have to have made a mistake somewhere along the way. Once we find that mistake, we can destroy them."

"You'll find that mistake." Micah believed that with everything he had in him. How could a team of amazing people like Prey's Cyber Team not find what it took to destroy the trafficking ring? While he was biased and absolutely thought that Teresa was the most talented on her team, he knew they were all talented and hardworking. He'd seen it with his own two eyes over the last few days.

They'd find that mistake, but right now, his job wasn't to push them harder, it was to take care of the woman who owned his heart.

"Come on, time for bed," he urged, leaning over to close the lid of the laptop that sat on her lap.

With a sigh, Teresa nodded and allowed him to scoop up the laptop and set it aside, then pull her to her feet. "Would you … if it's not too much trouble … do you think maybe you could …?"

Smoothing a stray lock of hair behind her ear, Micah leaned down to touch a kiss to her forehead. "You can ask me anything you want, pretty girl, and the answer is going to be yes."

She chuckled. "You should be careful making that promise, I could get creative."

"Get as creative as you want."

Another chuckle. "Well, this time I wasn't going to be creative. I was just wondering if you would sleep in my bed tonight?"

"Sleep or *sleep*?" he asked. Micah was up for either or both, but he never wanted to do anything that made Teresa uncomfortable, so he had to know what she needed from him tonight.

Cheeks bright pink, her gaze skittered away before resolutely returning to meet his. "Both."

"Go get ready for bed, and I'll check everything is locked up tight and meet you there." After pressing another kiss to her forehead, he nudged her in the direction of the bedroom.

Once she was gone, he checked the front door was locked, then all the windows. It would be next to impossible for someone to climb through one of them, but when they were talking about Teresa's safety, he wasn't going to take any chances. After he'd confirmed they were safely tucked in, he brushed his teeth, stripped out of his clothes, grabbed a bottle of massage oil and a condom, then headed for Teresa's bedroom.

Inside, she was laid out for him, her delectable body naked, and his eyes drank in the sight of her. She was so beautiful, not just on the outside but on the inside, too. So strong, so dependable, so responsible, always carrying the weight of the world on her shoulders.

Not tonight, though.

"Can't do your back since you can't lie on your stomach yet, but how about a massage?" he asked as he approached, holding up the bottle of oil.

"Sounds delightful."

He couldn't agree more. Settling on the end of her bed, Micah poured some of the oil into his hands, then picked up one of her feet. They didn't talk as he massaged her foot then worked his way up her leg, easing out the tension in her muscles. They didn't need to. Tonight was about helping Teresa relax so she was ready for him, her mind firmly in the present and not in the past.

When he finished with her first leg, Micah couldn't resist a touch. Just a small one. Brushing the pad of his forefinger along her center, he found it already wet for him. Teresa watched him through heavy-lidded eyes, desire etched into her features.

"I kept it," she whispered when he picked up her other foot and resumed his massage.

"Kept what?"

"The video. I was going to delete it, but ... I couldn't."

There was no need for her to explain what video she was talking about, and he loved that she'd kept it. A reminder whenever she needed one that she was still a sensual being, that those men hadn't taken that from her.

"If you want ... I could send it to you."

His gaze snapped to hers. "You'd do that? Trust me with something like that?"

"I know you'd never hurt me on purpose, Micah. Not like that. Never like that. What happened was a horrible misunderstanding, and I wish you'd handled it better, talked to me. I can't deny that there's still some pain left, and there will probably be a little scar left behind. But I'm healing more every day, and I don't just mean the wound on my stomach. I know you wouldn't do anything with that video other than watch it, and ... I kind of like that idea."

Micah groaned. "Pretty girl, do you have any idea what it does to me when you say things like that?" It wasn't just that he was impossibly hard as he thought about being able to watch Teresa get herself off whenever he wanted, it was that she was offering her trust as such a beautiful gift that it stirred up the emotions inside him, driving him wild.

"I know what you do to me." Her legs began to

move restlessly on the bed, and he could see the evidence of her arousal glistening on her center.

"Can I taste you, pretty girl?"

Teresa's eyes darkened with desire, and she gave a shaky nod, her legs already opening wider, ready to accommodate him.

Grabbing her hips, he eased her further down the bed until her knees bent over the sides, then knelt in front of her. Wanting to be mindful of her injury, he kept his hands on her hips as he leaned in and swiped his tongue along her wet center. While he knew it couldn't actually be true, she tasted sweet, like happiness and sunshine, like love and laughter. Like his future.

A moan tumbled from her lips, and the sound spurred him on. He wanted her panting and desperate, begging and pleading, then screaming his name as pleasure tore through her body, leaving her breathless and thoroughly sated.

It didn't take him long to figure out that she liked it when he circled her bud with the tip of his tongue, then moved to echo the movement around her entrance. Alternating between the two, above him, Teresa's head began to move against the mattress, her hands clawing the covers, as pleas fell from her lips.

"Please, Micah. More. More. Please, please, please, more. I need …"

"Know exactly what you need, pretty girl." Keeping one hand on her hip, with his other he dipped two fingers inside her, spreading her open so this time he could plunge his tongue deep.

Teresa's head came off the mattress as she gasped,

then dropped back down again when he began to thrust into her at an almost frenetic pace. She was close, he could feel it, see it in how desperate her movements had gotten, in the high-pitched quality of her voice as she begged for her release.

More than happy to give it to her, Micah closed his lips around her bundle of nerves and sucked hard. Watching her fall apart as her orgasm hit was the most wonderful sight in the world, and he kept sucking on her bud as she rode out the wave, wanting it to be so good for her.

"Mmm," she moaned as she came down from her high. "That was everything I've always heard it was supposed to be. Thank you."

"Don't thank me for worshiping your body the way it deserves," he told her as he moved to sit behind her on the bed, his hands under her arms to very gently pull her back so they were both sitting with her propped against him. Grabbing the massage oil, he poured a little more on his fingers and then started work massaging out the kinks in her shoulders and neck.

"Feels so good," she murmured, her head tipping forward to give him better access.

"You're always so tight here, so busy carrying everyone else's burdens. It was my job to carry yours, and I failed you." Micah didn't doubt that the weight of guilt he felt about the past would always rest heavily upon him. Which he deserved.

"You're here now," Teresa whispered.

"If you give me a chance, pretty girl, I'll never let you down again."

"I want to, Micah. But I'm scared," she admitted.

"Come here, pretty girl." Turning her around so she was facing him, he grabbed the condom he'd brought with him, and ripped it open, sliding it on, then lifting Teresa and lowering her down onto him slowly. "Even if you can't give me a second chance, I will still *always* be there for you. Any time, day or night, all you have to do is call and I'll come."

"I'm sure your bosses would love that," she teased. "Sorry I have to leave this highly sensitive and covert op because my ex-girlfriend needs something."

"The woman I love," he corrected, making her blush. "Even when I'm on the other side of the world, I'm still only a phone call away. I don't want you to ever have to carry another heavy burden alone again. Never again," he insisted as he started to move, thrusting up into her while holding her still so she didn't put undue pressure on her healing wound. "Never again."

Teresa's fingers clutched his shoulders as he thrust harder, more desperately, he needed her to understand how much he loved her and how sorry he was for abandoning her.

"Touch yourself, pretty girl. Need you to come first."

One of her hands dipped immediately between them, finding her bundle of nerves and working it with the same frenetic energy he felt. Her internal walls quivered, and a moment later she cried out his name as they clamped around him, setting off his own orgasm.

It flooded his system with so much pleasure he couldn't think straight. All he could do was feel, and pray Teresa felt it, too. The almost otherworldly connection that had always existed between them. It was like it was snapping back into place.

As the orgasm faded and he pulled out of Teresa, laying her down and disappearing to the bathroom to dispose of the condom and grab a washcloth to clean her up, he could only hope that's what the feeling had been. Once he'd cleaned her up, switched off the lights, and tucked them both in, something settled inside him as Teresa didn't hesitate to snuggle into his embrace as he pressed his front up against her side, spooning her as best as he could with her needing to sleep on her back because of her wound.

She was letting him in little by little, but was she ever going to be comfortable enough with him to let go of the fear and let him hold onto her heart again?

CHAPTER 17

May 7ᵀᴴ
    2:27 A.M.

A shrill shriek jerked her from sleep.

Confused and still half asleep, Teresa blinked open her eyes and lifted her head, trying to figure out what was going on and what the obnoxious noise was.

She'd been out like a light within minutes of lying down and snuggling into Micah's warm body. He'd always been so cozy. When they were teens and it was cold out, she'd always just tucked herself close and absorbed some of his body heat. Even though years had passed and there had been so much bad blood between them, it had been much easier than she would have guessed to curl up against him.

Because she was healing.

Like she'd told him last night, there was lingering pain, and there would likely be a scar left behind. They could never completely go back to how things had been between them when they were teenagers, but she was healing, and it was getting easier to let him in.

Now his large body moved beside her, seemingly waking with a lot more clarity than she had, because she felt him tense, and then he was flinging the covers back.

"Get dressed," he ordered, already searching for clothes for her and thrusting them at her.

"Dressed? Is that the fire alarm?" she asked, finally realizing what the sound was.

"Yes," Micah replied, his voice clipped as he found her a pair of shoes.

If she'd been wearing pajamas, Teresa would have been happy to just leave in them, but she was naked, and fire alarm or not, she wasn't going out of her apartment without clothing on. Shoving her legs into the leggings Micah had gotten, she realized with sinking clarity what was really going on.

"It's a trap," she said, standing and carefully easing the leggings up so the band didn't sit pressed against her healing wound.

"It is," Micah agreed. Since he wasn't bothering to shield her from the worry rolling off him in waves, she knew he wasn't just concerned, he was terrified.

"The guys are out there," she reminded him, grabbing the oversized T-shirt and pulling it over her head. "And you're here. They won't get to me."

Although she said the words to reassure Micah, they both knew they weren't necessarily true. While she would stick to Micah's side like glue, there would be a lot of people out there, and it would be far too easy for them to get separated.

Which was the point.

These people had decided to create chaos in order to flush them out and make an abduction attempt that much easier.

But she had no intention of making any of it easier for them.

As she shoved her feet into her sneakers, Teresa brushed a fingertip along the inside of her wrist. She was taking a huge gamble, and she knew Micah was going to be furious about it when he found out. But she wasn't going to leave herself vulnerable to an attack and reliant on anyone, even her team who she trusted implicitly, to luck out on finding her, it was part of the reason she'd insisted on going into Prey yesterday.

Both Eagle and Raven knew what she had planned, and if the worst happened, she had to believe that it would work out the way she hoped. The risks were high, but the potential benefit could be everything they needed to close the ring down once and for all, rather than just putting dents in its operation.

"I'm ready," she said as she straightened.

Giving her a quick once-over, Micah nodded, then they both hurried down to the living room. They paused only long enough for Micah to throw on jeans and a T-shirt, then put on his shoes, and tuck his weapon into his waistband, before he grabbed both their cell phones and shoved hers into her hand.

At the door, he paused, his large hands covering her shoulders, kneading a couple of times before pulling her close and crushing his mouth to hers in a fiery kiss that under any other circumstances would have wound up with them both naked and in bed again.

"I want you to call me, keep the line open, that way if we do get separated, at least we'll still be in contact," he ordered as he unlocked her door, and they both stepped out.

Teresa quickly brought up Micah's name in her contacts and called him. He answered, then he took hold of her hand, his long fingers holding firm to her own, and she prayed they weren't going to get separated.

Knowing they were walking right into a trap didn't mean they could avoid it.

They couldn't stay there so they were just going to have to hope for the best.

Her neighbors were streaming out of their own apartments, filling the hall as they all headed down the stairs by the elevator. They joined the throngs, and with each step they took, Teresa felt her anxiety rise.

Just minutes ago, she'd been snuggled in bed, Micah's comforting presence beside her allowing her to have pleasant dreams. In fact, she'd been dreaming of the two of them, they'd been right in the throes of passion when that fire alarm had ruined everything.

If she thought there were a lot of people in the hall, it was nothing compared to the number in the stairwell. Her building had fifteen floors, and she was on the ninth, so there were still a lot of apartments above them, which meant a lot of people all having to use the stairs to get out.

As they started down the stairs, Teresa was acutely

aware that any one of these people could be the enemy. They were here somewhere, if they weren't in the building, then they were outside it, just waiting for an opportunity to strike.

All about her, people bumped into her. Everyone was on edge, some people openly panicking, none of them knew that she was the cause of this. She doubted there was any real fire anywhere in the building, any real problem at all, but these people didn't know that, and they were acting accordingly.

It was slow going down the stairs, there were too many people, more than the stairwell was made to accommodate, so they had to trudge along with all the others, constantly getting pushed and pulled in all directions.

Throughout it all, Teresa clung to Micah's hand.

Not only was he her lifeline, her protection, but he acted as a buffer as much as he could, trying to keep her close so he took more of the bumps.

But the sea of people was like the ocean.

It pushed and pulled.

It had a mind of its own.

And sometimes it was almost impossible to handle.

They were almost down to the ground floor when she felt it.

A tiny prick against the exposed skin on her arm.

She knew immediately what it was, but whatever she'd just been drugged with was fast acting.

Already, her head began to swim, making it hard to focus.

Teresa tugged on Micah's hand, but with them being jostled as they were, he didn't seem to notice.

"Micah," she called, scared when her voice came out weak, not loud enough to be heard over the noise of the masses.

Then an arm wrapped around her from behind, and she was yanked away from her lifeline.

Whoever was taking her was moving quickly, taking them backward into the sea of people going down and into the door that took them to the second floor.

She saw Micah turn around, his gaze searching for her. Did he see her?

The door swung closed, and she tried to fight against the man carrying her, but the drug in her system made her clumsy, her limbs refusing to cooperate the way she needed them to.

"Teresa!" Micah's voice called from the phone she still clutched in her hand. "Where are you? Call out to me, tell me where to find you!"

"Micah," she called again, lifting the phone toward her ear. "Need you."

"I hear you, pretty girl, I'm coming, hold on for me."

"Hurry," she murmured just as the man carrying her swatted the phone out of her hand.

It landed on the floor with a clunk, her last lifeline snatched away.

Although her brain urged her to fight, to try to stop this from happening, to at least buy some time for Micah to find her, it was like she was watching her body from the outside, no longer in control of it.

She watched as she was carried inside an apartment and straight through it to the window. Watched as the window was shoved open and the man stuck his head out, calling to someone.

A man appeared below the window, and the man holding her maneuvered her through it, and then she was falling.

Maybe she screamed, she wasn't too sure.

The landing was soft and quicker than she'd been expecting as the man on the ground caught her.

Movement beside her was her abductor jumping out the window.

Since they weren't high up, he merely grunted as his feet hit the ground, and then they were moving again. With the flow of people streaming out of her building.

Once upon a time, she'd believed in safety in numbers, but tonight there was no safety to be found.

No one knew she was in trouble.

They likely just saw a guy carrying his partner out of the building, assumed she was sick, or hurt, or just panicked.

Police officers and firefighters were also filling the street, but there was no safety to be found from any of them.

A white van was waiting for them, and she was shoved into it, a man waiting inside jabbed her with a second syringe, and the world shimmered out of reach.

As the darkness descended, she prayed that her gamble would pay off, otherwise, her life was about to be over.

* * *

M<small>AY</small> 7th

2:37 A.M.

O<small>NE SECOND SHE WAS THERE</small>, clinging to his hand, the next she was gone.

Micah felt the surge of people around them, and his grip on Teresa's hand weaken as she was tugged backward.

He tried to reclaim his hold as her fingers left his.

Tried to turn around to see where she was, if need be, he'd haul her into his arms and carry her out of there. It might make him unpopular with the sea of people fleeing the building, but he didn't care about that.

All he cared about was Teresa.

They were going to go straight to Prey's office after this, and no matter how much she argued against it, she wasn't leaving until this ring was dismantled.

Managing to fight against the swell of people, Micah turned, scanning the heads, searching for the only face he was interested in.

"Teresa!" he yelled into his phone as he caught sight of the door heading into the second floor swinging closed.

Someone might have just fled through it and joined everyone else on the stairs, or if someone had deliberately pulled Teresa away from him, they might have disappeared with her through it. He was pretty sure there was no actual problem inside the building, whoever had triggered the alarm would know that, so they would know it was safe to hide out in one of the now-empty apartments.

The second floor was also close enough to the ground to jump out a window.

Glad he'd insisted on them having the phone connection as well as him holding her hand, he yelled into his cell, "Where are you? Call out to me, tell me where to find you!"

For a moment, there was nothing.

Then he heard it.

A frail wisp of a sound.

"Micah. Need you." Her words were faint, and he wondered whether there was a possibility that she had been drugged. She was still recovering, but she'd been doing much better, the infection clearing, her strength returning, and she'd been fine when they left her apartment a few minutes ago.

For something to have changed in that short time, it had to have been caused by something and drugs were the most likely.

"I hear you, pretty girl, I'm coming, hold on for me," he ordered as he fought his way through the people trying to push him down along with them. He had to get up to that door, his gut was telling him that's where Teresa had been taken.

"Hurry."

Following the whispered word, he heard a clunk like her phone had been dropped.

Dropped or forcefully taken from her?

Either way, it didn't really matter except to his own

mind because forcefully taken meant she was fighting, but dropped meant she might be unconscious, no longer able to help him get to her.

"Teresa! You still there? Answer me, pretty girl, tell me you're okay," he pleaded as he shoved people out of his way with more force than he usually would have used. But he was consumed with fear for his girl, it was all he could think about, it flooded his system, threatening to render him useless.

Making his way to the door, he flung it open, and his gaze immediately landed on the slight glow on the floor about three apartments down.

A phone.

Running to it, he could hear his own voice echoing from it as he called out Teresa's name over and over again.

Snatching it up, he found it was indeed her phone, and the door to the apartment it had been lying in front of was partially open.

Disconnecting the call, Micah shoved both cell phones into his pockets and palmed his weapon. There was no way he'd been leaving Teresa's place knowing they were walking into a trap without being armed, but he'd kept it out of sight as they'd made their way down the stairs, not wanting to cause additional panic and risk a stampede which could potentially cost lives.

Now he gripped his weapon in his hand as he carefully edged open the apartment door.

It was dark inside, quiet, and he could see curtains fluttering at the open living room window.

There was a chance it was a decoy, or that the homeowner had simply had the windows open already when they left and not thought to close them, but his gut told him that whoever had taken Teresa was no longer in the apartment. They weren't hiding, ready to take him out as well, last time they'd only abducted him along with Teresa because it was more convenient. This time around, trying to abduct two people would be an added burden that could get them caught.

Running to the window, he looked out, scanning the crowd for a glimpse of his girl.

Too many people. Too close together. Sirens of police cars and fire trucks swirled with the fire alarm, and the flashing of their lights made it more difficult to scan the sea of people for the only one he wanted to catch a glimpse of.

Or maybe it was his own fear that made it harder to focus.

Panic like he'd never felt before thudded through his system with each beat of his heart.

Terror like he'd never known before.

He'd been in life-or-death situations in his career as a SEAL. There had even been times when he had been positive he wasn't going to make it out the other side. He'd also lost friends and teammates, and knew the crushing grief of someone you cared about being snatched away much too soon.

But he'd never had anyone he loved in danger like this.

His teammates were like brothers, and he loved them, but in a very different way than the love he felt for Teresa. That love was all-consuming, it entwined their souls and made them one. Losing her would destroy something in him that could never be repaired.

As he scanned the gathered mass of people and didn't spot Teresa, Micah's hope began to dim.

Where was she?

"Teresa!" he screamed out the window. She'd sounded so weak on the phone, and he was sure that if she could have held onto it, she would have, because she knew it was a lifeline that could lead him right to her.

Just as he opened his mouth to yell her name again, he noticed something on the edge of the crowd.

A man was carrying a woman.

All he could see was a dark head resting against a shoulder, but it was all he needed to see.

Uncaring about anything other than getting to Teresa before it was too late, Micah threw himself out the window. He barely felt the jar as his feet slammed into the concrete below, because he was already moving.

Had to get to his girl.

Couldn't let them take her from him.

As he ran, Micah pulled out his cell phone and called Raven Oswald. He had no doubt that the men watching the building had already called in about the fire alarm, that more Prey operatives were already en route, but he needed them to know Teresa was gone.

"Micah? What's going on? Are you two somewhere safe?" Raven's voice came down the line almost immediately.

"No," he said, keeping his gaze locked on the man he'd seen carrying the woman as he dodged around a couple of little kids giggling about the excitement and not looking where they were going.

"What happened?"

"They got her. Maybe drugged her. Took her through an apartment and out a window. I'm following them, but they're too far ahead of me, and there are too many people." The next words he had to say almost clogged in his throat. He didn't want to say them. Didn't want them to be true. "I don't think I'm going to get to her in time."

The sense of failure that rushed through him as he admitted that out loud made him stagger. He was failing his girl all over again, and this time her very life was on the line.

"We already have the footage from the CCTV cameras running, we'll try to get a lock on her, anything you can give us to narrow down where she is will help," Raven told him.

"A van," he yelled, picking up the pace, forcing himself to run faster than he ever had before. "They're putting her into a van. Hey!" he screamed at the men still a good fifty yards or so ahead of him, with at least several dozen people blocking the way. "Put her down and get on your knees."

One of the men looked over his shoulder at Micah as Teresa was tossed into the van. The man searched the crowd, and Micah knew the exact moment he was spotted because the other man smirked as he joined the others in the van and slammed the door shut behind him.

"No!" Micah yelled. He lifted his weapon, but there

was no way to get a clear shot at the van to disable it without risking hitting one of the many people milling about.

Instead, he was forced to stand there and watch as the van disappeared, taking Teresa away with it.

She was gone.

He'd lost her.

Failed her.

Let her down when she was counting on him.

Again.

CHAPTER 18

May 7ᵀᴴ
    8:39 A.M.

Hammering inside her skull nudged her from the hazy, dreamlike state she'd been trapped in.

Teresa blinked as she opened her eyes, trying to clear her vision.

Everything was blurry, almost as if she were under-water, only she knew that she wasn't.

When she went to lift her hand to rub her eyes, attempt to clear them, and found that she couldn't move it, she realized with a horrible sort of sinking feeling in her stomach what had happened.

Abducted.

Again.

The trafficking ring's ploy to get to her by setting off the fire alarm at her building had worked. Someone had drugged her, pulled her away from

Micah, thrown her out a window, and then put her in a van.

She would have sworn that she'd heard Micah calling her name right before she was passed off to someone in the van, but maybe that was more wishful thinking than anything else.

He did know she was gone, though, she remembered hearing his voice through the phone. He'd likely been not far behind her but not close enough to do anything to prevent her from being taken.

A heavy amount of fear pressed down upon her, but there was also a whole lot of anger.

A ton of it.

More than she would have guessed.

If asked, Teresa would have believed that terror would be the dominant emotion flooding her system, but she would have been wrong. It was definitely there, and she knew that at any moment it could spike and take over, but the anger was so much stronger.

Anger that these people put money over human life. Anger that they took advantage of desperate people who were prepared to do things they normally wouldn't to save their life or the life of a loved one. Anger that they believed they could just snatch innocent people off the streets and cut them open to sell off their organs.

And anger that they'd ruined her second chance with Micah.

Even though she'd told him she couldn't make any promises about the future, the more time she spent with him, the clearer that future had become, the easier it had been to see past all the pain and betrayal. To see

JANE BLYTHE

that as she peeled back the protective layers she'd used to bury her heart, love still hid beneath them.

Micah Hart wasn't just her first love, he was her only love because he was her true love.

It was crazy to think that while she'd spent the last decade hating him for leaving her when she needed him the most, the love she'd once had for him was still there. It hadn't gone anywhere, it had just been buried too deep to find.

If it had survived everything she'd been through, and if she could see it peeking its way back out, finding its strength again with each apology Micah offered, each small thing he did to try to make amends, then she owed it to herself to see it through. To open her heart again, let Micah in, and see if there was still hope for them.

Now these people were trying to ruin that.

They had the worst timing. She was only just realizing that she did want to at least try with Micah. If things didn't work out, then they didn't work out, but she didn't want to go through the rest of her life with regrets.

For so long she'd just been playing things safe. Always trying to look at things logically and weighing up the pros and cons to make the most informed decision she could possibly come to.

But love wasn't logical. It didn't make sense. It wasn't something you could arrange neatly in a box.

It was wild and messy, but it was in that wildness and messiness that it found its beauty.

Love couldn't be controlled, and it couldn't be caged.

When it came down to it, even if it was the scariest thing she would ever do, she wanted to give Micah a chance. He was trying to fight for her, trying to show her how much he still loved her and how sorry he was. Even though they couldn't go back, they could go forward.

If she could get out of this alive.

"I hate you all," she yelled out as loud as she could. Her voice was a little scratchy from being drugged, and it wasn't quite as strong as she would have liked given the sincerity of that sentiment, but it felt good not to be passive.

Just because she couldn't save herself didn't mean she had to just lie there and take whatever they dished out. She hadn't last time, and it had felt great to fight back however she could, and she wished she'd bitten clean through that doctor's finger and severed it completely. If she got another chance, she was going to do whatever damage she could. They had her, they could operate on her again, they could even kill her, but they couldn't break her.

Nobody got to do that.

The only one who could break her was herself, and she had no intention of breaking.

So far in life, she'd survived a lot, but somehow, she always managed to come out the other side. Battered and bruised, not quite the same as she'd been before, but still there, still standing.

The same was going to be true this time around.

If her plan didn't work and she wasn't rescued, then she would die knowing she'd created whatever havoc she could.

"In case you didn't hear, I said I hate you all," she screamed again, then looked around the hospital room with irritation. There were things she could use as weapons lying right around her, yet they had her tied to the bed so she couldn't get to them.

"We heard you," a woman who looked to be in her late fifties snapped as she breezed through the door. The woman was dressed in a doctor's coat, with a stethoscope hanging around her neck, her light brown eyes were narrowed, and her lips pursed into a thin line.

"Good." She eyed the woman defiantly as she approached the bed. One thing she knew for certain from the work she and her team had been doing looking into the ring, and from what she'd learned from Ava and Isabella, as well as her own time spent as one of the ring's captives, was that none of the medical personnel were to be trusted. They weren't all here by choice, and some of them could maybe be persuaded to help, but she couldn't rely on that.

Besides, this woman didn't appear to be here under duress.

"I'm glad we were able to get you back. Thanks to you and your team's constant interference, we have to keep shutting down branches and trying to scramble to set them up in other places."

"If you're waiting for me to cry you a river, you're going to be waiting one heck of a long time," Teresa informed the older woman.

"Things can go easy for you here, or hard, up to you," the woman said, the arrogance rolling off her so strong Teresa literally rolled her eyes.

"Yeah, yeah, got it. You guys really care about me, and you want to make my stay with you as pleasant as it can possibly be. Course you do. In case that wasn't abundantly clear, that was sarcasm." The more Teresa talked back to the woman, the more empowered she felt.

Their goal was to strip her of power, strip her of humanity, and treat her as nothing but a collection of organs they could sell for profit. Well, she was going to spend every second of her time there reminding them that she was a human being, and if they wanted to murder her, they had to admit to themselves that was what they were doing.

"You think being a sarcastic brat is going to save you?" The woman scoffed.

"Nope. Not at all." If anything was going to save her, it was the little trick she had up her sleeve. And if it didn't work out, she had no doubt that sooner or later, Prey would find the head of the ring and destroy them. "But you have to know Prey isn't giving up, and we always win."

"This isn't some movie where good triumphs over evil."

Teresa laughed. "Oh, lady, don't you know, movie or real life, good *always* triumphs over evil. It's not a matter of if Prey is going to close you down, it's only a matter of when."

Muttering under her breath, the doctor proceeded to check Teresa's vitals, and as she watched the woman work, her gaze fixed on her own wrist, praying that the small device inside would remain undetected. It was her gamble, something she'd been working on for a while now, but it was still in the early stages, in fact, this was the first time it was being trialed.

It was still a prototype, still just something she worked on in her spare time, but she was putting her entire life in its hands.

* * *

MAY 7th
10:16 A.M.

"YOU LET HER DO WHAT?" Micah roared.

While his tone of voice didn't indicate it, he was very much aware of who he was yelling at. Very much aware of the money and power Eagle Oswald and the rest of his family wielded. They wielded it for good, taking the fortune they'd inherited and turning it into a billion-dollar company that saved lives.

They did a lot of good, but Eagle had connections everywhere, and Micah knew if the man so chose he could end his career with a single word.

The idea scared him, but not as much as knowing he could lose Teresa.

And what he'd just learned sounded very much like she'd gone back to her apartment with the idea of playing bait.

Without consulting him.

Not that she was obligated to talk through any ideas she had with him, they weren't a couple anymore, weren't even friends, although it definitely felt like something was building between them again, but he thought she would have mentioned this. At least clued him in because he was her bodyguard, and everything to do with her safety was his business.

But she hadn't told him.

Hadn't told anyone other than Eagle and Raven, if the expressions on the faces of the rest of her team were anything to go by.

"I didn't *let* her do anything," Eagle said mildly, seemingly unperturbed by Micah's attitude, which he supposed was a good thing and meant he wasn't going to lose his job for confronting the billionaire retired SEAL.

"Teresa talked to both of us about her idea and we both agreed that it was a good one," Raven added, her tone a little less arrogant than her brother's. "While we had all hoped it wouldn't come to this, Teresa knew the risks, and she was prepared to take them for a chance at bringing down the trafficking ring once and for all."

"That's not on her shoulders," Micah growled. Yes, her team was working toward that goal, and yes, she now had several personal reasons to want the organ trafficking ring destroyed, since they had gone after her and the people she cared about, but it wasn't on her to end it.

Knowing she was out there, alone, no doubt drugged, possibly hurt, there was a chance they had even already put her under and removed another one of her organs, was enough to make him lose his mind.

Good idea or not, he didn't care. All he wanted was for Teresa to be safe.

The opposite of what she was right now.

"Teresa felt like it was. This was her idea, I did not push it onto her, and neither did Raven. She wanted to use the fact that the ring is currently fixated on her to our advantage, and I thought her plan was a solid one, so I decided to trust her." Eagle looked him directly in the eye as he spoke those words, and Micah had no doubt it was a challenge.

If her boss could trust her, why couldn't he?

Maybe because Eagle wasn't emotionally invested in Teresa the same way he was.

Sure, Eagle cared about every single one of his employees, everything he'd ever heard about Prey suggested they were a family, and that their founder and CEO would go to the ends of the earth for any one of them.

But it wasn't the same.

Micah was desperately in love with Teresa. He wanted to spend the rest of his life making up for his bad decisions twelve years ago, and treat Teresa like the amazing queen that she was. To do that, she had to still be alive.

He could handle—barely—her kicking him out of her life, but he couldn't handle losing her.

Couldn't handle knowing she wasn't out there some-where chasing the happiness she deserved.

"I do trust her," he snapped.

"Then have a little faith," Eagle told him.

"That would be easier to do if her tracking implant wasn't a prototype. If it had been tested before and we knew for certain that it was going to work. But we don't know anything. She could have deliberately put herself in harm's way without any options for us to find her," he said desperately.

"She was confident that it would work," Raven assured him.

"Then why haven't we heard anything from her yet?" If Teresa's new tracking device was going to work, she could have activated it any time in the last eight or so hours.

That was almost how long it had been since they'd been awakened by the fire alarm.

There were so many things he wished he'd done differently.

Starting with refusing to leave her apartment. If there really had been a fire, it would have taken a while for it to reach them, and by then his backup would have been there, and they could have surrounded Teresa as they got her out, made sure nobody could get to her.

Although knowing what he now knew, that Teresa had been prepared for a second abduction attempt, he thought it was unlikely she would have agreed to stay.

Was there anything he could have said to convince her not to do this?

His heart insisted that there was. That if he'd known of her plan, he could have found the right words to say to plead with her not to put her life on the line. To show her that there was another way to bring the ring down that didn't involve her willingly allowing herself to be taken.

His head knew that was a lie.

There was nothing he could have done to change

Teresa's mind. She was too stubborn, and once she got an idea in her head, it was next to impossible to dislodge it.

"Any number of reasons," Raven reminded him. "Maybe they've kept her unconscious. Maybe they have her restrained in such a way that she can't access the tracking implant. Its whole design is that it remains inactive so that it can't be detected. To activate it, she needs to be able to hold her finger above it so that it can read her fingerprint and turn on. As soon as she can do that, we'll know where she is."

"And if she can't get to it?" There were so many variables. So many things that could go wrong, and that was terrifying.

"She will," Eagle said with more confidence than Micah could muster.

"And if it doesn't work as she intends it to?"

"It will," Raven said, echoing her brother's confidence. "If I didn't think her tracker was ready to be field tested, I would have told her no and insisted that she remain here with the others. I believe in what she's been working on, and this wasn't something she whipped up overnight. She'd been creating it for almost a year now, working on it in her spare time. It was already almost ready to be tested, and while I didn't think we'd be testing it on her under these circumstances, it was her baby, and this is what she wanted to do with it."

Of course it was.

Teresa had never met a situation that she didn't feel responsible for.

It was something he both loved and hated about her.

It was amazing that she always wanted to be everyone's hero, take care of them, look out for them, and protect them, but it always came at great personal cost.

This time that cost could be her very life.

"I believe in her and that's why I went to bat with Eagle for her," Raven continued. "I do know how terrifying this is, Eagle does too. We've both been where you are right now. I lived through hell for a decade when Cleo was taken, and Olivia was snatched right from this very building."

Eagle growled at the mention of his now wife's abduction. Usually, Olivia helped run the Cyber Team with Raven, but lately she'd been helping set up a second Cyber Team at Prey's West Coast offices, leaving Raven solely in charge there for now. But he had no doubt that if Eagle's wife had been there, she would have agreed with Raven's assessment to trust Teresa and the tracking device she'd created.

"Nathaniel has been through this with Ava, and Tobias with Isabella, and I specifically requested that Rocco's SEAL team be on standby because not only are they familiar with the trafficking ring, but they've also gone through similar things with their now wives," Raven informed him. "No one is telling you this is easy, but we are all on your side, and we are asking you to just have a little faith in Teresa. She's smart, and she's brave, she wanted to do this, and I suspect part of the reason was because of you."

"Because of me?"

Raven nodded. "These last few weeks she's been forced to confront her past. I know what that's like, and I know that sometimes you reach that point where you're ready to let it all go and take that leap of faith into the future, knowing there are no guarantees. That's how it was for me with Max, and I think that's how she feels about you. She's ready to jump, but to do that, she needs to eliminate this threat to her happiness."

Of course, Micah was so proud of his girl for being committed to facing this situation head-on and being willing to put it all on the line.

But the line was her life.

How was he supposed to deal with it if she wasn't rescued in time and died because he was back in her life, and he'd worked hard enough to earn a second chance, one she would do anything to grab hold of?

CHAPTER 19

May 7th
  11:04 A.M.

"Hrmph," Teresa muttered in annoyance.

She'd been working on trying to get to her tracker for hours now, but the way her wrists had been bound to the bed was making it impossible. The spot she'd chosen to embed it under her skin was right on the inside of her wrist at the base of her hand. She had a small scar there from an accident as a kid, so she'd thought if anyone should search her, they would assume it was just the scar if they were able to feel the tiny chip.

Not that she thought that was likely. It was too small, and these people had no reason to assume she would be using a tracking device. Although they should, since they'd already made it abundantly clear, first with Ava, and then with Isabella and some of the other nurses held captive with her, that they were relentless in pursuing those they deemed adversaries for whatever reason.

The problem was, the leather strap locked around her wrist was covering the tracker. Whoever had done it up had done it tight enough that she couldn't push it down to get her finger over the tiny device to activate it. Without a clear read of her fingerprint, it wouldn't turn on.

If it didn't turn on, nobody was going to find her.

By now, Micah would know about the tracker, and her plan to use it should she be taken a second time. It wasn't really about playing bait, she hadn't *wanted* the trafficking ring to get to her again, but she had wanted to be prepared in case it happened.

And she wanted this whole mess finished because it was standing in the way of her future.

A future that had disappeared after her rape when Micah cut himself out of her life, but had slowly come back to life over the last few days. If anyone was going to stop that future from happening, it was going to be her and no one else.

Certainly not an organ trafficking ring.

No one was going to steal her future from her this time. Not her dad's untimely death, not her mom's need for support, not Arthur's medical issues, not Simon and his criminal activities, not Micah deciding he got to make decisions for both of them. No one was deciding what her future looked like but her.

She was in control of her own life.

For so many years, she'd sacrificed everything she had to give to other people, but not this time. This time, she'd fought for her future, made her own choices, knowing they might not work out the way she wanted, but still willing to try.

It was die doing everything within her power to destroy the trafficking ring, or survive and try things with Micah. If they didn't work out, then maybe the two of them could be friends again. At least she'd know there would be no unanswered questions hanging over her head. No what ifs, no could haves, or should haves, or would haves.

When the door to her room opened, she saw a young man walk through it. He looked to be a few years younger than she was, maybe in his mid-twenties, and from the black eye he was sporting, she was going to take a guess that he wasn't here by choice.

Perfect.

Exactly what she needed.

"I have to get you prepared for surgery. I'm sorry," the young man added as he approached her bed, refusing to make eye contact with her.

Darn.

She'd been hoping for longer before they were going to put her under the knife again. She should have expected this, though, they'd likely already matched her organs with someone on their buy list. The ring was losing ground every time Prey raided another of their facilities, they had to move quickly if they wanted to keep their business operational.

"It's okay, it's not your fault," Teresa assured the man.

Surprise widened his eyes as his gaze snapped up to

meet hers. "Normally they … they think … they blame me."

"I'm not them. I know about the ring, and I know they force some of the doctors and nurses to do their dirty work. They abducted my friend and kept her for seven months, trying to force her to comply. Is that what they're doing to you? Making you work here? Are they hurting you when you try to say no?"

What she needed the most right now was an ally, and this young man could be it. All she needed to do was gain his trust, then convince him to release her hand long enough for her to activate the tracker. Then all they had to do was wait for Prey to arrive.

Slowly, the man nodded. Then quickly spun in a circle as though expecting someone to pop up after having witnessed his confession. When he reassured himself that no one was there, he hurried over to her side, leaning in close as he whispered. "They tricked me. Told me it was a legitimate job, it was meant to be well-paying. When I got here, they locked me in a room, put an ankle monitor on me, and told me what they wanted me to do. I told them no, but they don't care."

"How long have they had you?"

"What day is it today?"

"Umm …" Teresa's mind whirled as she tried to figure it out. "It was May 7th when I was taken, and I don't think they've had me more than twenty-four hours."

"They haven't," the man confirmed. "They took me in early April, so I've been here a month."

"They hurt you." She nodded at his face and the

darkening bruise, which was recent if the swelling in his eye was anything to go by.

Another nod. "I keep telling them this is wrong, but they never listen. All they care about is money. Well, *she* cares about more than money, but the rest don't."

"Who's *she*?" Teresa asked. Could he be talking about the woman in the skirt suit with the bun that both Ava and Isabella had mentioned?

"Ms. Tilly," he whispered, leaning in even closer.

"Is she the woman who runs the ring?"

"She's the one who offered me the job. I did some work for her, real work, legitimate work, taking care of her daughter. Her daughter is sick, with some genetic issue that causes her organs to start shutting down. Ms. Tilly has already lost her husband and three sons to it. She was determined not to lose her daughter as well."

"That's why she started the ring? Organs for her daughter?"

"I think so. She's very determined, she loves the money and power as well as keeping her daughter alive. But I never would have signed up for this." The man's voice grew urgent. "I thought it was another job like caring for her daughter, if I'd known what they wanted me to do, I swear I would have turned the job down."

"Shh," she murmured. "I believe you. If you'd turned it down, they would only have kidnapped you anyway. What's your name?"

"William."

"William, I'm Teresa. I think you know that already." When William nodded, she continued, "Do you also know that I work for Prey Security?" Another nod. "I knew the ring would try coming after me again, so I came prepared."

"Prepared?"

"I have a small tracking device implanted under the skin of my wrist. It's something I was working on. It remains inactive until my fingerprint wakes it up. Only my fingerprint will activate it. But to do that, I need you to loosen the binds on my wrist."

"I can't," William hissed, shaking his head desperately. "If they know I helped you, they'll hurt me."

"They'll hurt you either way," she reminded him. "Prey knows I have this tracker on me, they're waiting for me to turn it on so they can come. Sooner or later, they could decide to switch you from nurse to patient. They could take your organs as easily as they're taking mine. This is our only hope. Yours as well as mine. Prey will come, and if you know information about how to get in touch with Ms. Tilly, then they can shut down the trafficking ring for good."

"Will I … will I be punished for helping them?" William asked.

"No. Absolutely not. You aren't here by choice, and you were coerced into working for them. You'll be treated like all the other nurses and doctors who were rescued, like the victim that you are. Please, William. All you have to do is loosen the strap long enough for me to activate the tracker, then you can prep me for the surgery like you were sent in here to do."

She had to find a way to convince him to help her.

If she didn't, she would undergo this surgery, and then another and another, the ring would keep taking from her until there was nothing left. Convincing this scared young man to help her was the only thing that was going to save her life, his life, and the lives of all the other innocent men and women the ring had trafficked.

* * *

MAY 7th
    12:19 P.M.

THE WORDS BLURRED as Micah read them over again.

DEAR MICAH

I DON'T KNOW how you found out about what happened. Was it your dad? Did one of his colleagues mention that his son's girlfriend's name had popped up in a case? Did you read one of my messages or listen to one of my voicemails and then decide to block me?

I DON'T UNDERSTAND why you're not here.

I NEED YOU.

DON'T YOU GET THAT?

. . .

YOU'VE ALWAYS BEEN the one who takes care of me. That sees that even though I can handle whatever life throws at me, sometimes it still gets to be too much, and I feel like I'm going to get crushed beneath it all. Whenever that happens, you're always there. You help lift me up so I can keep going, keep doing what my family needs me to do.

BUT I'M scared I can't handle this. What if this is the thing that breaks me?

Is it my fault you won't come? Am I too broken for you now? Too damaged? Too dirty?

I FEEL DIRTY. So filthy. Every time I look at myself, I'm disgusted. I keep taking showers, but it doesn't make me feel clean. I scrub and I scrub, but I can't get the feeling of those boys touching me off my skin. Do you think it will stay forever?

I'M SO mad at you for leaving and blocking me, but I still want you so badly it hurts. I hate that. Hate myself for needing you when it's clear you don't want to be here. Maybe you never loved me the same way I loved you.

. . .

YOU WERE SUPPOSED to be my forever, now I just have to hope you won't be my destruction.

~~Love~~, Teresa

PS – I wrote love accidentally because it's how I always sign messages to you, but I don't think I can love you anymore, not after this. You made a choice for both of us, and now I have to live with the consequences too.

TERESA HAD WRITTEN the letter in her favorite purple pen, her handwriting so familiar because she used to love to write him little handwritten notes and hide them in his pockets for him to find later. There were a few spots where the ink had smudged, presumably because she'd been crying when she wrote it.

Now he was the one crying.

Asking one of his friends to go into his house, find the letter, and stick it in the post to get to him had probably been a bad idea.

Especially now when he was sitting in a helo flying out to where Teresa's tracker had been activated.

But he had to know.

Had to understand her pain on a level that was unsensitized by time, maturity, and a desire, despite everything he'd done to her to spare his feelings.

Reading the letter was the only way, and as much as it gutted him to read Teresa's words, he was glad he'd done it. He deserved to suffer for what he'd put her through, and there was no better way to do that than to read her heartbreaking questions. Feel her pain as she tried to figure out what her life was going to look like following her ordeal.

The only comfort he could take from it was knowing that his abandonment hadn't destroyed her. It had made her stronger, more determined, braver, and fiercer. But that in and of itself hurt, too, because in the process she'd had to harden her heart a little, learn to be a little tougher, and not love with abandon.

"We're going to find her," a voice spoke as a hand landed on his shoulder.

Micah looked over to see that Cole "Rex" Kingston was watching him closely. The man was part of Blake "Rocco" Wise's SEAL team, and this team had already gone in to rescue Nathaniel and Ava after the two were stuck in Mexico following Ava's escape from the traffickers. The team had then participated in both rescues of Isabella, although in the first one, they hadn't known she was a victim of the ring and had thought she was there willingly.

Now they were there again, ready to go in and help rescue the woman he loved.

As much as he appreciated the man's optimism, he couldn't seem to muster any of his own.

The opposite in fact.

It felt like even if they got to Teresa in time, he still wouldn't get to keep her in his life. Knowing how badly he'd hurt her was one thing, but traveling back in time and seeing how much she was hurting in the aftermath of her assault was another.

Pain crushed him. Not physical pain, that could be much more easily handled. Emotional pain was a whole other story. His, hers, it all melded together into one white hot ball of agony wrapped tightly around his heart.

"Don't give up on her yet," Rex urged.

"I changed something fundamental in her because I was too much of a coward to talk to the girl I loved," he said softly, knowing the words were heard not just by Rex but by the whole team and the pilot because they were all mic'd up. Micah knew that even if he'd confronted her with his accusation, he would have hurt her, but he would have been able to apologize immediately and stick by her side through everything.

"You messed up, no one is saying otherwise," Beckett "Ace" Morgan agreed. "We all heard what happened between you two when you were teenagers, but you're also fighting to show her how sorry you are and make things right."

"Yeah, I'm doing a great job of that. She got abducted twice while I was right by her side." The one person he'd wanted to save the most in his entire career, and she was the one he had failed the most.

"These people are determined, you know that. And Isabella was snatched while she was with Tobias," Decker "Gumby" Kincade reminded him.

It didn't help.

Tobias had a serious back injury that had ended his

JANE BLYTHE

Delta Force career, Micah had no such excuses to fall back on.

He was just a failure.

"Way I see it," Mark "Bubba" Wright spoke up, "you have two options. You can allow your guilt and regret to swallow you up and eat you alive, or you can be the man you wished you were for your girl back then. Give in or fight for her? What are you going to do?"

"Fight," the word came out automatically, but it was true. He'd already let Teresa down in the past, failed to give her what she needed, and been selfish and prioritized his own feelings and needs over hers.

Not a mistake he would make again.

"Exactly what we wanted to hear," Rocco told him, tossing him a grin.

"Teresa seems like the kind of woman who faces her fear head-on, who pushes through and does what she has to do despite it," Forest "Phantom" Dalton said. "Do the same for her. Push through that fear, don't give in to it. Fight for her every day for as long as it takes. She's already fighting for her future, fight alongside her, not against her."

Micah took those wise words to heart.

Fighting alongside his girl and not against her was exactly what he needed to do. Teresa had been willing to put her very life on the line to try to bring the trafficking ring down so she could have the future she wanted. He had to fight with that same determination.

When the pilot announced that they were approaching the place where Teresa's tracker indicated she was being held, they all prepared themselves. Teresa was being held in international water not too far off the US coast, there was no way they could approach undetected in the middle of the day, so they were going to jump from the helo as close to the boat as they could get and hope they could get on board before the guards had a chance to slaughter everyone.

A risk, but their best way to get to Teresa and the other victims who were no doubt there as well as quickly as possible.

"If nobody minds, I'm going to pass on being in the room when Teresa is rescued," Rex said, amusement dancing in his tone, and they all laughed. So far, Rex had managed to get a black eye from Ava and a hit to the groin from Isabella when he participated in their rescues. Micah knew the guys were never going to let him live it down, but the man seemed to take it all in stride and see the humor in it, as well as pride for the two women who had fought for their lives with everything they had to give.

As he prepared for the jump, Micah looked at the letter in his hands. Teresa hadn't wanted him to read it, but he was glad he had. Now he had to decide what to do with it. Holding onto it would be like clinging to a stumbling block that would get in the way of the future he wanted.

Ripping the paper into pieces, when Rocco opened the helo door, Micah leaned over and let them fall. It was time to let go of the past and be the man he should have been back then, the man Teresa needed him to be now.

CHAPTER 20

May 7ᵀᴴ
12:21 P.M.

This was it.

Teresa was lying in a hospital bed, just like she'd been last time when these monsters had removed part of her liver.

Like last time, she watched as the anesthesiologist approached, a syringe in his hand.

She wanted to fight, or at the very least come up with some sort of snappy retort that would show these people she wasn't afraid of them.

Only she was.

Terrified in fact.

But she'd made a promise to herself not to give in to that fear and let it consume her. So to that end, since she couldn't come up with a sassy remark, she merely held the gaze of the man standing beside her bed, ready to put her to sleep so he could steal her organs.

Just because they didn't want to see her as a human being, one just like them with hopes and dreams for her future, plans and goals, didn't mean she wasn't. And she wanted them to be reminded of that, even though she knew it wouldn't change anything.

The drug was injected into her IV, and almost immediately, she began to feel sleepy.

Even though she knew she would wake up on the other side of this operation, they weren't going to kill her just yet, when there was so much more money to be made keeping her alive as long as possible and harvesting as many organs as they could, she wouldn't wake up the same as she was right now.

When consciousness returned, she would be missing another organ.

One she could live without, but it would still be a piece of herself gone.

Pushed into oblivion by the drugs, the world faded to black around her, but at the very last second, she could have sworn she felt a small sting on the inside of her elbow. Right where her IV was connected.

There was no time for her to examine the feeling, try to figure out what it was, or wonder if she'd merely imagined the whole thing, because she passed out.

Only then there was more pain, a sharp stabbing one in her stomach right where her partly healed wound was.

"Stay still, don't move," a voice murmured close to her ear, but the words took a while to penetrate.

Why was someone telling her to be still?

And who did the voice belong to?

It was familiar, yet she couldn't seem to place it.

More voices spoke around her, chattering away too fast for her to be able to make out the words.

The energy from them seeped into her mind, though.

Panicked, angry, scared.

That's how the voices sounded, but she still couldn't figure out what was going on.

"Can you hear me?" that same voice spoke, this time low and hurried. Urgent.

Try as she might, her head was still too stuffy to be able to use her brain properly. Everything was fuzzy, and she wasn't sure what was real and what was just an illusion.

"I need you to wake up, we don't have much time. I think … I think someone is coming for us, but I'm afraid they're going to kill us before we can be rescued. I won't let that happen. But I really need you to wake up," the voice finished, desperation bleeding into the tone.

Someone coming for them?

Rescue?

The trafficking ring.

The surgery.

It all came filtering back in as the fuzziness in her head receded enough that she could focus again and access her memories.

She was supposed to be unconscious, put to sleep so she could be operated on. Why was she awake, and what had been the pain in her stomach?

Blinking open heavy eyes, she saw the nurse standing beside her. William, the one who had loosened the strap binding her wrist to the bed so that she could activate the tracker. That had been a couple of hours ago, so by now there was every chance that Prey was already mounting a rescue.

"Coming?" she asked. Her throat felt dry, and her voice came out scratchy, but William nodded, relief evident in his dark eyes.

"Yes. I wasn't going to let them operate on you, so I knocked out the IV, not enough to be noticeable but enough that it wouldn't really knock you out. I … didn't really have a plan for after that, but I was hoping you'd have an idea?"

Yeah, he looked hopeful all right.

Misplaced hope, because her brain was barely functioning. She'd gotten enough of the drugs to temporarily knock her out, but she'd obviously woken right as they were about to start the operation. That had to have been the pain in her stomach.

Lifting her head, Teresa looked down her body.

Saw she was mostly naked, the hospital gown she was wearing bunched up around her breasts.

There was blood on her stomach, running in rivulets down her sides, but it wasn't enough that she had to be concerned about blood loss.

"You saved me," she murmured.

"Maybe? I'm not sure yet. We have to do something," William said, already undoing the rest of the leather straps, then tugging down her gown to cover her as though modesty was what she was most worried about right now.

Did she want all these people to see her naked body?

Of course not.

But she'd rather live.

"Where are they? You said something about someone coming?"

William nodded. "Just as they started, there were shouts from outside. Apparently, there's a helicopter flying over us."

"Prey," she murmured in relief as she pressed her palms to the mattress and pushed herself up. Her head spun for a moment, and she had to clench her eyes against the sickening feeling, but hope was also bubbling to life inside her.

If Prey was coming, then rescue was just moments away.

But then the memories of the ship Ava had first escaped came to mind. When the trafficking ring realized Ava was gone, they had slaughtered everybody on board. Not just the innocent men and women they had abducted to cut open and steal their organs, but all the doctors and nurses had died, too.

Everyone.

By the time the rest of Nathaniel's SEAL team had reached the boat, there hadn't been a single survivor.

That wasn't happening this time around.

"We need weapons," she said as she opened her eyes and swung her legs over the side of the hospital bed. "If they come back, there's every chance they're going to kill us before we can be rescued."

The nod William gave was resigned. He knew that, too. Whether because he'd been told already what had happened on that ship a few months ago, or because the surgeon had said something before leaving, she wasn't sure, but she was glad they were both on the same page.

"Weapons, right." William stood and walked around the room.

While the young man looked for something to defend themselves with, Teresa stood on shaky legs. She was determined to do whatever it took to remain alive, to fight for her life with everything she had. She just had to hope her body was up for the task.

After being restrained on the bed for hours, her limbs felt weak and heavy, but since there was no time to worry about it, she shuffled over to William, who was holding up a couple of scalpels.

"Best we've got," he told her.

"It'll do if we act quickly," she said, taking one of them. The metal was cool against her palm, the blade small. If this was going to work, they were only going to get one chance at it.

Since William was looking at her expectantly, Teresa knew she would have to take the lead.

"We'll wait by the door. We kill whoever comes through it." She said the words confidently, like her heart was hammering against her chest. If Prey was already on board, she had no doubt that they would be able to prevent her or William from killing them, so the safest bet for them, their best chance at living, was to act immediately.

Although he nodded, William paled, and she hoped he could do this.

No sooner had they both scurried over to stand by the door than it swung open.

A single figure stepped through it, and just like she'd planned, Teresa didn't hesitate.

With a smooth slashing motion, she lifted the scalpel high and then brought it down, aiming for the person's neck. The sharpness of the blade was perfect for slicing through the skin there, and a single cut at the carotid artery would sever it and leave the person bleeding out, unable to be saved.

Unprepared for an attack, believing that she was still unconscious on the bed and that William was watching over her, the female surgeon was an easy target.

One slice and it was done.

Blood squirted out, then began to stream down the woman's neck.

Shock widened her eyes, and her hands flew to her wound as her gaze landed on Teresa.

The woman tried to speak but couldn't. She stumbled and then fell.

Dying.

Teresa had killed her.

Knowing it was either her or them didn't stop the nausea churning in her gut. She'd taken a human life.

Fighting against the nausea, knowing that she couldn't dwell on what she'd just done because there was more danger waiting for them out there, she turned to William and nodded at the door.

Together they crept out of it, and as she walked

slowly along the corridor, Teresa prayed that Prey would hurry up and arrive because she wasn't sure that she and William could kill enough people on their own to survive.

* * *

May 7th
    12:25 P.M.

WATCHING the torn pieces of paper flutter toward the ocean below was oddly cathartic.

Micah knew it wasn't really wiping the slate clean and having a fresh start, but it felt like it was.

There was always going to be his choices between them. Even if Teresa did want to give him a second chance, things would never be exactly the way they'd been in the past, the way they could have been if he hadn't messed everything up.

But they could still be good. The two of them could still be happy together. He would love her with every fiber of his being, and he would support her for the rest of their lives. He'd take care of her the way he always should have, and they could build the family they'd once planned.

Actions had consequences, and both he and Teresa had been living out the ones that came with his choice for too long now. It was time for him to step up and be the man Teresa had always deserved.

Seconds later, he jumped from the helo. It was

something he'd done dozens of times before. Usually, he got a rush of adrenaline as he floated through the air, confident in his abilities and those of his team. It was a different team with him today, but he trusted them as much as he trusted his own, and he knew that they could take on whoever was on board that boat and win.

But this time, there was an element of fear he never usually experienced, because he'd never gone into an op with someone he loved in need of rescuing.

Cancelling out that fear was determination.

Never before had a mission been so important.

Vital.

His life had always been tied up with Teresa's, and he wasn't going to fail his girl ever again.

About halfway between the helo and the softly rolling waves of the sea, something caught his eye. A little scrap of paper caught on a breeze wafting along beside him.

It was pure instinct to reach out and grab it.

Stuffing the small scrap inside his suit, he readied himself to hit the water.

That second where you were thrust deep into the water, momentum propelling you along, had always been his favorite. Obviously, given his career choice, Micah had always loved the ocean, loved the wildness of it, the freedom you felt when becoming part of this massive force of nature. Teresa loved the water, too, and she needed more moments of fun and adventure in her life. Maybe he'd see if she wanted to jump with him one day, or maybe even try out skydiving.

But first, he had to rescue her and bring her safely home.

With smooth strokes, he brought himself up to the surface, close to the boat, the heads of Rocco and his team popped up as well, and like a well-oiled machine, they made quick work of reaching the boat and making their way on board.

The vessel was much smaller than the one Nathaniel had set out to tag that night when he found Ava unconscious and alone in a lifeboat. That one had been a former cruise ship, and while this one had also been used for cruising, it was much smaller, something that wouldn't usually travel vast distances across the ocean.

Which made their job that much easier.

There were fewer places someone could be hiding, and with the trafficking ring taking hit after hit lately, he had to hope there weren't many guards on board.

It would be too much to hope for to have zero guards, though, and there would be enough to make fairly quick work of killing the innocents on board. The helo was obvious, flying across the clear blue sky, so they knew they did not have the element of surprise on their side.

Still, Micah was surprised that they made it all the way to the top deck without a single shot being fired.

That was as far as they made it, though.

The moment his feet hit that deck, bullets began to fly.

It seemed like the guards on board had decided to group together and try to pick him and the SEAL team off as they approached.

A plan which might have worked had those men had the same level of training and experience that he and the men on Rocco's team had. This was literally how they made their living. They stopped bad guys as Teresa's brother Arthur had gushed when he'd gone with her to visit with Arthur and her mom the other day. They eliminated threats, and right now, he'd never faced a bigger threat than those trying to hurt his girl.

Taking cover, he and the other SEALs all fired back. It would help to have some intel, how many guards there were, what training they had, how many innocents there were on the boat, if those who were victims of the ring were already dead, or were perhaps being slaughtered right at this very moment.

That thought filled him with a cold sort of rage he'd never experienced before.

Of course, Micah hated every single target his team had ever been sent to kill or capture, they were all evil people, and the world was a better place without them in it. But that sort of hatred was a little more detached, it wasn't personal, it was a job, one he'd signed up for, and one that he was good at and enjoyed, even though it was hard and required him to constantly put his life on the line.

These people had made things personal, though, they'd deliberately gone after the woman he loved, so this hatred was different. It infused him with a determination he knew couldn't be squashed. Wouldn't abate until his girl was safe in his arms where she belonged.

The shots being fired at him and the others began to diminish until they stopped altogether.

Slowly, they approached the spot where the guards had gathered, a spot that was now filled with several dead bodies. Eight, he counted.

Leaving one of the others to secure the bodies, confirming they were all dead and no longer a threat, Micah made his way down into the boat. It was quiet down there, there were no shots, no shouts, no anything.

Eerie was the only word he could use to describe it, and that made his stomach drop.

Were they already too late?

No.

He couldn't accept that.

Wouldn't.

With Rex, Phantom, and Gumby at his six, they proceeded to begin clearing the boat. Every door they opened, he expected to find Teresa waiting for him behind it. Each time she wasn't there, his anxiety crept another notch higher.

Where the hell was she?

Some of the rooms were empty, others weren't. There were men and women in some of the rooms. Strapped down to beds, their eyes wide with fear, when four men dressed in dive suits with weapons in their hands came storming through the doors.

Micha left it to the others to calm down the victims, he needed to find Teresa.

Only she didn't appear to be anywhere.

How was that even possible?

The tracker she had with her had worked. It had been activated, and it had led them to this boat. He'd been given no intel to indicate that had changed in any way, and yet they'd searched all the rooms, and she hadn't been in any of them.

"Where is she?" he demanded of no one in particular.

"Has to be here somewhere," Rex assured him.

"Yeah? Then why haven't we found her?"

"Maybe she went up here," Gumby suggested.

The SEAL was pointing to a smaller staircase than the one they'd used to work their way down to each floor. That one had been the main one, but this one appeared to be for the use of the crew, well, at least when the boat was a working cruise ship.

It was worth a shot.

Anything was.

So long as he found his girl.

Taking the steps three at a time, it wasn't long before he was back up in the fresh air on the top deck, only this time right at the back of the boat, the opposite end to where they'd boarded. This space of open deck was separated from the rest by a small room that had once been a bar and small kitchen serving passengers as they relaxed up there.

Now he scanned the space.

Empty.

Again.

Was it possible that Teresa had already been killed and her body thrown overboard? The ocean was smooth today, so her body wouldn't have traveled far, especially if she'd only been killed once the helo arrived. The tracker only told them her location, not her condition, so it was a possibility.

Then he spotted movement.

A flutter of something white.

"Teresa?" he called out, hurrying toward it.

"Micah?" her voice called out, and the relief of hearing his name falling from her lips almost took him to his knees.

"The others have got the remaining crew and medical personnel in custody," Phantom told him as he saw Teresa's face as she peeked around the corner from where she'd obviously been hiding.

This was it then. They'd found Teresa, she was safe, alive, possibly hurt, but she was up there when everyone else was still tied to their beds, so he knew that she was mostly okay. Physically, at least.

"You're here," she murmured as she took a step closer.

"You're alive," he said at the same time.

She smiled at him, but the smile quickly wavered as she turned her head slightly, obviously looking at something that he couldn't yet see, something—or probably someone—still hidden by the small structure.

When her gaze snapped back to his, her eyes were wide with fear, and she took a step toward him.

He was still closing the distance, but before he could reach her, haul her into his arms, stand between her like a human shield, a body came flying out of nowhere, tackling Teresa and taking her over the edge with them, plummeting toward the ocean below.

CHAPTER 21

May 7TH
   12:32 P.M.

The water was a lot colder than she'd been expecting.

While Teresa tried to take a breath before she went under, the shock of being knocked over the side of the boat, right when she thought it was all over and she was finally safe, meant she lost precious seconds.

Seconds that might turn out to be the difference between living and dying.

A mere ten seconds or so after she and William had left the small surgical room, they'd heard the first of the gunshots.

Knowing that meant Prey had arrived, that they were on the boat with her, had almost had her bursting into tears.

But she'd held them back.

Prey might have arrived, but it hadn't guaranteed

her or William's survival. She had no idea how many guards were on the boat, or how many medical personnel. She'd asked the young nurse, and he'd told her there were only half a dozen guards, and a dozen and a half doctors and nurses. According to William, about a dozen of those were here by choice, and the other half dozen were like him.

Add in another two dozen or so patients like herself, and she knew there was no way she could protect them all. While she hadn't had a firm plan in mind, she'd kind of been thinking they would go room to room and amass whatever army they could. Some of the victims would be in no shape to get out of their beds and arm themselves, but surely some of them would be.

Scalpels might be no real match for guns, but at least they were something, and she had felt better clutching hers in her hand. Without their own little army, there was no point in doing anything to try to help the Prey people who had boarded the boat.

When she'd asked William if he knew a place they could hide until it was safe, he'd suggested taking the back stairs up to the top deck. Apparently, there was a little building up there that had at one time been a bar and kitchen back when the boat had been used for its intended purpose.

That idea had seemed as good as any, so they'd crept up those stairs, both holding onto their scalpels like they were the only thing keeping them alive, and hidden.

Eventually, the shooting had stopped, but since they had no way of knowing which side had come out on top, they'd stayed right where they were. Teresa would bet everything she owned, gamble her entire future on the fact that Prey would win, but there was always the slimmest of slim chances that something could have gone wrong. If that was the case, she would have thought their best bet would be to jump overboard. The helo that had brought Prey would have still been out there and might have spotted them.

Even if it hadn't, she'd rather die at sea than on this boat.

Now dying at sea seemed like it might actually be a possibility.

Right as she'd been about to run into Micah's arms, relieved beyond words to see his face, and those of the SEAL team who had helped rescue Ava, and then Isabella. They might not be Prey, but they were on the same side, and they were every bit as skilled and experienced as any of her Prey family.

There was no one she would rather have heard calling her name than Micah.

If he was there, then she was going to be okay.

At least she thought she was.

Since Micah and a couple of the other guys were up there, she had assumed that meant everyone on board who was a threat had been taken care of. The guards were likely all dead, and the doctors and nurses were restrained.

But one of them wasn't.

The snarky doctor from earlier must have hidden up there as well, like the coward she was.

For whatever reason, the woman must have realized it was over, that she was about to be caught and would have to face the consequences of her actions, and decided that it was a better idea to throw herself at Teresa and take them both overboard than to just turn herself in.

Maybe she thought that if Teresa was with her, the others couldn't shoot at her. Which was likely true, Micah and the others wouldn't risk hitting her so they would need a clean shot, which would be difficult to get with them both tangled together.

It wasn't just that the cold was a shock to her system that had her momentarily freezing, or the fact that she'd never been out in the ocean like this before, so far away from shore. Not only was that terrifying in and of itself, but so was the fact that the woman who had taken her over the edge didn't seem to be content to let it stop with that.

She was trying to drag her further down.

Trying to drown her.

How the doctor thought that would help anything, Teresa had no idea. Maybe the woman wasn't thinking clearly at all. Whatever the reason, if she didn't snap out of her stupor soon she was really going to die.

Die with Micah and a team of SEALs literally right above her.

No.

You are not going to die.

Not here and now.

Not like this.

Not when you can get back the future you once thought was a sure thing.

The little pep talk helped a bit, and she finally

managed to claw her way through the shock causing her system to freeze and get her body and brain back in sync. Micah and the others might not be able to safely shoot at the doctor, but it wasn't like they were going to just stand up there and watch her try to break away from the woman's hold.

They were going to do something about it, which meant she had to as well.

While she hadn't been able to draw a proper breath before they went under the surface, the doctor obviously had, because her arms were still wrapped tightly around Teresa's chest, and she was actively pushing them both deeper and further away from the boat.

She couldn't let that happen.

The boat was safety.

Everything else was wide open, empty ocean.

Or not so empty.

Now was not the time to worry about sharks coming to get her. Honestly, they were the least of her worries right now. The deranged doctor trying to kill her was topping that list.

From the way her lungs burned, and her brain tried to convince her to open her mouth and take a breath even though she knew there was nothing but water for her to inhale, Teresa knew that the doctor wasn't actually all that far away from succeeding in her goal.

It was now or never.

She'd lost her grip on the scalpel somewhere along the way, either on the deck as she was falling, or as her body hit the water, so she no longer had a weapon. Her arms were pinned by her sides, but that didn't mean there weren't parts of the woman she couldn't reach.

Groin. Teresa had taken enough self-defense classes at Prey to know it was a great area to aim for if you were being attacked by a man. It was how she'd almost escaped those two men who tried to snatch her outside the deli that day she'd been saved by Micah.

That strategy worked on a man, but there was no reason it couldn't work on a woman, too. No guy wanted to be hit there, but it was a sensitive spot for a woman, too.

Curling her fingers into a fist, she rammed them between the woman's legs.

Underwater or not, she heard that howl of pain, and the arms around her suddenly loosened.

Shoving away from them, desperate to get back to the surface and take a breath, Teresa thought she was in the clear when something, a fist, a foot, a head, she wasn't quite sure what, rammed into her stomach. The blow to her partially healed wound that had then been cut open again had her seeing stars, the edges of her vision going black.

No.

Can't pass out now.

Unconscious means drowning.

Refusing to give up, Teresa kicked and swung at the hands that tried to claw at her. She wasn't going to die down there when Micah was somewhere close by. Maybe he was even in the water with her, trying to find her beneath the surface.

She had no idea how long it had been since she went

overboard, it felt like many minutes, but it was probably mere seconds since she'd hit the water and been taken under. After all, she was still holding her breath, and she wasn't experienced at doing that for long periods of time like Micah would be.

Her fist connected with something, and the presence beside her disappeared.

Thinking she was in the clear, she began to kick her legs with everything she had, needing to get to the surface so she could breathe in oxygen instead of water before her body's instincts took over and tried to make her take that breath where there was no air to be found.

When something snapped around her arm, she didn't hesitate to lash out all over again. She wasn't dying down there. She had too much left to live for.

* * *

May 7th
12:34 P.M.

By the time Micah reached the edge of the boat, Teresa had already gone under.

Tossing his weapon onto the deck, he swung a leg over at the same time Rex came up beside him and did the same.

"You're being daring," he said as he swung his other leg over and held onto the railing with his hands, surprised he could make any kind of joke at the moment. But he had to do something to try to break through the terror threatening to clog his mind and body and render him useless.

"I know, right?" Rex replied, shooting him a huge grin before they both let go.

This drop into the water was so much shorter than the one jumping from the helo had been, and a couple of seconds later, he plunged beneath the water. It was still pretty calm, the waves small, but Teresa had been caught by surprise, and it seemed like whoever had knocked her over had done so with the purpose of killing her.

For what reason he had no idea, it certainly wasn't going to save them. If anything, it was only going to make their situation worse. Now instead of simply being arrested and forced to face the consequences of their actions, there was every chance they were going to wind up dead.

Maybe that was the point. Suicide by cop. Well, by SEAL.

"Try not to get hit again," he told Rex, before he dived under the water, heading for the spot where he thought Teresa and her attacker would have landed.

As he went under, he heard Rex laugh, and his fear receded a little. The water wasn't rough enough to drag Teresa too far from the boat, and he'd all but followed her in, so she'd been in the water less than thirty seconds longer than he had. Unless her attacker was wielding a weapon—and he suspected she wasn't because if she was, they would have had a hostage situation more like when Isabella had been rescued—killing Teresa with her bare hands while trying to remain afloat would be next to impossible.

His girl was not dying today.

With strong, firm strokes, he swam through the water, scanning it for signs of movement that would indicate two people swimming to the surface. The fact that Teresa hadn't immediately come up for air upon landing told him that whoever had knocked her down was trying to keep her under. His girl was a good swimmer, but she was hurt and had been knocked over unexpectedly. He wasn't sure how big a breath she'd been able to take or how long she'd be able to hold it under these circumstances.

When he caught sight of something moving slowly in the water, his heart stuttered in his chest.

It was a body, he'd seen enough of them to know that. And it wasn't moving on its own, tossed about by the gentle waves.

Was it …?

No. Couldn't be.

Quickly closing the distance between it and himself, Micah didn't stop to examine whether it was Teresa or her attacker, nor did he waste time checking to see if the person was still breathing. Their only chance was to get to the surface, and if there was no pulse, start CPR, awkward to do in the water but not impossible. If it was the woman who had taken Teresa overboard, he didn't care about saving their life, but if it was his girl …

Water streamed down his face as he broke the surface, pulling the body up with him.

A couple of yards away, Rex's head also popped up, and he wasn't alone.

"I'm three for three," Rex called out, his tone amused and slightly tinged with pain.

"Three for three?"

Rex shifted slightly so that Micah could see that his friend was trying to keep hold of Teresa, who was struggling against him even if her movements were clumsy and uncoordinated.

Relief slammed into him, and he let out a choked laugh. Teresa was alive. Well, enough to be trying to fight off who she obviously thought was the woman who had knocked her off the boat.

Glancing down at the dead woman he still held onto, because there was no way she was alive when she hadn't made any attempts to get away from him, or to get herself up to the surface, nor had she taken in any breath now that there was air again, he saw it was Teresa's attacker. Not his girl. She wasn't hanging dead in his arms.

Touching his fingers to the woman's neck, he confirmed that she was deceased, then quickly dragged her along with him as he swam toward where his friend was trying to soothe Teresa, who was still fighting against him.

"Here, take her," he said, shoving the dead body at Rex as he reached for Teresa. As much as Micah would love to just leave the body out there and let the ocean dispose of the woman, he wanted this to be a clean op. He also didn't want to waste time later having to retrieve the body. He wanted to calm his girl down, get her out of the water, then get her back home.

"Avery is going to have a field day with this one," Rex said, clearly amused even as he rubbed at his jaw with one hand while holding onto the dead body with the other.

"She's going to think it's hilarious," he agreed as he smoothed a hand down Teresa's wet hair. Immediately, she stilled, as though sensing it was him beside her, and she no longer had to fight for her life. "Shh, pretty girl, it's me, you're safe now."

"Micah?" As he smoothed her soaked locks out of the way, her big brown eyes blinked at him then immediately looked around. He knew the second her gaze landed on Rex, and she realized he must have been the one to pull her up, because she suddenly looked sheepish. "Did I hurt you?"

"Yeah, you did, and it was awesome," Rex gushed. "Nothing I love more than seeing a victim kicking butt."

His words surprised a giggle out of Teresa. "I'm sorry."

"I'm not," Rex assured her. "You did the right thing. You didn't know who I was, and you acted accordingly."

"Thought you were her," Teresa murmured, glancing at the body.

"She can't hurt you anymore," he assured his girl. "Come on, let's get you back to the boat."

"Is William okay?" Teresa asked as he carefully shifted his hold on her so he could swim them both more easily.

"William?"

"The nurse who saved my life. He untied me so I could activate the tracker, and then he knocked out my IV so that I woke up when they were going to operate on me," she explained.

"I'm sure he's fine, we knew to be prepared for some of the doctors and nurses to be victims," he reminded her.

When they reached the boat, the others helped him get Teresa back up to the top deck. By the time he joined her, she was lying on her back, propped up against some blankets someone had collected, with one draped across her. She was shivering from the cold, unlike him, she wasn't wearing a specially designed dive suit, she was virtually naked, and water was streaming off her hair and puddling beneath her.

"You okay?" he asked, dropping to his knees beside her and cupping her cheek in his palm.

Immediately, she leaned into his touch. Tears shimmered in the brown depths of her eyes, but he knew Teresa well enough to know she was going to do her best not to let them fall with an audience. Always so strong, so determined, so stubborn. His girl didn't show weakness to anyone.

But it wasn't weak to be shaken after you'd almost died, to have survived hell all over again, to be grateful that you were alive.

"I-I'm okay," she whispered.

"She's hurt, they tried to cut her back open," a young man hovering close by spoke up. Micah assumed he was William.

Lifting up the blankets, he spotted the red staining

the hospital gown that was thoroughly soaked and sticking to her skin. Someone handed him a towel, and he pressed it against the wound, making Teresa wince. While there was enough blood for him to know the wound was serious and would have to be tended to as soon as they got medics there, it wasn't gushing blood in a way he had to worry about her bleeding out on him.

"You scared the life out of me with this little plan of yours," he told Teresa as he kept one hand pressed to her wound, and with his other tucked the blankets up and over her again to try to prevent her from going into shock.

"Sorry. I didn't want to scare you, but I had to take advantage of it if they got their hands on me again. It worked, too," she said, her gaze shifting to the young nurse. "He knows the woman running the ring."

All eyes snapped to William, his own included. The young man's cheeks heated, and he shuffled nervously from foot to foot, but he nodded his head to confirm what Teresa had just told them.

"You did it, pretty girl. Because of your bravery, we're going to demolish the trafficking ring. I'm so proud of you."

The smile she gave him was watery, but it was still a smile. "Then you better hurry up and kiss me."

"Nothing I'd rather do." As his lips pressed against hers, Micah felt a weight lift off his shoulders. Teresa didn't seem to blame him for her getting caught, and while he hated that she'd been in danger, her plan had ultimately worked out and paid off. As soon as the ring was no longer a threat, he was putting all his effort into convincing his girl he would never let her down again.

CHAPTER 22

THE QUIET AS she stepped inside the empty apartment had Teresa letting out a breath.

She hadn't realized how badly she needed some peace and quiet until this moment.

The whole day had been a whirlwind of activity, and it was hard to believe that it hadn't even been twenty-four hours since she was snatched in the stairwell of her apartment building after the fire alarm was set off.

That seemed impossible, and yet it was true.

In the last twenty-four hours, she'd been abducted, drugged, tested her tracker and found out that it worked as intended, almost been operated on, escaped, hidden as gunfire raged around her, been thrown off a boat, almost drowned, and then been rescued all over again.

After that, she was checked over by medics, received

stitches, and gave her statement over and over again to different people who all asked the same questions. Then there were the happy, angry reactions from her friends and teammates when she got back home. They were furious with her for putting her life on the line, while also admiring her bravery, and being relieved she was alive and relatively unscathed.

It hadn't felt brave while she was doing it, but she was so glad everything had worked out the way it had. So many things could have gone wrong, and if any one of them had, she wouldn't be standing there right now, drinking in the peace of the quiet apartment.

"How're you doing?" Micah asked from behind her.

As much as she'd been ready for a break from the others, appreciating them wanting to celebrate with her that she was alive, and that they finally had a name they could use to bring the organ trafficking ring down, but overwhelmed, that didn't extend to the man standing behind her.

When his hands landed on her shoulders and he began to knead the tense muscles there, Teresa sighed and let her head fall forward, giving him better access. While she'd been given a mostly clean bill of health, she was achy all over, her muscles tired and full of tension.

"I'm okay, just tired," she murmured, allowing his magic fingers to work the stress out of her a little bit at a time. Honestly, she could stand there like that forever. It didn't matter that the restitched wound in her stomach ached, or that exhaustion pressed down upon her. Tired as she was, Teresa wasn't quite ready to go to sleep yet.

"Want me to get some waterproof bandages so you can take a bath and then go to bed?"

"I took a quick shower when we got back here." Since she wasn't stupid enough to tempt fate again, not now that they had a name to work with, Teresa had moved into one of the apartments at Prey. This was where she'd stay until the ring was dismantled, then she, Ava, and Chelsea could discuss what they wanted to do next. She wasn't sure she could go back to living in their old place, and besides, Ava was with Nathaniel and was only waiting for the ring to be brought down before she made decisions about her future.

And now she had Micah to think about.

"I don't want to take a shower, I do, however, want to go to bed," she told Micah as she turned around so she was facing him.

There was no other word to describe the look in his eyes when he looked at her other than love. If you'd asked her a month ago if Micah loved her, the answer would have been a resounding no, and he never had.

Now she knew differently.

Part of her would always wish he'd handled things differently back then, but the other part, the bigger part, was just grateful to have been given this second chance.

A chance she didn't intend to squander.

"Take me to bed, Micah," she whispered as she placed her hands on his pecs, stroking gently, and pushed up onto her tiptoes so she could feather kisses along his stubbled jaw. The pain in her stomach wasn't going to ruin this moment for her. She was alive, Micah had come for her, and together they were going to find a way to straighten out the past into something they could build a future on.

"Trying to talk you out of it is pointless, isn't it?" he asked as he smoothed a lock of hair behind her ear.

"Totally pointless," she agreed, moving her lips to the pulse point in his neck and sucking lightly, making the bulge pressed against her stomach harden a little more.

"Then I guess I'm taking my girl to bed."

She squeaked as he scooped her up, automatically wrapping her arms around his neck. "You could sound a little more excited about the idea," she teased.

"Oh, pretty girl, if you weren't hurt, I would spend hours devouring you." His lips found the same spot on her neck she'd just been lavishing attention to on his neck, and she sucked in a breath as it seemed to send a bolt of heat straight between her legs.

"Yes," she said on a breathy moan, "let's do that."

A laugh rumbled through Micah's chest as he took her into the bedroom. Their bedroom for as long as he was there, because she didn't want to waste any more time apart. She knew that sooner rather than later, he would have to go back to his team, and she'd have to make the same choices Ava did about what her future looked like. Stay there and do the long-distance thing, or possibly see about transferring to the West Coast Cyber Team, Olivia Oswald was currently setting up.

For the moment, she didn't need to think, didn't need to get stuck in her head as she often did, all she had to do was feel.

Micah had always brought color to her life. His presence made her world brighter, calmer, easier, and a happier place to be. She'd missed him more than she had allowed herself to acknowledge, and she was so grateful to still have a shot at the future she'd always dreamed about.

"We'll have to do this carefully, pretty girl," Micah said as he set her on her feet. "I won't hurt you. Never again. Never again," he repeated as he began to very gently remove her clothing. Each brush of his knuckles against her skin made her hotter, and by the time he had her naked, she wouldn't have been surprised if she spontaneously combusted, that's how hot she felt.

"You won't," she assured him, framing his face with her hands and tugging him back up so she could touch a kiss to his forehead, and then press her lips to his.

He kept the kiss slow and sensual, not rushing things, letting his tongue sweep inside her mouth. As he kissed her, his hands roamed her body, skimming up her sides, kneading her breasts, tweaking her nipples, before dipping between her legs.

She was already wet for him, and she moaned into Micah's mouth when the calloused pad of one of his fingers slipped inside her, stroking deep, then slipping back out again to circle her bud. It seemed to pulse along with each beat of her heart, and she shifted, trying to get him to move quicker.

Instead, he laughed and stepped back. "So impatient," he teased as he stripped off his own clothes, tossed a condom onto the nightstand, and then piled up the pillows against the headboard. "Carefully," he said again as he helped her get situated, taking care to ensure she had plenty of pillows to rest against, and she was partially upright so he didn't have to worry about pressing against her wounds.

"Feels like coming home, doesn't it?" she asked with a content sigh as he knelt between her spread legs. "I mean I know we never did this before, but this, being with you, it gives me the same feelings you always used to give me. Home, safety, strength. When you're here, I know I don't have to handle everything on my own."

"Never, pretty girl. Never on your own again," he said as he thrust two fingers into her.

Each thrust was impossibly lazy, and each one managed to brush against that special spot inside her that had desire building steadily. As his fingers pumped into her, and his thumb circled her bundle of nerves, he alternated between watching her, a smile on his lips, kissing her, and suckling on her breasts until her nipples were tight little buds.

Not wanting to be left out, Teresa grabbed his thick erection, circling it with her fingers and running her palm up and down its impressive length. Each time she got to his tip she paused to run her thumb over it before stroking back down again.

"Now, Micah," she urged. Her orgasm was building, and she knew from the way he was twitching in her hand that he was close, too. "Want to come with you inside me."

"Okay, pretty girl." Grabbing the condom, he quickly tore the package and slipped it on, then he lined up and pushed inside her with one smooth thrust.

A gasp tumbled from her lips at how full she felt, so

perfectly and deliciously full that she almost came immediately. Somehow, she held back a bit, wanting to build this feeling inside her until it reached a peak higher than the heavens.

Even though his thrusts were careful, his desire not to hurt her still on his mind even as she knew his climax was rushing up to meet him, Micah's lips found hers, and he worshipped her with his mouth the same way he was worshiping her with his body.

It came on her slowly, she was climbing, climbing, climbing, then all of a sudden, pleasure burst inside her and she was falling. Falling and falling. Ecstasy lit her body alight and burned brightly as it refused to be doused. Burning on as she clung to Micah, needing his steady presence in the fiery light of passion.

By the time it finally began to fade Teresa knew.

This was where she was supposed to be.

* * *

May 8th
9:11 A.M.

WAS THERE anything more beautiful to look at than his girl sleeping peacefully?

Given everything Teresa had gone through in the last couple of weeks, Micah thought there absolutely was not.

Stunning as she'd been spread out beneath him last night, her skin flushed with arousal, her eyes bright and dancing with need, internal muscles clamping around him, squeezing him perfectly and shoving him toward an earth-shattering climax, he liked this more.

Because of the peace on her face.

There were no furrows in her brow, no tightness around the corners of her mouth, she wasn't having bad dreams, and she wasn't worrying about anything.

This was how he wanted her to always be.

No more pain, no more suffering, no more shouldering the load alone. He was there now, and while they still had a lot to figure out, he knew they would have those conversations and make things work.

Now, though, he slipped from the bed and crept out of the room, careful not to disturb her. It had been close to midnight by the time they were both in bed and asleep, and although she'd had about nine hours' sleep, her body needed a whole lot more. No work for Teresa today.

Even if she fought him on it.

She needed a full twenty-four hours to recuperate from yesterday. Actually, she needed a whole hell of a lot more than that, but he was pretty sure that was about all she would feel comfortable allowing herself. It was better than nothing, and he intended to make sure she spent the day doing absolutely nothing but sleeping, relaxing, and taking care of herself.

In the kitchen, he bustled about preparing breakfast in bed. He'd made sure that the kitchen was fully stocked before they got there so they wouldn't need to leave for any reason.

Well, he was going to have to sooner than he'd like.

His team only had a week left of leave before they had to be back, and he was pretty sure that even with the revelation they'd gotten from the young nurse, a week wasn't enough to close out this case.

A name was game-changing, but it wasn't magic, it didn't fix everything, but it was the beginning of the end, and his girl had done that.

He was so proud of her, he could feel the emotion clogging his chest. Every time he looked at her, he wanted to drag her into his arms, pepper kisses all over her face, take her lips and kiss her until neither of them could breathe, and tell her over and over again how amazing she was.

Since Teresa didn't love excessive praise, she probably wouldn't like it, but tough. She *was* amazing, and he *was* incredibly proud of her. Not that he ever wanted her to put her life on the line like that again. From here on out, he wanted her tucked safely away in front of her computer, not taking risks that could get her killed.

Once he had the French toast made, he piled up two plates and set both on a tray. Then he added glasses of orange juice, a bowl with some sliced fruit, and a vase with a single white hyacinth, Teresa's favorite flower.

Balancing the tray, he headed back for the bedroom. He hated that Teresa was stuck in this bland apartment. It was serviceable, but it wasn't homey, and she deserved something that made her feel comfortable as well as safe. Hopefully, it wouldn't be much longer until the case was wrapped up and she could go home. Wherever home wound up being for her.

Maybe it would be with her friends again, or … maybe she'd want to create a home with him.

It was a lot to hope for given their past, but he wanted it nonetheless. For now, it would have to be on the West Coast, at least until he retired, then if she wanted, they could move back here or stay there. Honestly, Micah didn't care where they lived as long as they were together.

He'd hoped to find Teresa still asleep when he returned to the bedroom. Had planned on waking her with a kiss, just like Sleeping Beauty or Snow White. But he didn't find her all tucked up under the covers, instead, she was standing up, wearing his discarded T-shirt from yesterday, and over by the dresser with something in her hands.

"You were supposed to still be asleep," he informed her as he set the tray on the dresser and wrapped his arms around her from behind, tugging her back so she was pressed snug against him.

"Woke up and you weren't there, so I was coming to find you," she told him, tilting her head to the side, likely so he could trail a line of kisses down the column of her neck, which was exactly what he did.

"Made you breakfast," he said, stating the obvious since she could clearly see the tray set out before her.

"What's this?" Turning in his arms so she was facing him, her hair all sleep ruffled, her eyes still slightly puffed, she was so adorable he couldn't help leaning down to touch a kiss to the tip of her nose before he looked at what she was holding out to him.

As soon as he saw the small, crumpled piece of paper, he knew what it was.

"Don't be mad," he started.

"You know in the entire history of language, never has anyone started a conversation that way, and the other person has managed not to get mad," she teased. There was amusement dancing in her eyes, but there was trepidation there, too.

"It's not bad, not really. The letter you sent me all those years ago, the one I never opened, the one I told you that I'd kept, I asked one of my teammates to go into my place, get it, and send it to me," he admitted. It wasn't that he thought he'd done anything wrong, well, not exactly, but Teresa hadn't wanted him to read the old letter, and he didn't want to upset her.

"You shouldn't have done that," she said with a sigh, letting her forehead drop forward to rest against his chest.

At least she wasn't shoving away from him.

That had to be a good sign, didn't it?

"I absolutely should have. I let you down, pretty girl, let them pull you away from me the other night. I could have lost you." It was something he didn't like thinking about, because he knew anything could have gone wrong and she wouldn't be in his arms right now. For the rest of his life, he was probably going to feel guilty about not insisting Teresa stay there or not keeping a better hold on her. More guilt for him to shoulder.

"But you didn't lose me," Teresa reminded him. "I'm right here."

"Yeah, you are." She'd lifted her head, so he brushed a quick kiss to her lips.

"I didn't want you to read it," she whispered.

"I know, pretty girl, but I needed to. It was good for me, I had to see your emotions as they were back then. I can't explain it, I just … had to. I had it with me on the helo when we came to rescue you. I tore it up, threw it out, ready to focus on the future instead of the past. But as I jumped, I found this piece in the air. It was like it was waiting for me. *I need you*. Of all the pieces I could have found it was this one. The reminder that I need, for both the past and the future. You needed me back then, and I wasn't there. That won't happen again. I swear it."

Needing her to know how serious he was, Micah dropped to his knees in front of her, his arms circling her waist, careful not to hold too tight and hurt her wound.

"I promise you, pretty girl, I will *never* let you down like that again. That's why I kept that piece of paper when I found it. Why I'm going to keep it on me every day for the rest of my life. My promise to the only woman I've ever loved, the only woman I'll *ever* love."

"I love you, too, Micah." Her fingers curled into his short hair, gripping him just tight enough to sting, and when he saw tears brimming in her big brown eyes, he pushed to his feet, scooping Teresa into his arms as he did.

"That makes me the luckiest man alive. I don't deserve your love, your forgiveness, or this second chance, but I won't ever make you regret giving them to me. I will cherish you the way you deserve forever. I'll be the man you need me to be."

"Yeah, you will," she agreed. "And I'll be the woman you need me to be. A team. That's what I want for us. To face life and all its challenges and craziness together."

"Together." Just the way he wanted it. "Now you need to eat, then I need to check your wound, don't want it getting infected this time around, and you going all tough girl and not telling me."

"Actually, I think you're forgetting something."

"I am?"

"Kiss me, Micah," she said with a laugh.

That sound was the most beautiful one in the world, and as he crushed his lips to hers, Micah knew he really was the luckiest guy in the world to be able to enjoy it for as long as he lived.

CHAPTER 23

"We're going to be late." Teresa huffed as she and Micah stepped out of the apartment door into the corridor that led to the elevators.

"Two minutes," he countered as he closed the door behind them.

"Two minutes now, but we still have to walk to the elevator, wait for the elevator, take the elevator, then get off the elevator and to the office. Can't believe I've never once been late to work when I lived across the other side of the city, and yet I'm going to be late when I'm staying right in the building."

The sound of Micah's laughter filled the hall, and his arm wrapped around her shoulders, tugging her into his side. When his lips touched a kiss to her temple,

Teresa found herself melting against him even if she was a little annoyed he'd made her late.

Originally, she had only planned on taking a day off before going back to work. Now they had a name, it was even more important than ever to dig into it, gather every bit of intel they could find, but she'd wound up taking two days off instead.

Not that Micah had to work all that hard to convince her.

Resisting spending the day with orgasms and cuddles was all but impossible. Especially when Micah was the one delivering both.

But now she had to go back and work with her team. Her stomach still ached, but it wasn't too bad, and there were no signs of infection setting into the wound, Micah was keeping a close watch on that. She was tired, and emotionally she was still at the box everything up to deal with later stage, but since she was staying at Prey, if it got to be too much and she needed a break, she could always head back downstairs and take one.

When they reached the office a couple of minutes later, Micah still had his arm around her shoulders, and Teresa realized how easy it was to lean into him. She was always going to be the kind of person who was independent, struggled to ask for help when she needed it, and liked to do things herself, but knowing that Micah was there, that he *wanted* to be there, made all the difference.

"Hey, you should have taken a few more days off," Ava rebuked, although her friend hurried over to give her a hug.

"Because you took a whole bunch of time off after you got hurt," Teresa shot back.

"You should both still be on leave," Chelsea piped up. "Tobias should be off with Isabella, too."

"That would leave only you and Josiah," Teresa reminded her. From the look her friend shot the injured SEAL, Chelsea wouldn't mind that all too much. While she hoped her friend got the happily ever after she wanted, none of them believed that Josiah would ever be ready for a relationship. Certainly not marriage and kids like Chelsea dreamed about.

Still, sometimes miracles happened.

The man standing at her side, his fingers absently stroking her shoulder, was proof of that. Never in a million years would she have guessed that this would happen. Yet here they were, together, willing to work through their issues and build a steady foundation for a relationship.

Maybe if it could happen for her and Micah, it wasn't totally outside the realms of possibility that it could happen for Chelsea and Josiah, too. Although she would not be holding her breath.

"And, Raven," Teresa added, glancing over at her boss, who was smiling at all of them.

"I understand why you're here, why you're all here. Sometimes the best thing to do when the world feels out of control is focus on what you can control," Raven said. Of all of them, her ordeal had been the most horrific because it had lasted an entire decade. Teresa didn't even want to imagine not having your child with you for most of their childhood, not even knowing if they were dead or alive.

"Exactly." She nodded her assent. That was exactly why she felt like this was where she had to be. This case was personal for all of them, and she had no intention of hiding in a bed and leaving the others to work on it. Especially when they finally had a name. "What did you guys find out about Ms. Tilly?"

"Desiree Tilly," Tobias informed her. "Once we had her name and all the information William provided us with, it didn't take long to work up a profile on her."

"She's forty-four years old, only child to a pilot and a dentist, both parents died within two years of each other, not long after she was married. Her husband had a rare genetic condition that caused his organs to spontaneously fail. Amyloidosis. It's hereditary, and it was passed along to all four of their kids," Chelsea explained.

"What does amyloidosis do?" she asked as Micah guided her over to the table and pulled out a chair for her.

"Affects proteins," Ava replied. "They're called amyloid fibrils, and they damage organs and can lead to organ failure."

"Which is what happened to her husband about four years ago," Tobias added.

"Unfortunately, all four of their children were more seriously affected than their father. Their firstborn son died at two when a liver transplant failed. She was pregnant with their second son at the time, and he was also born with the condition. Their third son came along two years later, and both boys got sick around the same time, and unfortunately, both died while waiting for transplants," Ava informed her.

"So within a couple of years, Desiree loses her parents, then three of her four children," Teresa said, it was enough to push anyone off the deep end.

"Daughter was born ten years after their third son passed away. At first, things looked hopeful, but then she got sick as well," Chelsea continued. "That seemed to be the catalyst for everything. Husband died within a year of the diagnosis. It was like he just gave up, the guilt of what his children went through because of his genes was too much. After that, Desiree sold off his family's business, which was running a luxury cruise company, and kind of disappeared."

"She decided to ensure that her daughter didn't die while waiting for a transplant," Teresa said softly. It was a heartbreaking situation, because in one sense, she could understand Desiree Tilly's helplessness and desperation. Knowing what she'd already lost, the woman likely felt like she had nothing to lose. There were no guarantees that her daughter would get the transplants she'd likely wind up needing if they just put her on a list. Instead, she set out to make sure there was no chance her daughter would die waiting for a life-saving organ that might never come.

Not that any of that excused the woman's behavior.

Having lost three of her four children and her husband, Desiree Tilly knew the heartbreak that came with the death of a loved one. Yet the woman hadn't hesitated to inflict that same suffering on hundreds of families across the world as she kidnapped at will. Stealing from healthy young men and women to save the dying and profit from it at the same time.

Understandable but not excusable.

The woman had to be stopped.

"So we know who she is, and we know why she started the trafficking ring, but how are we going to stop her?" Teresa asked. All this intel was interesting, but in the end, she wanted Desiree Tilly in prison where she belonged, where she could never hurt another innocent person ever again.

"I'm going to go in undercover," Josiah announced, shoving away from his desk and stalking over to join her and the others at the table.

"You're going to what?" Raven asked as they all stared at Josiah in shock.

"Pretend to be dying. It's clear she's investigated us. She targeted Teresa and Chelsea specifically by having their apartment trashed. So she likely knows I was kicked out of the SEALs because I was injured. She might not know all the details, but we know what hospitals she has contacts at, and I bet anything if I went looking to purchase an organ and convinced her I was dying, I could set up a meeting with her."

"No." Chelsea said it like her word was law.

While Teresa absolutely got where her friend was coming from, these people were dangerous, and she'd feel the same way if it were Micah offering to go in and make contact with them, this plan might actually work. If Josiah could get a meeting set up with Desiree Tilly, they could bring the woman into custody, cut off the head of the snake, and end this once and for all.

"Yes," Josiah said simply.

"It might work," Raven said thoughtfully. "We can probably pull a few strings and set up some fake appointments with specialists for you."

"It won't work," Chelsea said, her voice sure and confident. "There is no way anyone would buy that a man like Josiah, who put his life on the line for his country, would go to a black-market organ trafficking ring to buy an organ to save his own life. But …"

"But what?" Josiah snapped.

"They might buy that that he would do it for someone else. Someone he cared about," Chelsea continued, her gaze roaming the room, meeting all of theirs one by one. "If Josiah and I pretended to be in love, if we convince them that I'm the one who's dying and he's willing to do anything, even something illegal, to save me, they might buy that."

With his attention focused solely on destroying the organ trafficking ring, Josiah is determined not to let Chelsea break through the hold his past has on him in the fourth and final book in the action packed and emotionally charged Prey Security: Cyber Team series!

Rescuing Josiah (Prey Security: Cyber Team #4)

ALSO BY JANE BLYTHE

Prey Security: Cyber Team
RESCUING NATHANIEL
RESCUING TOBIAS
RESCUING MICAH

Prey Security: Athena Team Series
FIGHTING FOR SCARLETT
FIGHTING FOR LUCY
FIGHTING FOR CASSIDY
FIGHTING FOR ELLA

Prey Security Series: Artemis Team
IVORY'S FIGHT
PEARL'S FIGHT
LACEY'S FIGHT
OPAL'S FIGHT

Prey Security Series
PROTECTING EAGLE
PROTECTING RAVEN
PROTECTING FALCON
PROTECTING SPARROW
PROTECTING HAWK
PROTECTING DOVE

Prey Security Series: Alpha Team

DEADLY RISK

LETHAL RISK

EXTREME RISK

FATAL RISK

COVERT RISK

SAVAGE RISK

Prey Security: Bravo Team Series

VICIOUS SCARS

RUTHLESS SCARS

BRUTAL SCARS

CRUEL SCARS

BURIED SCARS

WICKED SCARS

Prey Security: Charlie Team Series

DECEPTIVE LIES

SHADOWED LIES

TACTICAL LIES

VENGEFUL LIES

CORRUPTED LIES

TRAITOROUS LIES

Saving SEALs Series

SAVING RYDER

SAVING ERIC

SAVING OWEN

SAVING LOGAN

SAVING GRAYSON

SAVING CHARLIE

Candella Sisters' Heroes Series

LITTLE DOLLS

LITTLE HEARTS

LITTLE BALLERINA

Broken Gems Series

CRACKED SAPPHIRE

CRUSHED RUBY

FRACTURED DIAMOND

SHATTERED AMETHYST

SPLINTERED EMERALD

SALVAGING MARIGOLD

River's End Rescues Series

COCKY SAVIOR

SOME REGRETS ARE FOREVER

PROTECT

SOME LIES WILL HAUNT YOU

SOME QUESTIONS HAVE NO ANSWERS

SOME TRUTH CAN BE DISTORTED

SOME TRUST CAN BE REBUILT

SOME MISTAKES ARE UNFORGIVABLE

<u>Detective Parker Bell Series</u>

A SECRET TO THE GRAVE

WINTER WONDERLAND

DEAD OR ALIVE

LITTLE GIRL LOST

FORGOTTEN

<u>Count to Ten Series</u>

ONE

TWO

THREE

FOUR

FIVE

SIX

BURNING SECRETS

SEVEN

EIGHT

NINE

TEN

Storybook Murders Series

<u>NURSERY RHYME KILLER</u>

<u>FAIRYTALE KILLER</u>

<u>FABLE KILLER</u>

<u>Christmas Romantic Suspense Series</u>

CHRISTMAS HOSTAGE

CHRISTMAS CAPTIVE

CHRISTMAS VICTIM

YULETIDE PROTECTOR

<u>YULETIDE GUARD</u>

<u>YULETIDE HERO</u>

<u>HOLIDAY GRIEF</u>

HOLIDAY LOSS - 12/2024

<u>Conquering Fear Series</u>

(Co-written with Amanda Siegrist)

DROWNING IN YOU

OUT OF THE DARKNESS

<u>CLOSING IN</u>

ABOUT THE AUTHOR

USA Today bestselling author Jane Blythe writes action-packed romantic suspense and military romance featuring protective heroes and heroines who are survivors. One of Jane's most popular series includes Prey Security, part of Susan Stoker's OPERATION ALPHA world! Writing in that world alongside authors such as Janie Crouch and Riley Edwards has been a blast, and she looks forward to bringing more books to this genre, both within and outside of Stoker's world. When Jane isn't binge-reading she's counting down to Christmas and adding to her 200+ teddy bear collection!

To connect and keep up to date please visit any of the following

There are many more books in this fan fiction world than listed here, for an up-to-date list go to www.AcesPress.com

You can also visit our Amazon page at:
http://www.amazon.com/author/operationalpha

<u>***Special Forces: Operation Alpha World***</u>
Christie Adams: Charity's Heart
Elizabella Baker: Challenging Luke
Linzi Baxter: Dangerous Rescue
Misha Blake: Flash
Anna Blakely: Rescuing Gracelynn
Julia Bright: Saving Lorelei
Cara Carnes: Protecting Mari
Kendra Mei Chailyn: Beast
Melissa Kay Clarke: Rescuing Annabeth
Gia Cobie: Saved from Revenge
Samantha Cole: Handling Haven
Cassie Colton: Rescuing Ryder
Jordan Dane: Redemption for Avery
D.M. Earl: Claire's Guardian
Riley Edwards: Protecting Olivia
Dorothy Ewels: Knight's Queen
Lila Ferrari: Protecting Joy
Nicole Flockton: Protecting Maria
Lea Griffith: Finding Ava
Desiree Holt: Protecting Maddie
Bree Hera: Trusting the Team
Rayne Lewis: Justice for Mary
JM Madden: Rescuing Olivia

A.M. Mahler: Griffin
Ellie Masters: Sybil's Protector
Trish McCallan: Hero Under Fire
Naomi McKay: Twist
KD Michaels: Saving Laura
Olivia Michaels: Protecting Harper
Annie Miller: Securing Willow
MJ Nightingale: Protecting Beauty
C.K. O'Connor: Delaney's Bodyguard
Danielle Pays: Defending Sarina
Lainey Reese: Protecting New York
Angela Rush: Charlotte
E.M. Shue: Discovering Tyler
Heather Slade: Code Name: Admiral
Dee Stewart: Fighting for Brielle
Lynne St. James: SEAL's Spitfire
Bella Stone: Rexar
Jen Talty: Shielding Jolene
Reina Torres, Rescuing Hi'ilani
LJ Vickery: Circus Comes to Town
R. C. Wynne: Shadows Renewed
Amanda Zook: Freeing Camila

Delta Team Three Series
Lori Ryan: Nori's Delta
Becca Jameson: Destiny's Delta
Lynne St James, Gwen's Delta
Elle James: Ivy's Delta
Riley Edwards: Hope's Delta

Police and Fire: Operation Alpha World

Freya Barker: Burning for Autumn
Jane Blythe: Salvaging Marigold
Julia Bright: Justice for Amber
Gia Cobie: Saved from Revenge
Leyna Cohan: Embracing Juliette
Nicole Craig: Justice for Francesca
Danielle M. Haas: Crossroads of Betrayal
Deanndra Hall: Shelter for Sharla
Reina Torres: Justice for Sloane

As you know, this book included at least one character from Susan Stoker's books. To check out more, see below.

SEAL of Protection: Alliance Series
Protecting Remi
Protecting Wren
Protecting Josie
Protecting Maggie
Protecting Addison
Protecting Kelli
Protecting Bree (Jan 6, 2026)

Rescue Angels Series
Keeping Laryn
Keeping Amanda (Nov 4, 2025)
Keeping Zita (Feb 10, 2026)
Keeping Penny (May 5, 2026)
Keeping Kara (July 7, 2026)
Keeping Jennifer (TBA)

The Refuge Series
Deserving Alaska
Deserving Henley
Deserving Reese
Deserving Cora
Deserving Lara
Deserving Maisy
Deserving Ryleigh

SEAL Team Hawaii Series

Finding Elodie
Finding Lexie
Finding Kenna
Finding Monica
Finding Carly
Finding Ashlyn
Finding Jodelle

Eagle Point Search & Rescue

Searching for Lilly
Searching for Elsie
Searching for Bristol
Searching for Caryn
Searching for Finley
Searching for Heather
Searching for Khloe

Delta Team Two Series

Shielding Gillian
Shielding Kinley
Shielding Aspen
Shielding Jayme (novella)
Shielding Riley
Shielding Devyn
Shielding Ember
Shielding Sierra

SEAL of Protection: Legacy Series

Securing Caite (FREE!)

Securing Brenae (novella)
Securing Sidney
Securing Piper
Securing Zoey
Securing Avery
Securing Kalee
Securing Jane

Delta Force Heroes Series

Rescuing Rayne
Rescuing Aimee (novella)
Rescuing Emily
Rescuing Harley
Marrying Emily (novella)
Rescuing Kassie
Rescuing Bryn
Rescuing Casey
Rescuing Sadie (novella)
Rescuing Wendy
Rescuing Mary
Rescuing Macie (novella)
Rescuing Annie

Badge of Honor: Texas Heroes Series

Justice for Mackenzie (FREE!)
Justice for Mickie
Justice for Corrie
Justice for Laine (novella)
Shelter for Elizabeth
Justice for Boone

Shelter for Adeline
Shelter for Sophie
Justice for Erin
Justice for Milena
Shelter for Blythe
Justice for Hope
Shelter for Quinn
Shelter for Koren
Shelter for Penelope

SEAL of Protection Series

Protecting Caroline (FREE!)
Protecting Alabama
Protecting Fiona
Marrying Caroline (novella)
Protecting Summer
Protecting Cheyenne
Protecting Jessyka
Protecting Julie (novella)
Protecting Melody
Protecting the Future
Protecting Kiera (novella)
Protecting Alabama's Kids (novella)
Protecting Dakota
Protecting Tex

New York Times, *USA Today* and *Wall Street Journal* Bestselling Author Susan Stoker has a heart as big as the state of Tennessee where she lives, but this all American girl has also spent the last fourteen years living in Missouri, California, Colorado, Indiana, and Texas.

She's married to a retired Army man who now gets to follow *her* around the country.

www.stokeraces.com
www.AcesPress.com
susan@stokeraces.com

Made in United States
Cleveland, OH
09 September 2025

20273348R00184